CLOSER

ALSO BY K.L. SLATER

Safe with Me
Blink
Liar
The Mistake
The Visitor
The Secret
Closer

CLOSER
K.L. SLATER

bookouture

Published by Bookouture in 2018

An imprint of StoryFire Ltd.

Carmelite House
50 Victoria Embankment
London EC4Y 0DZ

www.bookouture.com

ISBN: 978-1-78681-665-8
eBook ISBN: 978-1-78681-664-1

For my lovely mama x

THEN

She knows it's her. She knows this before they even pull her tiny body out of the oily black water.

Dread squirms in her stomach and she wills herself not to vomit at the side of the quay.

Not here. Not in front of all these people.

Someone drapes a scratchy pale blue blanket around her shoulders. Someone else presses a plastic cup of hot tea into her hand.

But neither kindness stops her from shaking, or brings back what she has lost.

There are concerned, hushed whispers all around. The sounds blend into one swishing echo in her ears, like dry leaves swirling against asphalt on a breezy autumn day.

She holds her breath against the ripe smell of the water, closes her eyes against the rawness of the hopeless dread that hangs above them all.

'Why don't you wait inside, love?' a policewoman says softly. 'There's no sense in standing here in the cold. It might be a while and… you don't need to see her the moment they find her. Not like this.'

'I'm not going anywhere.' Her voice sounds cracked and hard, a brittle shell that tries in vain to protect the soft belly of her agony. She plants her feet a little further apart in an effort to stabilise her trembling legs and says, 'I have to be here when she comes out. I'm her mother.'

The policewoman nods and takes a step back, merging back into the small crowd of concerned onlookers.

Mercifully, there are no rubberneckers here, no jackals. They're all people who can and want to help. Police, medics, the underwater search divers, the quayside staff... Their faces are full of the same dread too. Just diluted.

But there is also a tangible anticipation in the air. A drowned child is undeniably tragic, but is nevertheless a major event in this sleepy seaside town where graffiti on the pier is the most high-profile criminal act that's occurred in the last few months.

She knows the people here will go home at the end of the day. With drawn, troubled expressions, they'll tell their families, over food, about this terrible, terrible tragedy. They will frighten their children with this example of what the water can do if you take risks.

In a day or so, they'll accept a drink on the house in the local pub with the feature bar that overlooks the quayside.

They'll hang their heads on the street when there's another pat on the back for the awful job they've endured.

Some of them will dream about the web of burgeoning blue veins that almost pop through the child's skin as they pull her from the water. Her bulging eyes and swollen, distended tongue will visit some of them for many nights to come.

But at some point, perhaps not too long afterwards, they will tell themselves: *Enough*.

They'll recite silent prayers of thanks that their own children are intact and they will begin to forget. This terrible day and the dead child will become a story to recount on suitable occasions. A sadness they feel that is sometimes allowed to air in order to warn others.

And, in time, they will get on with their lives once again.

She starts as raised voices sound. People surge forward around her.

The police officer appears next to her again, lays a comforting hand on her upper arm.

A shout. Water splashing as they pull something small out of the terrible wetness.

A collective groan of grief.

She drops the cup of tea. Scalding drops of liquid pepper her hands and body and she is grateful that it helps her to focus.

She recognises the soft hair that she used to brush until it shone. Now it sticks to her bony shoulders like thin, wet ropes. The fragile hands splayed like limp starfish. And her rosebud lips, the perfect Cupid's bow too impossibly pale against the sickly bluish-white pallor of that ten-year-old face.

Yes, she tells herself. This is the broken body of her poor dead daughter.

CHAPTER 1

Emma

Now

I pull up outside the dance school in my new, shiny bright red Toyota.

Well, not exactly *brand* new. My budget wouldn't stretch to that, so it's second-hand. But the way the car slides into the parking space with ample room to spare is a novelty, and I breathe a sigh of relief that I no longer have to park Shaun's enormous Audi within the designated white lines.

I check the clock on the dashboard and am gratified to see that I've arrived a good ten minutes early. Maisie will still be in her ballet class. I turn Smooth Radio down low, rest my head back and close my eyes.

Like every other parent I know, my life seems to consist largely of work and ferrying Maisie to her hobbies, particularly since she joined the dance school about a year ago.

Today is Monday, which in our world means ballet. It's jazz and tap on a Friday, and she's just started freestyle disco on Tuesday nights, which my mum has reluctantly agreed to pick her up from. That's before we get to performance art at the church hall a couple of times a month.

My mum has been retired from her job as a school librarian for three years now. Her life is busy, not least with catching up with old friends and trying out her own new hobbies. She's fond of saying, with a chuckle, that she doesn't know how she ever found the time to go to work before.

She was already helping out with driving Maisie around, and so I tried to appeal to her sympathetic side when Maisie announced she'd also like to go to the new disco class.

'You see, I can't just finish work every day at five o'clock sharp any more, Mum, not now I've got the new job. More often than not it's six, sometimes seven before I even leave the office these days.'

'They'll come to expect you to work late every day if you're not careful, you know.' Mum pressed her lips together. 'I can pick Maisie up from the new class until she breaks up from school for Christmas, but I can't keep it up indefinitely, Emmeline. I've agreed to start a new line-dancing class with Kath in September and it's scheduled for Wednesday nights.'

Cantankerous Kath, as Shaun likes to call her, is Mum's best friend.

'Seriously? People actually still *do* line dancing?' I pasted a look of exaggerated horror on my face. 'I thought it had died out at least a decade ago.'

Mum's head whipped around and I quickly looked away so she didn't see me trying not to laugh. Served her right anyway, calling me by my full name, which I've hated since primary school.

Everyone calls me Emma these days. Except Mum, if she can help it.

But I have to admit, she's right about my hours. Since I started my new dream job, my working day seems to bleed later and later into the evenings.

It's what Shaun and I always expected. The new position came with so much more responsibility, but I knew it was crucial I proved myself from the off. After all, I love what I do and the extra time is no hardship; the long days at work fly by.

Like I told Shaun, it's best we think of overtime as an investment for the future, rather than unpaid hours.

'An investment in *your* future, you mean,' he said in that playful way he often tries to pull off when he's using humour to cover his irritation.

It's a shame he feels the need when everything is going so well at last.

You see, Shaun and I... we're not together any more.

Well, that's not strictly true. We are still – to all intents and purposes – very much together. We're just not together *like that*. We've called time on our marriage, on our emotional attachment as husband and wife.

Instead, we've devised a surprisingly amicable agreement, without consulting lawyers, or resorting to any outside interference at all, and it's working just fine for both of us. It might sound a cold and pragmatic outcome to some, and we're fully aware that it's far from the norm. But to us it feels a very adult, very modern and efficient arrangement.

I feel lighter inside than I have done for years.

On the surface of it, nothing has changed between us. We live together in a leafy suburb of Nottingham with our ten-year-old daughter. We get on well, like we did when our marriage worked. We like the same foods, the same TV programmes (with the exception of football), and we even share the same taste in music.

I like to think we're more like siblings now, or friends. Close friends who still feel an affection and consideration for each other.

The most important thing we have in common is our love for Maisie. And it was for her sake we made our unconventional pact in the first place.

'The extra hours I'm putting in are for Maisie's future too,' I responded to Shaun's jibe, and turned back to read about new legislation in the publishing of information about the gender pay gap.

To be fair, out of the three partners at Walker, Dent and Scott, one is female. But it hasn't escaped my notice that most of the actual lawyers are men, as were three of the four paralegals.

I allow myself a small satisfied smile. Seven weeks and three days ago, the company gained another qualified female paralegal: me.

I've worked so hard to get here, I'm determined nothing is going to get in my way now. Least of all Shaun's griping about my putting more hours in.

This company is not the first one I've worked at. I started my legal career at Clayton and McCarthy, a much smaller firm just outside the city. I had big hopes and dreams of forging a career path from humble beginnings there too.

But three years ago, after the trauma of what happened while I was employed there, and on the advice of my doctor, I took a few weeks' leave without pay. Looking back, I feel sure now that the partners must have been relieved when I gave them an easy way out. I also realise now that it probably made me look guilty of everything my colleagues were whispering about me behind my back.

But whatever they thought, I was not that person. I know that, my family knows that.

Once I'd made the decision to take some time out, I tried to relax and focus on the simple things that would hopefully bring back the balance in my life. I took up baking, cross-stitch, even yoga and Pilates.

Yet in time, being at home just seemed to make everything worse. The more I tried to relax, the harder it became.

I'd hear noises upstairs in the middle of the day when Shaun was out on a photography job and Maisie was at school. I'd put my phone down on the kitchen worktop, and when I went back for it, I'd find it had disappeared, only to turn up on the coffee table in the living room, convincing me that someone else was in the house.

Shaun would sometimes come home to find me curled up in a ball on the couch, or sitting in the locked downstairs loo, shaking and waiting for his return. Each time he'd trawl the rooms upstairs, and when he came down, his face creased with concern, he'd say gently, 'There's nobody up there, Em. There's nothing. Not even a spider.'

One day Maisie came into the bedroom to find me hiding behind the curtain in tears because I'd convinced myself a man had walked by the house twice and looked in with what I described at the time as 'worrying intent'.

Like many of my concerns at the time, it was just another foreboding feeling I couldn't shake. There was no real substance to it.

I had to admit then, finally, that my nerves were shot to ribbons.

'We need to get you away from the house and from that job,' Shaun said.

I didn't argue with his suggestion that we go away for a while. At that point, I would have happily moved somewhere else entirely to start again incognito. Without the stigma, the gossip, the accusing stares.

We booked a ten-night family holiday in Spain, and afterwards I did feel more positive and even agreed to undertake a few counselling sessions to try and deal with the guilt and remorse.

I resigned from my position as legal secretary at Clayton and McCarthy and took on a job in an independent clothing shop. Later, I worked in the ticket office of the Playhouse on Wellington Circus.

I only stayed in each post about six months, but it seemed to do the trick. It gave me some space and time away from the legal profession I still yearned to be part of but that still felt too close for comfort.

When the time felt right, I joined Walker, Dent and Scott and worked for a year as a legal secretary before Joanne Dent, the female partner, agreed that the company would sponsor me to study for the Graduate Diploma in Law, commonly referred to in the business as the GDL. At last, my dream of becoming a fully qualified paralegal was within touching distance.

'As long as you're sure you can manage the additional workload alongside your other commitments,' she said when she reviewed my application. 'And you realise you'll have to sign an addendum to your contract tying you to the company for two years following completion of the GDL? This training programme is a big financial commitment for us.'

'Yes and yes,' I said pleasantly, but it irked me that she'd alluded to my 'other commitments'. I felt certain she was referring to Maisie. I happened to know Joanne had a young daughter too – Piper attended Maisie's dance school – and so I found the snipe both irritating and surprising, coming from a fellow working woman. I'd expected more.

Still, it was all worth it. After two years of setting the alarm and working from five until seven each morning, then grafting for two to three hours after Maisie had gone to bed, I managed to pass my GDL with a very respectable 2:1 and qualify as a paralegal.

It was an amazing feeling.

Granted, the process hadn't been too great for my marriage, but after years of being told I'd never come to anything worthwhile, it was a very sweet moment indeed.

More importantly, it felt like I'd put the trauma I'd gone through at Clayton and McCarthy firmly behind me.

'I hope Dad is turning in his grave,' I said to Mum at the graduation ceremony as we stood with a glass of flat fizz and a nibble each.

'You were always oversensitive with him, Emmeline. Still are,' Mum said, biting into her prawn vol-au-vent. 'He never meant anything by it, the silly old fool.'

She'd called him a lot worse than that when he was alive. Night after night, when his drinking pals would take an arm each and drag him up the path at gone midnight, I seem to remember that Mum was often very *oversensitive* herself.

'It still hurt,' I mumbled, sipping my drink and wishing I'd asked Shaun to come instead of her. 'Whether he meant it or not, it's stuck in my head all these years.'

'Perhaps you ought to be thanking him instead,' Mum said tartly. 'Maybe in a roundabout way it was your father who gave you the drive to achieve something in your life. Like you've done today.'

My graduation day was about the closest Mum has ever got to congratulating me.

Mum's never been very open with her affection. I can remember criticisms, pieces of advice and curt nods to acknowledge various achievements at school, but that's about it.

There's a lot of stuff that happened back then that we've never talked about.

I suppose some things are better off forgotten. For now.

CHAPTER 2

I open my eyes from my musing just as Maisie emerges from the dance school entrance.

I love moments like this, when she's completely absorbed in her friends, her life, and doesn't know I'm watching her.

Her face is ruddy from ballet class, her smile bright and alive as she skips down the steps clutching her new pink and silver dance bag Mum bought her last week. She spoils her.

Maisie is flanked by Sandeep and Zoe, her two best dance friends. She has a lot of categories of friends: school friends, dance friends and performance art friends. Several of them overlap.

Sandeep goes to Maisie's school but Zoe goes to an independent school out of town. Her family lives in the big house with a corner plot at the end of our street.

I'm on friendly terms with lots of the mums, but because of my recent studies and working full-time, I rarely find time to meet for coffee or tea at one of the many café bars in the centre of West Bridgford, as lots of them do.

Zoe shows the other two something on her phone screen and they collapse into giggles.

Then they're hugging and waving and going their separate ways. Sandeep's mum crosses the road to meet her daughter and waves to me as Maisie flies towards the car, her dark curls bouncing as she runs. The passenger door is wrenched open and suddenly she is next to me, breathless and vibrant, filling the small space with her zinging energy.

I kiss her on the cheek and start the engine.

'Good class?' I ask, checking the mirror and pulling out onto the road, sounding the horn as we pass the girls and their mums, who are deep in conversation.

As usual, I can't stay to chat, I have to get back home to work, but everyone looks up and waves as we drive past, including Miss Diane, who always steps outside to chat to the parents who collect on foot.

'Yes, it was a great class, Mum. And guess what? Piper Dent did all her steps wrong and tripped up and hit her head.' The delight in Maisie's voice is obvious.

'Maisie,' I say, elongating her name with mild reproach. 'It's not nice to gloat. Anyone can stumble, including you.'

An impish smile plays on Maisie's lips.

'But she wasn't using her eyes and ears, Mum. She told Miss Diane she already knew the steps and she didn't want to wait for the rest of us.'

Use your eyes and ears is a phrase the young and impossibly slender Miss Diane tells her dance students repeatedly. It has struck a chord with Maisie and she often uses it in jest to reprimand me or her father if she feels we aren't paying her full attention.

'Did Piper hurt herself?' I ask, thinking of Joanne's intolerance of people's mistakes at work and how that might translate into her role as a mother.

'She said her ankle felt sore and her head hurt, so Miss Diane said she couldn't join in with the barre exercises, which are her favourite. She had to sit on a chair and just watch for a while because of health and safety. The second we finished class, she ran out crying and her mum came back inside and said she wanted a word with Miss Diane.'

'Oh dear,' I say, feeling a pang of sympathy for the teacher.

I feel duty bound to mute my true reaction to Maisie's tale and say all the right parental things, but privately, I know just what a spoilt little diva Piper Dent is.

Joanne is a powerful influence in the area. As well as being a partner at Walker, Dent and Scott, she owns a portfolio of commercial buildings across the city, including the one the dance school rents.

We've all witnessed Piper, who is ten years old, the exact same age as Maisie, having a full-scale tantrum in the middle of the street. On one occasion, she emerged from the dance school raging, kicking her mother's gleaming white Mercedes, which is always parked on double yellow lines at the end of a class.

If Joanne happens to forget a post-exercise snack for her daughter, says no to an impromptu sleepover request or a trip to McDonald's after class, there is always hell to pay.

I can't imagine what it must feel like to be usurped by one's ten-year-old daughter. For all Joanne's professional achievements and tough nature in her court cases, she seems thoroughly incapable of handling the girl.

Piper turns up to the modest dance classes each week wearing the most exquisite tulle creations, sparkling with hand-sewn crystals. The cost of such garments I can't begin to hazard a guess at.

At the end of class, she's often to be found outside, twirling and preening whilst a circle of girls, including Maisie, look on in awe, dressed in their own rather dull dance uniform of grey leotard and pink tights.

Rumour has it that at the beginning of the autumn term last year, Miss Diane plucked up courage and broached the subject of Piper wearing the dance school uniform. She was apparently told in no uncertain terms to never mention it again or she'd be looking for new premises for the studio.

So I can kind of understand Maisie's glee in Piper coming unstuck; my daughter is only human after all.

'There's a banana and a carton of orange juice in the glove compartment,' I tell her. 'Just to keep you going until we get home.'

'Ooh good, I'm starving.' She clicks it open and takes out the food. 'Mum, can you, me and Dad all watch a film together again tonight, like we did yesterday?'

She glances at me. She has detected something is different at home, but isn't quite sure what. Shaun argued that she was old enough to understand our decision, but I managed to convince him to wait a while. 'Until the dust settles a bit,' I suggested.

'We'll not be watching a film tonight, but we will again at the weekend,' I tell her. 'Your dad is cooking tea and he'll be with you later while I'm working.'

'Working where?'

'In the spare room.'

A faint scowl settles on her forehead as she finishes peeling her banana and takes a bite without answering.

The traffic lights change as we approach and I slow down to join the queue. While we wait, I turn to Maisie.

'You like spending more time with your dad during the week, don't you?'

'Yes, but…' She thinks for a moment. 'I'd like you to be there, too.'

'I will be there, only I'll be upstairs. And I'll see you before you go to bed.'

She looks out of the window and I can no longer see her face.

I've promised myself I'm not going to feel guilty about this. It's a far better arrangement than we had before and I'm confident Maisie will soon get used to it.

Shaun and I now rota the whole week, alternately caring for Maisie during weekdays and scheduling one family activity at the weekend. Simple things like watching a film or walking around the nearby park and feeding the ducks together.

It's all stuff we never seemed to manage to get around to doing before. Up until now, the majority of Maisie's care fell upon me, while Shaun got to disappear at least three nights a week.

He works as a freelance photographer and currently gets most of his paid work from a small local newspaper. He also sells some of his photographs to photo libraries, magazines and other periodicals.

When I first met him, he fostered ambitions to get regular work for one of the big nationals. Sadly, over time, he seems to have trimmed down his expectations to the extent that he no longer believes he'll get there.

'Social media has killed journalism,' he complains regularly. 'Nobody wants good old-fashioned reporting any more. By the time you've got the lowdown on a story, some eighteen-year-old kid working for a news website has already tweeted it together with a pic emailed in from a member of the public.'

That said, the truth of the matter was that he often scooted out of the house at a moment's notice when he heard about a scoop. This resulted in me getting behind on my studies on occasion, leaving me no choice but to make up the time at weekends, scuppering any chance of family time.

Maisie has lost out before, but this way, we all win. Especially her. It's a much fairer arrangement and it seems to work on all levels despite it being contentious in the eyes of some.

OK, I'm talking about my mother.

I haven't told her everything, but I had to tell her *something*. The bare bones of it.

'I've never heard anything like it,' she said curtly when I tried to explain. 'You two need to sort yourselves out and make it work. Me and your father were married for forty years and it wasn't all wine and roses, I can tell you that.'

It's true that Shaun wasn't as keen as me in the first instance, but even he has now admitted the extra time he's spending with Maisie is paying dividends.

'I feel like I'm getting to know her on an emotional level I didn't really have before,' he told me. 'I do miss us, Emma, you and I. But I can't deny there are advantages to what we've done.'

From my own point of view, I feel less tired, less stressed, and without question, I'm less snappy now with both Maisie *and* Shaun.

We share the housework, having drawn up a rota for duties like the laundry, cleaning the house and food shopping. Theoretically we were supposed to share this stuff before, but somehow it always seemed to fall to me to fill in on the numerous occasions Shaun forgot or was called away on a local story. Now, it all feels far more equitable.

Aside from the bickering between us, mostly about his career, I'd always encouraged him to keep at it, to keep trying. It was the waste of talent that bothered me. I just couldn't understand his lack of ambition. It annoyed and concerned me in equal measure.

On top of that, we could have done with the money any extra work might bring in. We've always managed, but it would have been nice to have a little spare after we'd paid the household bills.

'You need to find a way of getting the stories other people miss,' I suggested on more than one occasion. 'Sniff them out like a terrier and be ready and waiting for the big snap. Don't worry about stepping on other people's toes, just go for it.'

Just a few encouraging words, I thought at the time. I didn't have a clue he'd actually take any notice of them.

But the last couple of weeks, there's been another development I didn't expect. Something that could complicate and scupper everything we've planned to achieve a stable and balanced home life.

I think Shaun may be seeing someone else.

CHAPTER 3

I turn left onto the driveway and shut off the engine.

'I like our house, it's got a nice friendly face,' Maisie says, leaning forward and looking up wistfully.

I smile and follow her appreciative stare. I know what she means. The house is nothing special, just a red-brick Victorian semi in Ladybay, a desirable area – according to local estate agents when we bought it – located just three miles from the city.

It has attractive symmetrical windows and a smooth brown PVC door with stained-glass panels. The small front lawn is edged with neat borders and we have two terracotta pots containing topiary trees, which Maisie herself helped us choose, that perfectly frame the entrance porch.

She particularly loves her bedroom, which overlooks the long, narrow garden at the back and, crucially, has a walk-in cupboard complete with shelving for all her soft toys.

'I want to live here forever,' she sighs, and looks at me. 'Promise we can?'

Icy fingers tickle the back of my neck. I can't lie to her.

She can't know how close Shaun and I came to splitting up and selling the house. It was one of the options we discussed before deciding there was a better way – until Maisie is a little older, at least.

'Well, we've no plans to leave it any time soon,' I say briskly, opening the driver's-side door. 'Now, make sure you've got all your stuff and let's go and see what Dad has rustled up for tea, shall we?'

I walk up the short path, push the front door and am surprised to find it locked. Rolling my eyes, I fumble in my oversized handbag for my keys.

It's happened a few times in the last couple of weeks: Shaun isn't home when he's meant to be and reappears at his leisure with no offer of explanation. The whole point of our new arrangement is that we're supposed to have parity in our parental duties, each of us giving Maisie equal shares of our time.

Just lately, Shaun seems to be either unwilling or unable to grasp this fact.

Inside, the house is quiet. At this time of day, Shaun would usually be home and watching the news headlines on television. Seeing as it's his turn to make tea, I would at least expect to hear him pottering around in the kitchen.

For the last couple of weeks, I've had the distinct feeling he's being distracted elsewhere.

'Hello?' I call out into the silence. No response.

'Where's Dad?' Maisie frowns as she follows me inside. 'I thought he was supposed to be looking after me tonight while you're working?'

'Perhaps he's had to go out on a quick job,' I say lightly, making a real effort to swallow my irritation. She's had to listen to enough sniping between us over the last year. 'Close the front door behind you, poppet.'

I toss the car keys on the console table in the hallway and glance around there and in the kitchen for a note, but there's nothing.

Perhaps I've been too willing to believe Shaun is as invested in our new arrangement as I am. We only agreed on this week's rota yesterday and he seemed more than happy to look after Maisie tonight. He volunteered to, in fact.

'I'm starving,' Maisie grumbles. 'Can you make tea tonight instead, Mum?'

'Course,' I say. 'Go and get changed out of your dance gear and I'll rustle something up.'

When I hear Maisie skip lightly upstairs, I ball my fists and let out a silent scream.

Tonight, I'm scheduled to listen to a company webinar about very important legislative updates as well as new case law. I'm due to give an outline of my findings in the morning at our 8.30 staff meeting.

I know Joanne sees it as a chance to appraise my analytical skills and gauge how I can communicate my findings effectively with the team. For me, it's a valuable chance to impress her and the other two partners in my new capacity as paralegal.

And Shaun knew this. He bloody well *knew* it.

Joanne had given me an entirely reasonable seven days to listen in to the session. I'd initially planned to do it over the weekend, but Shaun had to pop out to shoot a local football match on Sunday so asked me to cover his usual time with Maisie.

'I'll cover the whole of Monday evening when you get back from dance, so you'll have plenty of time to get done what you need to,' he assured me.

He might at least have texted me to say he'd be home late or something, I grumble silently to myself.

I grab my bag, realising I haven't actually checked my phone for a while. Maybe he has sent me a text. On the second foraging attempt, I find it wedged right in the bottom corner beneath a mountain of useless stuff: school letters, empty headache tablet foils, tissues… the list goes on. It's rubbish I'm always meaning to throw away.

The screen lights up instantly and I see I have indeed missed a call, a text *and* a voicemail.

I listen to the message, praying it's not Shaun saying he'll be out all night. But it's not from my husband at all.

'Hi, Emma, it's Joanne from the office.' My boss's clipped, efficient tone fills my ear. 'Listen, we've just had a big job come in, it's all hands on deck here. This is going to be the perfect chance to flex your new paralegal muscles.' She pauses, as if she's trying to control her excitement. 'If you can get in by six tonight, I'd be immensely grateful. Otherwise, I'll have to get one of the other paralegals in… OK, thanks.'

I immediately speed-dial Shaun three times, but each time it goes straight through to voicemail. I wonder if he's run out of battery, because he never turns his phone off – even in the cinema – in case new jobs come in. He usually just turns the ringtone to silent if he doesn't want to be disturbed.

I stare into space as my fingers rake through my hair. I feel light-headed with frustration. I swear, it will be all I can do not to go for his jugular when he finally gets home.

It's 5.35 p.m., but I still have time to get into the office on Mansfield Road by 6. It's only an eleven-minute drive from home if there are no delays. I pick up the phone again and call my mother's landline. She lives on the way into the office, on Radcliffe Road. It'll be easy to drop off Maisie and then whizz across the city if Mum is around.

The phone rings but then goes to voicemail. I leave a harried message.

'Mum? I have a bit of an emergency at work, they need me to go in urgently and Shaun is out.' I take a breath, aware that I must sound a bit manic, speaking so fast. 'I can't stress how important this is, Mum. Can you call me back right away, please?'

I also call her mobile phone. Again, it rings and I leave another message.

That's all I can do for now, and it's killing me.

CHAPTER 4

'Mum, when will tea be ready?' My daughter stands at the door, her face grim as she registers that nothing is yet being prepared. 'I'm starving and you said—'

'Yes, yes. I know what I said. Here.' I open a cupboard and throw her a packet of crisps. 'Eat these and tea will be ready in ten minutes.'

She regards me suspiciously through narrowed eyes. 'A snack *before* tea?'

'I know,' I say, ashamed of breaking one of my own healthy-eating rules. 'But I know how hungry you are and something important just came up.'

Maisie tears open the bag and pops a crisp into her mouth.

'What just came up?'

'Don't talk with your mouth full,' I say, pulling a packet of fish fingers out of the freezer. 'Something unexpected has cropped up at work and I'll have to go into the office when your dad finally decides to come home.'

'I'll be OK watching TV, you know,' she says, licking a salty finger. 'Until Dad gets back, I mean.'

I place three fish fingers on a baking tray and hesitate.

'I'm ten now, Mum. And I can call you if I need to. I'll be fine.'

I chop half a sweet potato into small wedges and drizzle over olive oil as I think it through.

Maisie is right. She's very sensible and I'm sure Shaun will be back soon. There have been a couple of instances lately when he's disappeared off doing his own thing, but to be fair, he's usually reliable. He probably won't be very long; he'll have just got held up somewhere.

Maisie waits for my decision, holding her breath. She'd love nothing more than for me to treat her as a grown-up.

You should stop worrying so much, give her a bit more space. Shaun's frequent observation rings in my ears.

'I'll see,' I say, sliding the baking tray into the oven. 'Maybe Dad will be back before I have to decide.'

'OK…' She draws the word out as she slinks off down the hallway, the resignation audible in her voice.

I stand by the sink and stare into the garden. The lawn has stopped growing now and the beech hedge at the bottom is beautiful in its fully burnished winter foliage. The garden has always been Shaun's job, but I guess under our new sharing arrangement, I'll have to show willing come spring.

I pick up my phone and call him again. It goes straight to voicemail.

I text Joanne.

Just trying to sort childcare. Should be there v soon. Emma.

I don't really know why I just did that. It's looking highly unlikely that I'm going to get cover for my daughter. Several of Maisie's friends live close by, but I'm not on a drop-in basis with any of their mums; play dates and sleepovers are always pre-planned.

Deeper friendships are made and developed at pick-up and drop-off times. I'm always rushing in and rushing out again, no time to dally or talk about the next meet-up for coffee and cake.

It would be seen as a bit rich for me to ask more of the other mums when I clearly can't give anything back myself.

So I exist on a civil, pleasant level with them that never moves beyond that.

It's suited me up until now. Three years ago, when I was desperately trying to recover from everything that happened, I naturally became more withdrawn, more insular. My social life has never properly recovered.

I glance at my watch. Please, *please*, let Shaun come home soon, I pray silently. Or let Mum at least call back.

If I leave in ten minutes, I can still get there for six, the time Joanne said she'll wait until. If I lose this job to one of the other paralegals, it will be an amazing opportunity missed. I just can't let that happen.

Waiting for Maisie's fish fingers and wedges to cook feels like forever, but in a few minutes, I'm carrying her tea into the lounge on a tray.

She's showing me her school reading book and explaining something about the story. I nod, my mind a blur and unable to actively listen.

There's been no sight or sound of Shaun or of Mum, and a glance at my watch tells me it's now my last chance to leave in time to get to the office for six.

Maisie is settled at last, eating her tea and watching television. She has her reading book and the phone nearby if she needs me. She can lock the back door behind me and keep the key in the lock in case she has to get out of the house in an emergency.

Shaun should be home any time, and anyway, I'll only be an hour or two, tops.

This is a brilliant chance for me to impress Joanne Dent and make my mark on a high-profile case, securing a glowing career that will have a positive impact on my family.

It's a no-brainer, surely… if I can only convince myself to leave my ten-year-old daughter alone in the house.

CHAPTER 5

Val

Everyone remembered their own childhood differently and it wasn't something you necessarily had control over. Val realised that.

If her own dear mother was alive today, she'd probably recall things in a way that Val herself had an entirely different recollection of.

But she worried that with her own daughter, Emmeline, it was more than that. She was prone to *imagining* things. She had this tendency to exaggerate events and hold them in her mind until needed; like a weapon to use against others.

Something to rest blame on when the mood took her.

Over the years, Val had read articles in various newspapers about how adults, after embarking on therapy, had 'recovered' memories of apparent abuse that other family members denied ever happened.

These adult children had believed in their recovered trauma so completely that some had gone on to immediately estrange themselves from their now elderly parents.

It wasn't quite that dramatic with Emmeline, thank goodness, but it still worried Val that her only daughter demonised her father in such an aggressive way. As the years marched on, it seemed to only get worse as Emmeline's 'memories' became more vivid.

It was true that Eric had not been perfect as a husband or a father. Val was the first to admit it.

He drank too much and often staggered home inebriated after yet another lock-in drinking session down the Dog and Duck, his local pub.

He had the manners of a pig at the dinner table and he'd been known to bet away bill money down at the bookies, leaving Val in a state of desperation when threats came in to cut off the electricity and water yet again.

But it had to be said that Eric was also a grafter and had been so all his life.

When he and Val first met, like most of the men in the small Nottinghamshire village, he'd worked at the nearby Bentinck pit, mining coal. They got engaged quickly, and within three years, they were married with a newborn baby daughter, christened Emmeline Rose. Unlike some men at that time, Eric had been happy they had a girl.

'I'd never wish that black hole on any of my kids,' he said, studying the dust on his knuckles, ingrained so deep it could no longer be scrubbed off. 'And I can rest assured now that our lass won't have to.'

Eric had worked his way up to the coalface by that time, and the family enjoyed the fruits of his labour. They moved from a long, narrow terraced house on an unmade road in Annesley Woodhouse, to a nice three-bedroom bungalow on Cavendish Crescent. There was a neat private garden at the rear, and the front faced onto fields and the village hall.

Val felt like the lady of the manor as she found herself the envy of her friends and family, who all still lived in houses like the one she'd just left.

Eric had turned thirty by this time, which was young for a man to reach the rank of face worker. It was the best-paid non-managerial role in the pit and required the miner to crawl in the tiniest, most claustrophobic and dusty spaces. In return, the job provided the highest salary and unlimited overtime opportunities.

Valerie, five years younger than Eric, enjoyed a certain status in her own family and amongst the local people.

As a couple, they were working hard and doing well in life. They took an annual holiday and kept a comfortable home with all mod cons, and that was what the people around them valued most in those days.

So although there were things Val might have changed given the chance, she hadn't got a lot to complain about, certainly compared to some of her friends who hadn't been so lucky in their choice of partner.

Yet to hear Emmeline talk, she'd been dragged up on a rough estate and told she'd never amount to anything.

That wasn't how Val remembered it at all. Eric had been keen on discipline and Val hadn't always approved of his methods. She also knew that she herself had been a hard taskmaster at times. But it had come from a good place; she wanted Emmeline to be the best she could be. It was a hard world out there and it had been up to them to prepare her for it.

If Eric had seemed overly critical of their daughter, it was only grounded in the belief that she had the wherewithal to make something of herself.

Therefore, when Emmeline announced she'd decided to study sociology at university, he had not been at all impressed.

'Never mind all these flaming useless ologies, it's just utter nonsense they make up these days. You should at least go for something solid, like English, or maths, or science. You're a bright lass with the world at your feet, but sign up to study a load of twaddle and you'll never make owt of yourself, my girl. Mark my words.'

Val had been there the first time he said it, had heard it all *and* the positive intention behind it.

But it seemed Emmeline had only ever retained the last eleven words and had been obsessed with trying to prove him wrong ever since.

No matter what the cost to herself and her family.

In Val's opinion, that was how her daughter had got herself into a pickle at Clayton and McCarthy. Emmeline had fostered such great hopes for her career prospects there, seeing it as a chance to prove her father wrong.

It was one thing being ambitious, but to be ruthlessly ambitious… well, that was when things could turn nasty. As they had done for Emmeline.

Despite her insistence to the contrary, Val doubted her daughter was over it at all, even now. In some twisted way, the trauma of that experience had probably contributed to the break-up of her marriage to Shaun.

Emmeline thought she'd got it sorted with this daft 'split up but stay together' arrangement, but Val wasn't at all convinced.

Such things often appeared to work well at the outset, but emotions were tricky things. They couldn't simply be dampened down and controlled at will.

Val felt sure it wouldn't be long before there were ructions.

She just hoped and prayed that nobody got hurt in the process. Specifically her beloved little Maisie.

CHAPTER 6

Maisie

She lay in bed and listened to the *tick tock tick tock* of her pink *Beauty and the Beast* clock.

She was too grown up for it now. Last week when Sandeep came over for tea after school, Maisie slipped it into her bedside drawer before her friend could spot it. When Sandeep had gone home, she took it out again, because despite her embarrassment, she wasn't ready to get rid of it yet.

The alarm on it played the theme tune to the film and was set to go off at 7.30 each morning. It was only 6.45 right now, so she had plenty of time to lie here and think.

The rhythmic ticking soothed her. It felt reliable and safe.

Things seemed to be changing at home, although Maisie couldn't say precisely how. But things were definitely happening between Mum and Dad. Bad things.

Also, Mum had been acting a bit weird.

When she picked her up from dancing last night, Maisie spoke to her twice but she didn't reply, just stared out of the window as if there were other things on her mind.

Dad had come home very late last night. Maisie had finally dropped off to sleep after tossing and turning for what seemed like hours waiting for him. When she woke in the early hours, she heard her parents arguing in their bedroom. She put the pillow over her head and hummed her favourite Ariana Grande song over and over until they'd stopped.

Before Dad got in, her mum had been moody all night, trying to do her work on her lap on the sofa because he hadn't stuck to his promise to look after Maisie.

'I'll be fine watching television if you want to go and work up in the office, Mum,' Maisie had offered.

'It's fine,' her mum said tersely. 'Your dad might be happy leaving you to your own devices, but I like to know you're safe and cared for.'

That wasn't really fair. Usually Dad never left her on her own. It was just that he'd been out quite a bit the last two days.

He had peered into her room on his way to bed, and when he saw she was awake, even though it was massively late, he'd sat on the end of her bed and told Maisie some exciting news.

'I can't say too much at the moment, but life is going to get much better soon, poppet. Then there'll be nice treats in store for you all the time.'

Maisie wondered what the treats might be and if Mum would share in them too.

Best-case scenario would definitely be that they got her a dog, although in reality, she knew that unless her mum was planning on giving up work, it wouldn't be fair to have a pet as it would be left alone for too long.

Perhaps a holiday, then. Maisie had always dreamed of going to Disney World in Florida because nobody laughed at you for loving Disney films there; even adults could get away with acting like kids.

Excitement burned briefly in her chest, until she realised what a nightmare a holiday might turn into. Being stuck in a room with her parents shooting vicious looks at each other and hissing nasty things under their breath wasn't Maisie's idea of fun.

Maybe a family holiday wasn't the best thing to wish for at the moment.

Mum seemed to get so angry lately, so angry that Maisie thought not even Disney could make it all better.

CHAPTER 7

Emma

I wake up at midnight, and that's when I hear the telltale signs: the creaking of the third and sixth stairs, the suppressed cough, the landing light shining through a crack in the door.

Shaun is finally home.

My breaths immediately become shallow. It took me ages to get to sleep earlier, the fury and frustration coursing through my veins like wind through a tunnel.

In the end I decided I couldn't leave Maisie on her own; of course I couldn't. It was never a real consideration, I was just playing with myself, letting myself believe for a few hopeful minutes that I might still be able to fulfil Joanne's request and somehow get into work.

I can't imagine how Joanne, as a single mother, pulls it off. She probably has a vast network of family members to help her out. I've never known her call in because her daughter is ill or the childminder has let her down.

I waited and waited last night, willing my phone to ring, but there was radio silence. Shaun didn't answer any of my calls or texts. There was simply no response from him at all. Likewise, I heard nothing from my mum.

Finally I was forced to text my apologies to Joanne and say I wouldn't be able to make it in after all. She didn't reply.

'Anyone would think I'm five years old or something,' Maisie said moodily when I told her I'd be staying home. 'Carla Bridges' mum leaves her on her own every Saturday night until eleven thirty and *she's* in my class.'

I push the nugget of disturbing information from my mind. That can stay on Carla Bridges' mum's conscience. I don't want it on mine.

It occurs to me that a couple of months ago, if Shaun hadn't come home or sent word that he'd be late, I'd have been out of my mind with worry. I'd have had no problem creating a dozen awful scenarios as to where he might be: there had been an accident of some sort, someone had stolen his phone, he was lying in hospital unconscious…

But since our mutual decision to split, I've somehow subconsciously erected an internal barrier that prevents me from becoming as invested in his life.

I wonder now if that barrier has provided free rein for him to look elsewhere for a relationship.

It's not myself I'm worried about if he's spending time with someone else, but Maisie. This was to be a fresh start for her and her dad to spend some quality time together.

My fingers find the edge of the quilt cover in the dark and I twist the fabric tightly until it feels like it might tear.

I guess in the end we both wanted different things. We've always been polar opposites in our ambition: his ambivalence to his career, my obsession with my own. After a while, it was just easier to carry on on our own individual paths than to forge one together.

So now I'm able to evaluate the situation logically and calmly. Although I'm still fond of him, I no longer love him. Shaun is an adult, Maisie's father. A man who has recently made a willing commitment to our new arrangement and has sadly already let me down very badly.

Earlier, I just felt annoyance and an overwhelming sense of the unfairness of it all: that he could prove to be so unreliable at the exact time a perfect, rare opportunity arose to show my potential at work.

Unreliability wasn't a side of him I'd been used to seeing, but I can't help but wonder if he has already discovered a new sense of freedom.

At least Mum eventually returned my call at 8.30.

'Hello, love, do you need me to have Maisie?' she said breathlessly without waiting for an answer. 'I've just got back home from the cinema. Kath and I went to see this lovely film. I forget the title now, but it had that northern actress in it. You know, the skinny one with the red hair who was in—'

'It's fine now, thanks, Mum,' I say quickly, intercepting one of her lengthy rants. 'I just tried you on the off chance.'

'You said it was something to do with work. Was it important?' She sounds concerned.

You bet it was. It was incredibly important to me and my career.

I say, 'It's OK, Mum, it can't be helped.'

'Couldn't Shaun have looked after—'

'He was out for the evening.'

'I see,' she says in a tone that implies she is very aware that things have changed between me and my husband but grudgingly accepts I don't want to talk about it.

After Maisie went to bed, I ran a bath but was too fidgety to lie there for very long. I took myself off to bed at ten o'clock and forced myself to read. When I realised I'd started the same page for the third time, I gave up and just lay there in the dark, crying in frustration before finally dropping off.

I didn't sleep well, the words of Joanne's voicemail circulating endlessly in my mind.

And now, Shaun creeping in at just after midnight will surely put paid to any more rest.

I cock my head to one side and listen as his socked feet pad softly along the landing. They come to a stop outside my bedroom door.

Only a few weeks ago, it was *our* bedroom, but I already feel an ownership of it. Now, it's my own private space.

Annoyingly, I see I left the door slightly ajar, and so I keep my eyes closed and my breathing regular as he nudges it open a smidgeon more and light spills into the room from the landing.

No doubt he'll be dithering over whether to wake me to apologise or to relay an elaborate excuse he's thought up while driving back to the house from wherever it is he's been all evening.

I can feel the anger and frustration hurtling around my chest again like a squash ball. My fingernails cut into my palms under the covers but I continue to feign sleep because I don't trust myself to have a reasonable, controlled conversation right now.

Besides, why should I give him the satisfaction of getting it over and done with so he can have a good night's sleep knowing he won't have to face me in the morning?

I wait until I hear the door squeak closed again, until the soft pad of his feet carries him next door and into the spare bedroom where he now sleeps.

I turn over onto my back, hearing him cough. There's a dull thud as he cracks open the window for a little air.

Only then do I sit up, swing my legs over the side and click on the bedside lamp. The wall illuminates with a soft globe of light and I stare at the faint square of lighter paint on the wall next to me.

This is the spot where our framed wedding photograph hung for eleven years. I'd chosen it for our bedroom; it had been my favourite out of hundreds that the photographer took on the day.

Me in my pearl- and crystal-encrusted white dress, clutching a simple bouquet of calla lilies. Shaun in his navy suit and crisp white shirt with a dusty-pink silk tie that matched exactly the colour of our three small bridesmaids' dresses.

The photographer had managed to catch an 'unofficial' moment where we'd gazed at each other, our faces rapt in adoration.

The photo is in the bottom of the wardrobe now. I took it down a while ago, after Shaun and I had our talk and made our difficult decision.

A sudden thud rattles me back into the here and now as the bedroom door swings open wide and hits the wall.

'I knew you were pretending to sleep,' Shaun says triumphantly, leaning on the door frame. 'I only wanted to say I'm sorry about tonight.'

'*You* woke me up coming in, actually,' I say acidly. 'It would have been better if you'd stayed out all night, wherever it is you've been.'

He sighs, walks into the room and pushes the door closed behind him as if he still sleeps in here.

I fold my arms and watch as he strides over to the window, peers through the curtains at the inky night sky beyond and then pulls them back in place again.

'I mean it, I really am sorry,' he says. 'It couldn't be helped. It was… completely unavoidable.'

Oh, this is going to be a good excuse, I can feel it. But I'm not going to ask him anything about where he's been and what could have been so important he couldn't call or text to let me know.

I'm not going to make it easier for him in any way.

'Did you think about Maisie at all tonight?' I say instead. 'Had it slipped your mind that you'd agreed to look after her… that she might be left home alone?'

He swallows. 'Is she OK? I mean, you were with her, right?'

He glances at my phone on the bedside table.

'Oh yes, I was with her. You kindly made that decision for me.'

A muscle flexes in his jaw.

'The way you said it, I thought something had happened. I know we made an agreement, but—'

'If you were a single parent you couldn't just take off and leave her alone like that.'

'Point taken, but I knew you were home and—'

'You knew I was home and that I'd change my plans and step in despite our understanding that you would care for Maisie because I had to work. You didn't give a thought about any commitments I might have, just assumed I'd do what I've always done.'

During our marriage, I've obviously done a great job of teaching Shaun that my needs are not in the least bit important. I've taught him I can be relied upon to change my plans with zero notice, despite what we might have agreed.

I like to think I'm a progressive, independent woman, but clearly I'm fooling myself. I might as well be my mother, treated like something on the bottom of my dad's shoe for all those unhappy years.

'Look, don't be like this, Em.' Shaun sighs, as if I'm testing his patience. 'Something came up and I had to go. I just had to go, OK?'

Something came up.

I wonder what her name is, I think wryly, while hoping I'm way off.

'You knew I had to listen to the webinar to prepare for my meeting tomorrow.'

'Yours is not the only work that's important, you know.' He frowns, pursing his lips. 'I've said I'm sorry. Nobody died.'

'And if somebody *had* died, you wouldn't know about it because you made sure you were completely uncontactable.'

He actually smiles then and shakes his head, looks away as if he can't believe my drama. I scrunch my toes into the carpet. I feel so angry, I want to roar at him.

I open my mouth to let rip, and he puts up his hand.

'Wait,' he says. 'Just listen.'

I watch as his whole demeanour changes. His face is animated, his body tense with excitement.

'I accept I went back on our agreement, but if truth be told, I have no regrets,' he says simply, his cheeks flushing pink.

'What?' I shake my head at him. He's not drunk, but he's acting as if he is.

He steps forward and perches on the end of the bed. *My* bed.

'It's hard to know where to start, Em,' he says softly.

If he thinks I'm going to make it easy for him, he's sadly mistaken.

'Emma, I…'

I roll my eyes. Life's too short to dither like this.

'Just say it. I promise I won't judge you. We all make mistakes.' If he's been on some kind of dating site and taken someone out for a drink, then who am I to complain? So long as it's not anything serious. It's the upheaval to Maisie I'm worried about.

'Has someone said something?'

I frown. The back of my neck prickles. 'Said something about *what*, exactly?'

He takes a moment to breathe in, and then he speaks clearly and slowly.

'Emma, I'm seeing someone and… well, it's serious.'

My heart seems to leap into my throat and I stand up. I feel light-headed.

'Since when?' I manage.

'You've gone pale, Em,' he says. 'Sit down.'

I do as I'm told.

He walks over, sits next to me on the bed. Reaches for my hand.

'I know it must be a shock, but it was only a matter of time until we both moved on with other people, right? That's why that silly arrangement of yours was so unrealistic, keeping our lives on hold like that.'

'Silly arrangement of *mine*? We both agreed it was for the best and you know it.'

I snatch my hand away, fury coursing through my veins. I knew he was up to something. I bloody well knew it.

'Exactly how long has this been going on for you to call it *serious*? Who is it?'

'It's only been the last couple of weeks. Since we split. I… I was never unfaithful to you,' he stammers. 'I didn't plan for this to happen; it was just one of those instant attractions that knocks you for six.'

'Instant attraction,' I say faintly. 'Like we always said happened to *us*.'

I feel a pang of something in the middle of my chest: sadness, regret, jealousy… I'm not sure. Maybe all three.

'What's her name?'

His face turns grey, and it scares me; he's trying to hide something.

'Who is it?' I'm shouting.

Shaun stands up and takes a few steps away from me. He turns his hands over so his palms are facing upwards in front of him, as if I should back off because nothing can be done about it.

'It's Joanne Dent,' he says.

CHAPTER 8

'Emma!' Shaun dodges the pillow I launch at him. 'For goodness' sake, calm down!'

'You sly, underhanded…' I reach for a paperback and brandish it above my head, but my hand is shaking too much to throw it.

'Look, I didn't see the harm, OK?' He holds his hands up in the air to ward me off. 'The *Post* sent me to photograph some legal lunch and we just clicked. I'd seen her before at the dance school and… Well, at first it was just a chat and a coffee, and then…'

'And then what?'

'And then things moved really fast. Both of us were shocked. I felt out of control.'

I let out a bitter laugh. 'But not out of control enough that you'd just slow down and think about the consequences of you shagging my boss, is that right?'

'Emma! It wasn't like that. I'm truly sorry. I… I can't really explain it.'

I feel… *violated*. A strong word, perhaps inappropriate, but that is honestly the feeling that floods through me before other emotions swiftly follow.

'You do know Joanne's daughter is the exact same age as Maisie? What are the other dance mums going to say?'

'I don't care about them.' He is suddenly sure of himself, a quality he had when I met him but that's been missing for a long time. 'Surely it's a good thing that Maisie and Piper already know each other? There's more chance of them getting along.'

'Piper Dent is a spoiled little brat, and for your information, Maisie can't stand her.' I spit out the words like bitter pips. I don't care that I sound churlish, and that adults aren't supposed to speak that way about kids. It's true.

Shaun shakes his head slowly, as if there's no hope for me.

I take a breath and speak very slowly.

'Your selfishness could cost me my career, you do realise that? What woman wants the ex-wife of her new boyfriend hanging around the office? She'll fire me, employment law or not. They can always find a reason if they want to.'

'No! She thinks a lot of you, thinks you're very capable.'

'You've discussed *me*?' I snarl. 'Now that really is pillow talk at its worst.'

'It wasn't like that, Em. She said you've already told her we're not together as such.'

'Whatever.' I fold my arms and stare at the blank wall, rueing the day I confided in Joanne Dent. 'I have to get some sleep so I can try and squeeze some work in tomorrow morning. I was too busy making sodding fish fingers for tea, you see, so our daughter didn't go hungry. Just go. Please.'

He stands up, runs his fingers through his hair and shakes his head. Behind the bravado he looks dishevelled, his skin already shadowed with faint stubble. But he is still lit from within by a glow that, to my fury, my vitriol cannot dim.

'I want to be on my own,' I say before he tries to talk further.

A few minutes later, he's in the spare room. The door closes behind him and I hear the light switch click off on the other side of the wall.

Finally I let out the breath I've been holding onto like a safety blanket.

Joanne Dent. *Joanne Dent!*

Of all the women he could have chosen to start a relationship with, it had to be my boss. Just when my career is finally taking off after all those hours of studying, of making sacrifices and slow, steady progress. This happens.

A month ago, I remember loitering at the kitchen window, washing and drying a few glasses just so I had a reason to stand and watch as Shaun chased Maisie around the garden.

It was such a joy to witness the wild abandon of our daughter, squealing, half choking with laughter as her dad mimed clumsy ape-like moves, purposely moving slowly so that Maisie could escape each time he drew near.

Just a few weeks before that, Shaun seemed to have his head constantly in a photography book, spending hours each evening perusing online photo libraries, researching the best place to bank his own photographs to maximise the pittance he received each time one was used.

The most Maisie could hope for was for him to sit next to her, still engrossed in his own activities but pretending to watch *The Simpsons* with her. Maisie wasn't a massive fan of *The Simpsons*, but I noticed with an aching heart that she would put it on to tempt her dad to spend a bit of time with her, as she knew it was one of his favourites.

I was never in any doubt that Shaun loved Maisie with all his heart, of course he did. But his interest in photography always seemed to shout loudest and overtook his time with her.

I understood how being consumed by work felt, but as I had always been the parent who stayed home each night with Maisie, I had to curtail my time spent studying and working.

Our new arrangement had changed all that. It had given me more time for myself, and at the same time had gifted Shaun and Maisie the time to get to know each other again. And the real joy of it was that both of them had wholeheartedly embraced the chance to do so.

That's why in my moments of doubt, when I questioned the unconventional nature of our home life, I still had the unswerving conviction that our decision had been the best thing for all three of us.

That day, when I'd wiped the last glass and set it on the shelf behind me, I stood a moment longer, smiling as Shaun finally captured Maisie in a bear hug after deliberately wrong-footing her near the trampoline.

I watched as they laughed together, hugged, stood still to get their breath back.

As Maisie buried her head in Shaun's chest, I saw his face change. The smile melted away and an expression of pain took its place.

Now, I would admit that the arrangement to call time on our marriage was initially my idea but Shaun had readily agreed back then. He agreed with everything I suggested.

If it was what he wanted then, how could he do this? His actions will have consequences for all of us.

That day, when I'd watched my husband and daughter for a while out of the window, I'd forced myself to turn away, swallowed down the sour taste in my mouth.

Little did I know it was a portent of far worse to come.

CHAPTER 9

Joanne

If she had only realised exactly who the rugged, slightly nervous photographer was, Joanne would have approached the entire situation differently.

But she hadn't known. Not two weeks ago, anyway.

She shuffled paperwork around on her desk, just reorganising it, not actually processing any of it. She hated feeling distracted like this when there was so much work to get through.

She had been a full partner at Walker, Dent and Scott now for four years, and the time had flown by. It had always seemed to be the case that either very little happened in her life or, without warning, major events sprang up in super-quick time.

That was how it had been when she met the photographer, as it still amused her to call him.

She had no reason to complain about anything, told herself every day that life was good. She was now secure financially and Piper was growing up into a clever, gregarious young person whom Joanne felt proud to parent.

On top of this, she truly loved her work and, without wanting to sound boastful, knew she was damn good at it. Her rapid rise in the legal profession was testament to this.

She had built a first-rate team around her at Walker, Dent and Scott. The support team of paralegals and administrative staff served all three partners, but in reality, they all had their preferred staff.

Roy and Dan, the other two partners, often worked with men but Joanne, understanding that the glass ceiling really did exist in the legal world, found satisfaction in giving other talented females a chance to shine where she could.

As a result, she got to know some of her staff better than others, particularly the women. She had her own private office on the second floor but tried to move around the building as much as she could, not least because her personal trainer told her to do something active for at least five minutes of each hour for the sake of her thighs, if not her workload.

So she often heard the staff talking about their personal lives. It was hard not to take bits in as she walked around the office. Some of them seemed to do nothing but gossip all day long, but she tried not to get dragged down into disciplining staff like a schoolteacher. Anya was both the office manager and the partners' PA and that was her job.

Also, there was an unwritten policy that directed that the three partners should endeavour to separate themselves from everyday office affairs.

One of the functions of Anya's role was to relay any rumblings of discontent or personal problems the staff were experiencing so the partners didn't personally get drawn in but could be made aware.

Anya also liked a little gossip now and then when she brought Joanne's coffee through.

Joanne was vaguely aware that the newly qualified paralegal, Emma Barton, had a husband and a little girl, Maisie, who was around the same age as her own daughter. The girls attended the same dance school in town, in one of Joanne's own buildings, in fact. They often nodded to each other at drop-off or pick-up, but that was about it.

There were far more experienced paralegals in the team, but Joanne hadn't forgotten how Emma had Opened her heart in a recent professional development interview. She'd mentioned her marriage problems and admitted she was driven to because, growing up, her father had constantly told her she'd never make anything of herself.

That need to prove her worth had resonated with Joanne on a very deep level. It had been one of the many things she'd tried hard to bury years ago. Suffice to say, some things just didn't want to stay hidden, and that was a problem, because hers was a childhood she'd rather forget.

Unlike some other local legal outfits, Walker, Dent and Scott were not the kind of firm who threw glitzy parties that ended up in the 'Who's Who' pages of the glossy *Nottinghamshire Aspect* magazine. The most they did was take the staff out for a quiet lunch each year, usually at Hart's restaurant, a week before Christmas.

So although she knew he existed, Joanne had never met Emma's husband, Shaun.

This year, Walker, Dent and Scott had the honour of being chosen to host the annual legal conference for the East Midlands region. Roy and Dan had asked Joanne if she fancied organising the event, and she'd readily agreed. It was just her cup of tea.

She booked out the ballroom at nearby Colwick Hall. Once the ancestral home of Lord Byron, it was an ornate and impressive building set in extensive grounds on the River Trent. Joanne felt sure the legal eagles from surrounding towns and cities couldn't fail to be impressed by the hand-painted ceiling and majestic pillars. It was the perfect venue to cement Walker, Dent and Scott as the premier legal practice in Nottinghamshire.

She'd organised canapés and champagne for arriving guests and a four-course lunch served at white-linen-dressed round tables for ten.

Just as one speech was coming to an end, she'd spotted a couple of flashes from the back of the room. She'd slipped from her table and stalked over to the man in dark clothing clutching a fearsome-looking long-lens camera.

'Who are you and who do you work for?' she'd demanded in clipped tones, fearing he had been sent by a rival law firm intent on stealing her ideas.

'My name is Shaun Barton and I'm freelance.' He raised the palm of his free hand in the air, the width of his shoulders and muscular biceps not lost on Joanne.

She was trying to act fearsome, but there was something about this tall man, with his rugged good looks, his slightly arrogant stance but shy manner, that completely disarmed her.

'The *Post* asked me to come along to get a few shots for the *Nottinghamshire Aspect* magazine. Apparently someone asked if they could cover the event.'

'Oh!' Joanne felt the creases slide from her brow, and she smiled widely at him. 'In that case, carry on, thank you.'

She turned to walk away and then hesitated, two glasses of champagne lending her a little more sauce than usual. 'If you fancy a glass of champagne and a bite to eat, my table is over there.' She pointed with an oval nude fingernail. 'We had a no-show.'

Ten minutes later, Shaun Barton slid into the seat beside her, and he stayed there until the end of the afternoon.

The man was a tangle of interesting contradictions that, to Joanne's equal delight and annoyance, got her heart racing a little faster. It was a long time since she'd felt that.

Much later, back home and sitting on her balcony with a blanket wrapped around her shoulders, she poured herself a well-earned glass of Rioja. She had a warm glow of satisfaction in her chest, signifying a job well done and the fact that she had Shaun Barton's business card in her handbag.

*

The next morning, she drove to work, unusually pumped up with anticipation for the day ahead.

She smiled to herself mischievously, recalling Shaun's mesmerising blue-green eyes and forceful square jawline. They'd been unable to focus solely on each other as there was important networking to be done, especially for Joanne, as the event host. Still, they'd managed to engage in a little small talk and enjoy the invisible electricity that crackled between them.

The journey into work was swift, as she'd left the house earlier than usual, thanking her lucky stars that Piper was on a youth hostel trip in Derbyshire with school for the week. For once, events seemed to have conspired to help her, rather than hinder her.

She parked the car in the otherwise empty staff bays and stopped halfway across the car park to fish the office keys out of her handbag.

When she looked up, she saw Shaun Barton standing by the office door. He looked even taller and broader than she remembered. Her heart thundered in her chest and her mouth felt dry.

'Could you spare me a few minutes?' he said cautiously as she drew closer. 'I've come to apologise.'

CHAPTER 10

Joanne was aware that people often took her confident manner – sometimes bordering on bolshie – the wrong way. What they didn't realise was that it was merely a tool to conceal a multitude of deeply personal fears and anxieties.

She had been a meek child, overshadowed by Carmel, her older, borderline genius sister. Carmel had been the apple of her parents' eyes, and despite her best efforts, Joanne never really had a chance of getting anywhere close to her sister's academic achievements.

But Joanne was a bright girl, and she had a real knack for understanding very quickly exactly what made people tick.

At school, she realised that nobody ever noticed a wallflower. The shy, introverted children were left to wilt on the sidelines, whilst the more extrovert personalities stepped into the spotlight – and the teachers' favour – far more quickly.

She found it easy to assume these beneficial attributes, even though most of the time she battled with low self-esteem and anxiety. She could turn her appropriated personality on and off like a light bulb, and regularly did so to great benefit.

In later life, these qualities and ability combined to make her an astute and effective lawyer, able to build rapport with people from very different walks of life. So much so that she'd often wondered if her real calling should have been to become an actress.

Particularly at times like this, when her knees had turned to jelly and her guts to liquid.

She eyed Shaun coolly, took a breath in and swept past her visitor and up to the building, oozing confidence. In reality, her hand shook as she tried to get the key in the door, and every few beats, her heart bounced out of rhythm inside her chest.

Once inside, she asked him to take a seat while she made some coffee. She wouldn't usually offer refreshments to an unannounced visitor, but she badly needed some caffeine to try and kick this dreamy feeling of hovering above herself, as if she were watching a stranger.

She pointed out the comfy seats in the reception. He didn't move over to them right away, so she inched back past him, squashing against the mammoth curve of the reception desk, forcing her close enough to smell his lemony scent and see the shower-damp ends of his hair that curled into his strong, lean neck.

She filled the kettle and spooned coffee into two cups in the small kitchenette. She could hear him whistling and it made her smile.

He was so different to the men she worked with. Like her, they were probably operating with false images too. Suited and booted and using convoluted language to meet the clients' expectations of what a good lawyer should look and act like.

It was refreshing to meet a man who wasn't afraid to simply be himself, and act naturally in what for some would be quite an intimidating situation.

She found herself glancing in the small mirror on the wall behind the door, fingers flicking through her expensively high-lighted blonde wedge to inject a bit more volume.

She stared at the glass, blotting her lips together, wishing she'd used the more flattering peach shade instead of the plain nude gloss this morning. At least she'd worn her new Armani trouser suit, sharply cut to show off her slim figure at its best.

Get a grip! she hissed silently to herself as she moved back to the counter top.

This was exactly how it had started last time. Six years ago and yet it felt like a lifetime.

She recognised the power of the chemical attraction that manifested itself as a physical, magnetic pull between them.

The thought of how it had all ended before sent a shudder through her bones, and she closed her eyes against it. She'd worked so hard, rebuilt everything around herself, and there was Piper to think about... No. She couldn't allow their faces to shadow her thoughts for even a second.

But the past was in the past and it faded a little with each and every day. That was all that mattered.

She forced her mind to focus on the job in hand, sloshing a little milk into each cup before carrying the drinks through to reception.

Glancing at the wall clock, she noted it would be at least another twenty minutes before the other staff started to arrive for work. She felt relieved. The other partners would recognise him from yesterday's event and she didn't want to raise any eyebrows.

'Thanks for giving me a chance to explain,' Shaun said as she handed him a coffee.

Joanne sat down opposite him, purposely perching on the end of a cushion to show her long legs to their best advantage. She was curious as to what he wanted to apologise about.

He took a sip of his coffee and set it down on the low table next to a neat stack of magazines. Then he laced his fingers together and seemed to pause in thought for a few moments, before meeting her enquiring stare.

When he spoke, his voice sounded level and considered.

'I wanted to make something perfectly clear to you. My wife is Emma Barton. She works as a paralegal here at Walker, Dent and Scott.'

'Emma?' Joanne said faintly, as the connection registered. 'Oh... I see.'

She felt instantly deflated, her chest swelling with huge and unexpected disappointment. Although they hadn't had much time to chat last night, it should have been one of the first things he'd told her.

Shaun cleared his throat and looked away.

'I say "my wife", but we're not really together any more. It's... complicated.'

'It sounds it.' Joanne put down her own drink, not trusting her slightly shaking hand to keep it from spilling over her new trousers. 'But no harm done, I suppose. Strange you didn't mention it, though.'

'I don't know why I didn't,' he faltered. 'It must've had something to do with the chemistry between us.'

Joanne raised an eyebrow.

'I know you know what I'm talking about, but I was out of order. That's why I came in early to see you, to apologise. I didn't mean to mislead you in any way.'

'I see.'

A smile spread over his generous mouth.

'I wondered if you'd let me buy you a coffee after work. You know, to apologise properly.'

'Thank you, but I couldn't possibly accept. You're married to one of my staff.'

'It's just a coffee, and I told you, we're not tog—'

'Even so. I'm sure you understand it violates certain ethical boundaries for me.'

There was an awkward silence. Both of them could feel the electricity between them. Both of them knew not to mention it.

Eventually finding common ground in chatting about the warm weather that was predicted for the rest of the week, Shaun finished his coffee and left the building.

He turned back at the door.

'You have my card,' he said softly. 'If you change your mind about the coffee, that is.'

She nodded. 'Bye, Shaun.'

For a few minutes, Joanne sat alone in the pleasant space. The light flooded in through the Velux windows above her head and bounced off the waxy dark green leaves of the potted palms in the corner.

Shaun leaving like that was like the warm glow of the sun on her face suddenly fading.

But it was time to pull herself together. There was work to do.

She stood up and dusted herself down, berating herself for being so ridiculous. She would push this annoying photographer from her mind, and in a day or two, with any luck, she would forget he ever existed.

CHAPTER 11

Twenty-four years earlier

You've been locked in your room for a long time now.

There is no clock in here any more so you're not entirely sure how long you have been upstairs. But the light has faded outside and you know that soon it will be completely dark.

You can stand the hunger pains, the thirst and the boredom, but you hate the dark more than anything.

They removed the bulb ages ago as part of the punishments, and the shadeless pendulum hangs uselessly from the ceiling, reminding you of a hangman's noose. Sometimes, when you lie on your bed and stare at it, it seems to sway slightly, as if something unseen is moving it.

'Please, God, please help me.' You hug your knees closer to your chest. 'Please let me know you're here, God.'

You imagine a bright white light above your head, like you once saw in a photograph of the Virgin Mary. And for a few minutes, you feel a little better. Until the light fades a bit more and your heart begins to pound.

'I promise, if you keep me safe, I'll not steal any more biscuits from the jar,' you whisper into the shadows.

You always promise God things when you need Him the most, but once your punishment is over, you nearly always forget to follow through.

That's just the kind of person you are.

You really hope that God hasn't noticed, because you need Him now. You need Him more than ever.

CHAPTER 12

Emma

I arrive in the staff car park ten minutes earlier than usual and inspect my puffy eyes in the rear-view mirror.

I resorted to a darker eyeliner this morning in an attempt to define them, and also used some sparkling eye drops, but there's no escaping the bleariness.

I usually wash and style my hair every day; it's a thin and lifeless mess otherwise. This morning, though, I just couldn't face the palaver. Instead, I've scraped it back into a low ponytail at the nape of my neck and pinned back the wispy side bits with a couple of Maisie's glitter hair grips. Perks of being mum to a fashion-conscious pre-teen, I suppose.

Since qualifying as a paralegal, I've made a real effort to sharpen up my image, ditching the comfy skirts and trousers paired with tunic tops in favour of shift dresses with matching jackets and a couple of serviceable trouser suits in black and navy that I can brighten up with a silky blouse and heels.

Today, a far more casual outfit of baggy black trousers, flat pumps and an ill-fitting floral top has made a comeback. Damn Joanne Dent and her perfect image and perfect career. Overnight, the stuff I admired her for has started taunting me. I just don't know what the two of them are thinking, getting involved on a romantic level. It's messy. Very messy.

I heard Shaun leave the house at six this morning. I fought the urge to jump out of bed and scream out of the window at him.

This wouldn't be usual behaviour from me, but everyone has their limits and he's managed to push me well beyond mine.

It's my job to take Maisie to school for her breakfast club, leaving me plenty of time to get to the office for my start time of 8.30. I had thought Shaun might offer to take her in today, as a sort of peace offering. But no. He'd had no problem at all in getting himself out of the house and away from my planned scorn at breakfast. It was like he'd suddenly grown a pair overnight.

Then, unexpectedly, in he waltzed again at 7.40, just in time to take her.

'Get your bag, princess. I'll whizz you to school.'

'Yesss!' Maisie was delighted. She much prefers Shaun's roomy car and the fact that he's willing to play her favourite playlist at full volume all the way there, with no interrogation about last night's homework.

I've parked up at the far end of Walker, Dent and Scott's neatly marked-out staff bays, facing the hawthorn hedge that acts as a barrier to the pavement running alongside. The leaves look cool and green against the backdrop of a cloudy sky; it seems so simple and uncomplicated, compared to the difficult situation that awaits me inside the building. Like it or not, I'm going to have to face Joanne at some point today.

I close my eyes and allow myself a couple of deep, calming breaths before grabbing my handbag and walking across the car park as confidently as I can manage.

Joanne's office overlooks the car park. She might well be looking out of the window at this very second. Just the thought of it has the fury sticking in my throat like crushed nut shells.

I swallow it down. I can't afford to let this affect my career, and although it's a complication I didn't want or envisage, Shaun is effectively a free agent.

Damn him for rushing into it, though, after agreeing that a stable home life was of paramount importance to our daughter.

My chest feels tight and my legs seem a bit shaky as I move quickly towards the building.

I don't know if Joanne knows I know yet.

Working out how I'm going to play it is sending my anxiety levels sky high. It shouldn't be me that's on the back foot here. I've done nothing wrong.

As I approach the rear entrance, I glance up at Joanne's office window again, but it's shaded by a white slatted blind. Inside the cool building I pass the small communal kitchen on the right and climb the stairs to the first floor, pausing to stow my handbag in my locker.

This floor houses the admin staff, paralegals and the two trainee solicitors. The second floor belongs to the practising solicitors and the three partners, including Joanne's own smart glass office.

I'm not the only one who's in early today. Three or four people are already at their desks, looking busy, but I don't miss the lightning-fast look that two of the other paralegals shoot each other before smiling too widely at me.

When I turn on my monitor and log in, everyone seems very busy and yet there's this kind of crackle in the air. As if I'm the last person to learn what's happening between my husband and Joanne. I don't know, maybe I'm imagining it.

While my emails are loading up, I open up the webinar and put in my earphones. Maybe if I can scan the legal updates, I can somehow blag my way through the meeting. Joanne is razor sharp, so she'll know instantly that I haven't done the required legwork, but I'd do well to remember that the reason I didn't sleep well last night was because of her.

An internal message box flashes up on my screen.

To: Emma Barton
From: Joanne Dent
Emma, can you pop up soon as you get here pls.

I feel eyes burning into my back, and sure enough, when I turn quickly to glance around, everyone hurriedly looks back at their paperwork.

They know. They all know, I'm certain of it.

It feels like my skin is on fire. I push my chair back and stand up quickly, somehow knocking over the glass of water on my desk.

I stride over to the filing cabinet closest to me, snatch up the box of tissues next to a dusty pot plant and mop up the water as best I can. Fortunately it hasn't touched the keyboard.

After binning the soggy tissues, I send my monitor to sleep and head out of the office and up the stairs to the second floor.

If I turn around now, I know they'll all be staring open-mouthed, so I don't. I don't turn around; I just put one heavy foot in front of the other and propel myself closer and closer to Joanne Dent's office.

CHAPTER 13

'Come in.' Joanne's clear voice rings out when I tap on her office door.

I step inside. She is bent over a document, marking it with vicious scrawls and lines. She doesn't look up immediately.

Thunder roars in my head. The woman in front of me has deceived me, but she's also my boss. Fury battles respect and respect wins through.

'Morning, Joanne, you wanted to see me.' I'm striving for a confident tone, but I'm painfully aware I miss the mark by a long way.

There is silence apart from the sound of her pen slashing through words on the page and the hum of the air-conditioning unit from its position above the door.

The room is cool, bordering on chilly, but Joanne has shed her smart jacket and is wearing a thin, silky blouse with sleeves that end on her slender, lightly tanned forearms.

'There. That should do it.' She lays down her pen and indicates one of the chairs opposite her desk. 'Please. Sit down, Emma.'

I sit down and clasp my fingers together in front of me.

She looks at me. She's giving nothing away.

'I had a discussion with Shaun last night,' I say. 'He told me about the two of you.'

'I see.' There is a strange expression on her face, but no trace of regret.

'It's your business, of course. Shaun and I, we're not together any more. I think I mentioned that in one of our one-to-one meetings.' Her eyes widen slightly, as if she's surprised at my candour. 'We have agreed to physically stay together in the house for the time being, for Maisie's sake, but we've called time on our marriage. We've grown apart, you see.'

My words falter. I can feel my cheeks burning and I am suddenly annoyed that I'm helping to justify the two of them together. It should be her who is trying to placate *me*.

But Joanne doesn't offer me any platitudes or sympathetic noises. She just sits there, detached. Cold.

A sense of unfairness oozes into my chest. This is all Shaun's fault.

'I'd rather we get things in the open,' I offer. 'I don't want it to affect my working here.'

'If it makes it any easier, neither of us expected this to happen. It's not ideal, granted. But Shaun and my relationship has nothing to do with your job, Emma. The two things are completely separate.'

Are they, though? She is in a position of power at work. She could make life very difficult for me if she chose to.

I don't know what to say. Do I smile and act as if everything is OK, even though I'm personally furious at them both? Or do I tell her how I really feel?

She picks up her pen again and twiddles it in her fingers, looking thoughtful.

'I have to say, it's very bad timing.' I can't stop myself. 'Our marriage is over, but my concern is Maisie. Shaun agreed that stability at home was key in making sure she didn't suffer, and then I find out he's been… seeing you.'

'Obviously it's difficult for me to comment on that.' Joanne sighs and puts down her pen again.

'Of course, but you must see he's put me in an impossible position. We'd agreed a new arrangement, the criteria being that we do what is best for Maisie. But now I don't see how our amicable relations, our arrangement, can continue.'

I clamp my mouth shut. Despite working quite closely with Joanne for the past couple of months since I qualified, I don't really know anything about her personal life apart from that she has a daughter.

'I hope you don't mind me asking if a little bit of you hoped you two would eventually call a truce, give it another go?'

I'm taken aback by her forthright manner, but it's obvious she feels relaxed enough to be frank with me, and I choose to take that as a good sign.

If their relationship is as serious as it sounds, I need to keep on civil terms with them both for Maisie's sake.

'Not at all,' I say quickly, and I mean it. 'I wish him well in his life, but my daughter and my career are my priorities now.'

She gives me a genuinely relieved smile.

'I appreciate you coming to speak to me this morning, Emma. I admit it's not an ideal situation, but you can't always choose who you fall in love with.'

Fall in love? As far as I'm aware, they've only been seeing each other a couple of weeks!

'You seem very serious about each other, given that it's such early days.'

'I know.' She gives me a coquettish grin. 'Neither of us expected it to happen so quickly, but rest assured, the girls are our priority. We will tread carefully, but it's great they already know each other through dancing.'

'Yes.' My fingernails drive into my palms.

This is so weird. I just want to get out of her office.

'Let's agree now to put personal matters behind us in terms of the job.' She leans back in her sumptuous cream leather padded chair.

'Agreed.' My shoulders drop an inch.

'The reason I asked you to pop up here is that I have a couple of new cases beginning next week. If you'd like the experience and you've got a few hours spare, then I'm happy to bring you on board with them.'

'Yes! I mean thanks, Joanne. That would be amazing.' My cheeks flush a little when I realise I never gave her chance to say why she'd asked me up here in the first place. I'd simply assumed it was about Shaun.

I've never considered that anything remotely positive could come from this. She certainly didn't have to offer me the work; usually the more experienced paralegals get the interesting stuff.

Maybe our complicated personal situation can work after all.

She pulls a stack of folders towards her. 'OK, good. So, I want you to start by sifting through this lot, summaries of other similar cases from the national database. See if you can pick up any useful consistencies in terms of the circumstance and relevant outcomes.'

It's the kind of job that would usually put me to sleep, but on this occasion, it makes me sit up in anticipation.

'You'll be working closely with me on this, and happily, as we've had a higher rate of new case enquiries since I've worked on raising our company profile, it's possible you're going to be in at the deep end work-wise.'

'Music to my ears.' Maisie's face flits into my mind as I realise I'll need Shaun's support more than ever.

'It won't be a problem?' Joanne says hesitantly. 'Doing more hours… with your current personal circumstances, I mean?'

'Not at all,' I hear myself say. 'Whatever it takes. I've got my mum and friends to call on any time I need help with Maisie.'

Friends? If only that were true.

I've never a huge friendship group, but prior to starting my paralegal qualification, I had two or three good friends I saw regularly.

With the pressures of work, studies and my failing marriage, they stopped asking to meet up after my repeated rejections, and just sort of faded away.

I'm starting to realise that's what happens to relationships. If you forget to work on them, before you know it, they end up tailing off.

The twist is, my relationships with both Joanne and Shaun are key to my life. They both have a massive influence and I can't afford to get on the wrong side of either of them.

In other words, I'm between a rock and a hard place and I have no choice but to make the best of the situation.

CHAPTER 14

Back downstairs, a cluster of paralegals sit, apparently discussing paperwork, around one desk. As soon as I appear in the doorway, they stop talking and look up expectantly.

I paste a self-satisfied look on my face and make a big deal of plonking the armful of files Joanne gave me down on my desk.

'No rest for the wicked, eh?' I say, grinning over at them.

It was obviously my overactive imagination, thinking that everyone knew about Joanne and Shaun's relationship. There's no way they could know.

I busy myself clicking through emails, waiting for my heart rate to settle down. I can't help feeling relieved that I've cleared the air with Joanne; regardless of my opinion on what's happened, it wouldn't do to get on the wrong side of her.

Last year, her PA of eleven years, Penny, failed to put an important regional meeting of legal professionals in her diary, resulting in Joanne being mortally embarrassed when the head of the SRA, the Solicitors Regulation Authority, called her personally to express his disappointment in her no-show.

The next day, Penny announced, very reluctantly, her decision to take early retirement from the company, and a week later, Anya was appointed.

So I consider myself lucky she's held out the olive branch in terms of the job.

My phone lights up and I see it's a text message from Shaun. *Hope everything OK at work. Can we talk tomorrow?*

Joanne has confirmed my workload is going to be heavy with the addition of the new cases. Why should I let Shaun off the hook by asking him to move out? He can pull more than his weight to make up for what he's done.

After ten minutes or so, I pick up my phone and text a reply. *Yes. We definitely need to talk.*

And we will talk. Not about what *he* thinks, though.

CHAPTER 15

Joanne

It had been a long time since Joanne had felt a force of attraction as strong as she'd felt with Shaun Barton. She thought those days were behind her.

But instead of feeling uncomfortable, she found herself welcoming the excitement, despite the awkwardness of the situation when it came to seeing Emma each day at the office.

After Shaun had appeared at work a couple of weeks ago, she'd initially ruled out meeting him for coffee. Even though her heart was saying otherwise, her head took control and she'd baulked at the fact that he was married to one of her employees. It was simply too complicated.

But then, when Emma had been so frank about her personal life, she'd inadvertently confirmed to Joanne that Shaun had indeed told her the truth.

Joanne had known then that she *would* contact him.

It was now late morning. The hours had whizzed by in very positive and exciting meetings with the other two partners, in which they'd discussed the encouraging trend in new business enquiries. Thanks to raising the company profile in various ways, including hosting the recent East Mids legal conference, the Walker, Dent and Scott name was fast becoming synonymous

with quality, good-value legal advice and support, and winning
the last few cases had enhanced their reputation.

Although Joanne had contributed enthusiastically to the meetings that day, she wasn't able to give the other partners her complete
and undivided attention. An undercurrent of excitement flowed
through the afternoon, filling her with a delicious anticipation
she hadn't felt for years.

Just thinking about Shaun's strong, wide shoulders and his fresh,
citrusy smell made the entire surface of her skin buzz. Back in her
own office now, she pulled a pile of documents towards her and
picked up her silver Montblanc pen, trying to push thoughts of
him from her mind. Sadly, it seemed she was too late: her focus
on the mountain of paperwork she had to read through and sign
during the morning was now non-existent.

She sipped the coffee Anya had just placed on her desk and
allowed herself the luxury of thinking back to the morning she'd
decided she would meet Shaun after all.

She'd opened the slim top drawer of her desk and retrieved his
business card, tapping his mobile number into her phone.

'Shaun Barton.'

His voice sounded deep and smooth when he answered the call,
and her heartbeat seemed to relocate into her throat.

She opened her mouth to speak and found that her usual stoic,
professional telephone manner had simply evaporated. Instead,
she found herself stammering like a nervous schoolgirl.

'Hi… it's Joanne Dent. I… I'm ringing to say if your offer of
coffee is still open, then… well, I'd love to.'

'Fantastic,' Shaun chuckled, as if he'd expected her to call back
all along. 'Can we make it today? After work?'

He named a time and suggested Roast, a trendy local coffee bar
that specialised in fair-trade South American beans. She'd been
wanting to try the coffee there for ages.

She paused to gather herself.

'Sounds perfect,' she replied coolly, secretly delighted he wanted to meet so soon. 'I look forward to it.'

She'd left the office an hour early, telling Anya that the wisdom tooth she'd had so much trouble with last year was grumbling again.

'I've managed to get a cancellation at the dentist. Can you cancel my four o'clock appointment?'

She silently thanked her lucky stars Piper was still away on her school trip.

She didn't make a habit of letting clients down at short notice, but she wouldn't be able to concentrate if she stayed. Besides, she wanted to freshen up at home. She couldn't change her clothes – Shaun had seen her already that morning, and it wouldn't do for her to look as though she had changed specifically to impress him – but she could certainly spruce up her hair and refresh her minimal make-up; she never brought much with her to work in that regard.

She darted out of the building before one of the other partners thought of something vital for her to look at before she left.

The journey was blissfully quiet in the middle of the afternoon compared to her usual rush-hour battle at the end of the day.

Home was a two-bedroom flat in a leafy village, usually around a twenty-minute drive from the Walker, Dent and Scott offices in the city centre. Today, courtesy of leaving so early, she managed to do it easily in ten.

She aimed a remote fob as she drew close, and the electric gates opened, allowing her to smoothly turn her Mercedes SLK onto the long, tree-lined driveway that led up to Linby House.

At the top of the driveway, the wide tyres of the sports car crunched on gravel as she parked in her reserved spot next to the fountain.

She grabbed her handbag as she got out of the car, marvelling at how unencumbered she felt without armfuls of case files to lug upstairs. She was reminded that there was once a time when she had had more in her life than simply work. There it was again: the past she was trying hard to bury.

As she approached the red-brick building, she admired the domed turret and decorative brickwork of the Victorian house.

She had bought the penthouse apartment two and a half years ago. Penthouse was probably a bit too grand a word, but it was true enough that the flat did take up the whole of the top floor of the house, and she enjoyed the use of a larger balcony than the other five flats on the lower floors, which afforded her lovely views of the surrounding fields and woodland.

When she and Piper first moved here, Joanne had envisaged the two of them enjoying relaxed barbecues on the covered balcony during finer weather. It hadn't quite turned out like that.

Piper got bored easily with no television or computer to keep her attention. She took to wolfing down her food and swiftly disappearing back inside, leaving Joanne feeling all too aware she had no special someone to share her life with any more.

However many magazine articles she read extolling the benefits of being single and living alone, it didn't make sitting on your own watching the sunset with a glass of wine any less lonely.

She and Piper were close, of course they were. But Joanne was painfully aware that the child could not – and should not be expected to – fill the aching gap inside her.

Five years ago, she had made a pact with herself that she wouldn't begin a new romantic relationship for at least ten years.

The ten years bit hadn't been a period of time plucked out of thin air. Joanne had taken time to consider all eventualities and had consequently calculated it carefully.

Five years was enough time for things to still feel real and raw. She frequently awoke with a racing heart and skin clammy enough to dampen the sheet beneath her.

Five years was still a relatively short length of time for someone determined enough to dig around in her past and find a wealth of information.

Conversely, ten years seemed like a lifetime away; long enough for memories to fade, a good enough chunk of time for people to move away and forget the sharp detail of what had happened back then. Ten years was long enough to build a successful career, meaning she and her daughter would be financially secure.

Best of all, thanks to the ruling of the Court of Justice of the European Union in 2014, everyone had the right to be forgotten online. Joanne had taken full advantage of this development and was still working to effectively erase any mention of what had happened.

It was a work in progress, but she had every confidence her ten-year plan would soon be completed satisfactorily.

It was a small price to pay to finally feel free. A small price to stop anyone who might be out to dig up dirt.

CHAPTER 16

Later that afternoon, she'd parked her sports car in a spot just about a five-minute walk away from the coffee shop.

Glancing at her watch and seeing there was still ten minutes to go before her agreed meeting time with Shaun, she turned off the engine and pressed back against the headrest.

All things considered, she wasn't entirely sure why she'd agreed to meet him. The signs were already there – in the buzz that zipped through her veins like lightning, in the way her logical thoughts and confident manner were disrupted – that this guy was something special.

Joanne was only too aware she'd stepped inside the danger zone she'd promised herself she'd keep away from. The question was, could she indulge in a little dalliance and be strong enough to keep him at arm's length? She was still a couple of years off the end of her ten-year no-relationship period, and she knew she'd do well to keep this at the forefront of her mind.

She checked her handbag, satisfied her phone was in there.

It's not too late to cancel, the cautionary voice in her head whispered, but she swiftly pushed it away.

She was entitled to a little fun, wasn't she? And that was all this needed to be.

This feeling... this attraction, it was powerful. It was nice to feel alive inside again, and she found she didn't want it to end just yet.

Besides, she was in a far better place now. She felt like a whole new person.

On the rare occasions she allowed herself to venture back in her head, it felt like a complete other life. A life that was almost completely buried.

At precisely three minutes to six, she picked up her handbag, got out of the car and walked to the coffee bar. She'd be a couple of minutes late. Not enough to appear rude but just right to avoid looking over-keen.

She could see, through the smoked glass front, that the place was about half full. She spotted at least three small round tables free.

She opened the door and inhaled the heady smell of freshly ground coffee beans. The whoosh of the steamed milk and the gentle buzz of cordial conversation instantly loosened her tight shoulders.

She scanned the tables with a faint smile on her face, ready to wave to Shaun and make her way over. But it soon became apparent that he hadn't yet arrived.

She felt a wave of irritation. Joanne Dent wasn't accustomed to being kept waiting. At the same time, a faint thrill rumbled inside her at the fact that he wasn't a pushover who felt intimidated by her.

Heading for the table furthest from the door, she passed the serving counter and a small glass-fronted display unit. She glanced at the mouth-watering dainty pastries and wholesome-looking salad wraps inside, but she wasn't tempted. Her stomach, although empty after she'd skipped lunch, felt raw and unable to deal with solid food.

What a silly state she'd allowed herself to get into. They were meeting for coffee, for goodness' sake, she reminded herself. This wasn't a romantic date.

Her bottom had barely reached the wooden chair when the entrance bell chimed and Shaun's six-foot-two – she'd already estimated – frame filled the doorway.

She raised her hand and he smiled, and in a few long strides he was there at the table. He wore a close-fitting black T-shirt and jeans. She glanced down to see that his feet were clad in blue suede boat shoes with white stitching, and no socks.

Joanne felt overdressed rather than smart.

She stood, and he leaned forward and very lightly kissed her cheek. His lips felt like a firebrand against her skin and she sat down again quickly, feeling slightly dazed.

'I didn't get drinks,' she managed. 'I wasn't sure what you'd prefer.'

'It's OK, I'll order,' he said, reaching into his back pocket for a wallet. 'The espresso macchiatos are really good here, if you like your coffee strong. I'll get us a couple of pastries, too.'

'Perfect.' She nodded, appreciative of the way his back narrowed into a neat waistline as he turned back towards the counter.

When you were a single parent, you got used to making all the decisions, big and small. You couldn't really discuss things with a child; you just had to get on with sorting life out for the two of you.

So Joanne found it refreshing when Shaun didn't defer to her. She liked the way he assumed control.

She busied herself fishing in her bag for a tissue for something to do while she willed her cheeks to lose some of the heat she could feel burning there.

Merely a minute later, Shaun was back.

'They're bringing the order over.' He smiled, pulling out the chair right next to her rather than the one opposite.

'Great,' she said, breathing in his now familiar citrus scent. 'Have you come here straight from work?'

'Yeah, I've been doing a photo shoot with international athletes at Loughborough University.' He grinned, looking down at the table and shaking his head before looking back at her. 'Sorry, it's just… it makes a change from photographing lost dogs who found their way home, you know?'

'Local news is a bit like that, I suppose,' she laughed. 'I could probably put some contacts your way. If you make sure the magazine photos favour me.'

'You don't need special favours, you look perfect the way you are.'

It was a cheesy line, but she swallowed it, flushing with pleasure.

A young man wearing jeans and a white T-shirt with a long black apron appeared carrying a tray.

'Two espresso macchiatos and two Danish?' He began to put the glass cups down without waiting for an answer. The coffee and milk were cleverly layered in graduated colours and finished with steamed milk topped with froth hearts.

Joanne picked up the small silver spoon on her saucer and scooped up a small whip of creamy froth with a sprinkle of brown sugar. Then she took a sip of the strong, nutty brew and looked at him over her cup.

'I hope things sort themselves at home for you. The situation sounds difficult.'

Shaun took a bite of apricot Danish, chewing for a few moments before swallowing and answering.

'It's what we both want.' He shrugged. 'It's just Maisie I worry about. I have to make sure she's OK.'

'I'm sure she'll be fine,' Joanne said, looking at her pastry but not touching it. 'Kids are surprisingly resilient.'

She thought about Piper. Strong, confident and competent at most activities she put her mind to. They didn't talk about her father. Joanne wasn't sure why that was, but to her relief, Piper had never asked. It felt like an unexploded mine under her feet – she knew the day would come and it probably wasn't far off.

'Emma has always insisted that Maisie is more sensitive than your average child,' Shaun said, picking up his pastry again. 'But I agree with you. She's probably stronger than her mum gives her credit for. I guess we'll soon find out.'

CHAPTER 17

Joanne finished signing a batch of client contracts and sat back in her chair.

Weak rays of sunlight battled the slats of the window blind, projecting line grids on the opposite wall.

If she wasn't with Shaun, she was thinking about him. Things had moved along so quickly in the space of two weeks, it helped her process it to think back to how they got there so quickly.

That afternoon in the café, Joanne had felt relieved when the conversation grew lighter. She didn't really want to talk to Shaun about his wife and daughter. She didn't want to be reminded that Emma was her employee.

Instead, she tried to relax and enjoy listening to Shaun talk animatedly about his photography work. She found it a refreshing change to listen to career speak about something other than the legal industry in which she herself was utterly immersed.

'You've heard the phrase "a picture paints a thousand words", right?' he asked her after ordering them another coffee each. 'I think that's so true. In a good photograph, you can capture mood, feelings and emotions… Get it right and you can tell a whole story in a single snapshot.'

Joanne nodded, thinking about the handful of photographs locked in her desk at home. Photographs that showed a time when she was once happy, when she believed in a future that was never to be.

She hadn't been able to bring herself to burn them, but she would, one day. It was essential to erasing the past and an important part of her ten-year plan. It was the final piece of a jigsaw she was trying her hardest to destroy.

Shaun waved a hand in front of her face.

'You were somewhere else then. Care to share?'

'Oh, just thinking about what you said, that's all.' She grinned widely. 'And you're right. The best photographs don't need any words.'

'What about you? Do you get satisfaction from your job?'

'Of course.' She nodded, pressing her fingertips against the hot cup. She'd be climbing the walls later with all this caffeine. 'People turn themselves inside out, get into some pretty complicated situations. It's satisfying when you can help them sort through the tangles.'

'I bet.' Shaun nodded. 'I certainly don't want an expensive legal wrangle, so I'm trying to keep things civil with Emma.'

'Very sensible,' Joanne remarked.

'Not always easy, though.'

'Well, maybe you should get yourself a good lawyer.' She uncrossed her feet under the table and slipped off one shoe. When her foot touched lightly on his, they looked at each other.

'Shame I can't afford your services,' he said softly, his eyes sparkling with mischief. 'The papers are saying you're a hot-shot lawyer.'

'Maybe we can come to some arrangement,' she said slowly.

Her heart began to bang on her chest wall, but she ignored it. Kept her face impassive and her expression amused.

'A mutually convenient one, perhaps,' he suggested, leaning forward on his elbows and staring into her eyes across the table.

'I know an intimate little bar hidden away on a side street behind this place,' Shaun suggested. She didn't need encouraging; she wasn't ready to part company yet. Fifteen minutes later, they'd graduated from coffees to cocktails.

'Just so you know, my fee is usually more than a couple of cosmopolitans,' Joanne said, her head feeling slightly fuzzy from drinking on a virtually empty stomach. She had barely touched her Danish earlier. 'I'm not usually such a pushover.'

She swayed slightly in time with the slow tempo of the chill-out lounge music that enveloped the dimly lit bar.

'So you say.' He smirked. 'I could tell a mile off you're the kind of woman who appreciates a classy drink.'

She suppressed a grin and tried to look offended, failing on both counts.

'How very dare you! I'll have you know I'm a hard-working single mother who is—'

'Beautiful, smart and great company.' Shaun took a step closer to her, his muscular arm pressing into her side. She could feel the heat of his body through her thin silk blouse.

She looked up at him, and he bent his head towards her slowly, testing her reaction. She parted her lips slightly and blinked.

A jolt of electricity ran the length of her spine and goosebumps popped up on her forearms as he planted a kiss very lightly on her mouth before straightening up and taking a step back.

'Wow,' he breathed. 'Did you feel what I felt?'

She nodded, her eyes wide. 'And here was me thinking we were just going for a coffee after work.'

Joanne opened her eyes. Her heart sank and she closed them again at once.

Beside her, she could hear Shaun breathing.

A man. In her bed, here in her apartment.

What was she thinking?

She took a breath in, held it a moment or two and then released it very slowly. She had to calm down.

She'd done nothing wrong. She was an adult, a single woman. There was no chance of Piper walking in on them, given that she was still away. She hadn't got drunk and was in perfect control of her senses.

But in its own way, it was far more dangerous than that.

The virtual chemical reaction they'd both experienced was more powerful and real than any manufactured stimulant.

She'd only felt attraction like this once before, and she was still in the process of trying to erase the devastating consequences of it from her life.

Shaun stirred beside her, opened his eyes.

'Hello, gorgeous,' he croaked, flashing a pearly white smile that crinkled the corners of his cheeky eyes.

He turned on his side and propped himself up on his elbow to look at her.

'You OK?'

'I'm fine.' She turned her head and smiled weakly at him. 'I just feel a little dazed. Things moved a bit faster than I expected and now… well, here we are.'

'Here we are,' he echoed. 'Together. Bound by some sort of crazy magnetism I've never felt before in my life.'

'Me neither,' she said without flinching. 'The question is, what are we going to do about it?'

'Do?' He laughed. 'For a start, I'd say we thank our lucky stars we've found each other.'

'That aside, I meant what do we do about the fact that you're married to one of my paralegals?'

As soon as she acknowledged the elephant in the room, a growing feeling of discomfort began to rise from her solar plexus, succeeding in obliterating the glow she'd felt all evening.

'It's not as if me and Emma are still together; it won't be long before we're not even living in the same house any more.'

'But I work with her,' she said softly. 'I've already given her tasks on my new cases, so I can't avoid talking to her.'

'You've no need to feel guilty, Jo. We've agreed to part and our marriage is over. Emma wants that as much as I do.'

He'd asked her earlier in the evening if he could call her Jo and she'd nodded. She'd always hated anyone shortening her name, but when Shaun said it, it sounded sexy and showed her he'd sensed an intimate and well-hidden side of her that nobody else knew existed.

She sighed, bit her lip. 'It still feels wrong. Dishonest, somehow. I can't look her in the eye while I'm… secretly seeing her husband.'

He reached over to her with his free hand, traced a wavy line from her shoulder to her arm with a fingertip. She groaned softly, inching over towards him.

'You won't have to feel dishonest for long,' he said, cupping the back of her head in his hand and pulling her gently towards him. 'I've been around long enough to know we're going to have something special here. I'll tell her about us.'

CHAPTER 18

Emma

At the end of the day, after battling gridlocked roads due to an accident on Trent Bridge, I walk straight into the kitchen, where Shaun is preparing tea.

'You're earlier than I expected. Maize is at your mum's, so sit down, I'll pour you a glass of wine.' He nods to the counter, where the bottle of the full-blooded Rioja we bought in Spain last year sits open and breathing, next to two crystal wine glasses we received as a wedding gift. We'd left one bottle unopened, vowing to drink it when there was reason to celebrate. I'm pretty certain *this* wasn't what I had in mind.

'I'll just have some water, if that's OK,' I say tersely.

As a rule, I try not to drink alcohol and to eat a little more healthily during the week. It isn't always easy to stick to it and I probably won't manage it tonight. Judging by the smell emanating from the bubbling pan, Shaun has cooked his signature spaghetti bolognese, and annoyed or not, I'm not about to refuse *that*.

I sit down in the easy chair near the wall-mounted television. The news is on but thankfully has been muted. From here I have a good view of the garden, and it's nice not to have the hum of the office in my ears.

We had the extension done two years ago. Before that, the kitchen had been adequate enough but was a long and narrow space with no room for eating. I recall a happy, boozy evening, just the two of us in the lounge with the French doors thrown open, planning the new space we'd use for family living. I loved the idea that the person doing the cooking would easily be able to interact with other family members and guests, rather than be screened off from all the fun.

This was back in the days when we still used to have friends over regularly for a late supper of seafood risotto or Shaun's legendary spag bol, washed down with copious amounts of wine and followed by thick slices of my home-made lemon drizzle cake with good coffee.

We haven't done the friends thing for a long time now. Both of us so busy with work and… well, with life itself. And we soon realised that awkward questions from other people were far more easily avoided when we kept ourselves to ourselves.

During the past twelve months, I found myself avoiding the kitchen living space when I could. It was too open, with nowhere to hide when the bristling frustrations crackled like electricity between the two of us. They seemed to gather strength when I spent time in there with him.

But after we made the new arrangement, the animosity seemingly dissolved into thin air, leaving me, finally, with some space to breathe.

Until he started seeing Joanne, when it became apparent that the negative feelings hadn't really dissolved at all.

Shaun has barely been home in the evenings for the past two weeks. Looking back, I'm now realising that the way he walked around in a daze with a faint smile on his lips, should have made it obvious that he was in love.

At work, Joanne has taken to sending messages about the cases I'm working on through one of the other paralegals. I've barely seen anything of her apart from at the dance studio, where she appears briefly to pick up Piper, steering well clear of me.

I shift around, struggling to get comfy despite the soft cushions.

I can feel the old frustrations making a spectacular comeback, nipping at the edges of my thoughts.

'Forgive me for insisting about the wine.' He pushes a coaster across the coffee table and places a large glass of Rioja in front of me. I open my mouth to object, but he sits down on the adjacent sofa and speaks first. 'It's not a water night, Emma. I think we both need a glass of wine.'

There he goes again, thinking he knows what's best for me.

Despite myself, I pick up the glass and take a big gulp of the ruby liquid, allowing it to sit a moment in my mouth so I can savour the intense flavours of blackberry, cherries and, I think, the faintest hint of dark chocolate.

Shaun got me into tasting wine rather than just swilling it down. It was an interest we shared, for a while, at least.

I close my eyes and track the warmth as it slides down from my throat to my stomach.

My hand moves towards the glass again and I intercept it, tuck it under my thigh. I need to keep my wits about me.

'We talked this through at length. Our marriage… us, we're not working. You agreed, I agreed. We can't keep constantly going over it.'

He sighs and clasps his fingers between his splayed knees. He hangs his head and stares down at the tiled floor. He's thirty-six in a month's time, and I can see tiny glints of grey in the soft new growth of chestnut-brown hair at the nape of his neck.

'I want to do my fair share, Em, and I want to spend time with Maisie too. But I'm sorry, I just can't work around our current agreement.'

He's not sorry at all. There's a smugness playing around his mouth and eyes, and I stand up, suddenly furious.

'Fifty-fifty care for Maisie and fifty-fifty on the household chores. That was the agreement.'

His eyes appraise me coolly, but he doesn't speak.

'I'm not willing to do more than half, so I don't know how there's any flexibility.' I clench my fists to stop my fingers from trembling.

'I'm happy to do my share, just not every night,' he says, his manner infuriatingly laconic. 'I could have Maisie say on a Sunday, maybe Saturday afternoon. You should be able to get your work done then.'

He stands up, struts over to the glass doors like a peacock with his chest all puffed out, staring at his own reflection. Where is the man without any self-esteem, without any real belief in his own abilities? Where is the man I married, who used to irritate me with his lack of drive and ambition? Dithering about whether he was good enough to run an evening photography course at the local college, or staring wistfully at the full-colour spreads of the freelance photographers who worked for the big national newspapers.

'If they can do it, so can you,' I told him numerous times. 'You just have to believe in yourself.'

'I've realised that my time is now, Emma,' he says evenly. 'And I intend on making it count, whatever it takes. You need to understand that.'

'Well, whatever planet you're currently residing on, I have a wake-up call for you. You have a daughter who deserves your time and attention.'

'I've made a decision,' he says quietly, as if I haven't spoken. 'It's not something I've arrived at lightly, Emma. I want you to know that.'

I fold my arms. He has my full attention now, but he's stopped speaking.

'So… are you going to tell me what this momentous decision is or not?'

I'm not entirely sure what I expect him to say, but I think it may well involve me staying at home and looking after Maisie while he gads off on holiday with Joanne. I wouldn't be at all surprised if he announces he's going on a work trip somewhere.

I swallow hard at the thought. If he does say something like that, there's absolutely nothing I can do about it. He knows that I'll always be here for Maisie and that I have Mum to help out too.

All the equal care we've been striving towards was never real, not really. I see now that it's all too easy for him to take off and leave everything to me because there's always been an unspoken deal between us, as there must be with hundreds of thousands of other parents.

When the chips are down, the mother is the one who is expected to step into the breach.

Despite his initial confidence, Shaun is fidgeting now. Biting his thumbnail and tapping the toe of his shoe on the kitchen floor. I've known him long enough to recognise all the signs of his discomfort.

I widen my eyes. 'Well? I'm waiting.' I stand up and walk over to the kitchen counter.

'I… I'm moving out.'

His voice is calm and quiet. He stops biting his thumbnail. He presses his fidgety foot flat to the floor and stands very still.

I slide my hands out to the sides and grip the worktop behind me.

'I just need some space. I think we both need some space, Em.'

'You think *we* need some space?'

'Yes.'

'But we have our space, Shaun. Yes, we have a commitment to our arrangement, but after that, we have our own space to do whatever—'

'I just can't do it any more,' he says shortly. 'This stupid arrangement, I mean. I don't know what we were thinking of, or why you even suggested it.'

I lean back against the counter, feel the cool, hard quartz cutting into the bottom of my back.

'Well, I'll remind you. We were thinking of Maisie. Of how we can minimise the effect on her of us splitting up. And it might have been my suggestion initially, but you agreed with it. You agreed with all of it.'

'I know I did. But now… well, I've changed my mind.' He runs a hand through his hair. 'I'm allowed to change my mind, because it's not working. It just isn't.'

I laugh bitterly. 'I wonder why that is? There's a sense you're moving on to bigger and better things, perhaps?'

'I knew you'd be like this.' He shakes his head. 'I want us to stay friends, for Maisie's sake. I'm trying to make this as easy as I can, Emma.'

'Easy for you.' I feel the edge of the worktop grazing against my grasping fingers. 'Not so easy for me to effectively be a single mum to Maisie, keep this house running *and* my own career on track. While you flounce around like a lovesick sixteen-year-old.'

'I'll still pay my share of the bills,' he says.

'That's really good of you,' I remark. 'I don't need to remind you that in a court of law, you'd be expected to do just that. Where is it you're moving to?'

But of course I already know.

He looks at me and I look back at him. The air is thick with an awful silence that actually hurts my ears.

The love that used to bind us together has gone.

It's melted into thin air and left behind it a space big enough to accommodate just about every negative feeling you could name.

'I'm moving in with Joanne. I'm there most of the time now anyway.'

'Wow. How long has it been? Is it even three weeks yet? Sounds a considered, sensible decision.'

'What we have is very rare. I hope you find it for yourself some day.'

The draining board is full of dirty breakfast crockery waiting to be loaded into the dishwasher. He hasn't bothered to clear up before he starts to cook dinner.

It crosses my mind to take each piece and throw it as hard as I can at him.

'That's quite a turnaround in opinion after your determination to keep things stable for Maisie for the foreseeable,' I say, just about managing to keep my cool. 'You must be taking advice from someone who's got strong views on our marriage and our daughter's well-being.'

He looks down at his feet with a faint smile, as if I'm conforming to every bad thing he thinks of me.

'I'm not here to argue, Em. Just to tell you about my decision. We've already done the hard bit, agreeing that our marriage is at an end. This is just a change of heart about our living arrangements, that's all.'

'A change of heart for *you*, maybe. For me, it changes everything. I'll have a house and our daughter to look after. And tell me, are there plans for Maisie to play a part in your exciting new life?'

'Of course.' Two dark red spots are blooming nicely on his cheeks. 'Joanne and I are going to take the girls out for the day and explain it all to them.'

'Sounds like you've thought of everything, Shaun. You've certainly moved fast; made more decisions than you have in the whole of our marriage, in fact.'

My eyes bore into him and he looks away.

'Right, well, I'll pack a few things to tide me over until we can sort out the best time to—'

'You can take everything now,' I say.

'What? I can't do that.'

'I'll take Maisie out for the day after dance on Saturday morning. Get your stuff out then.'

'Emma. Why are you being so unreasonable about this?'

'Get what you need until Saturday and go,' I say, struggling to keep the tears at bay. 'I don't want you here when Maisie comes back with my mum.'

He sighs, shakes his head and then turns and leaves the room.

I sink down against the kitchen cupboards and bury my head in my hands.

My life is a failure. Just like my dad always said it would be.

I hear shoes shuffling on the floor and something being pulled from the coat cupboard. The front door opens and closes with a soft click behind him.

It feels like there's been a power shift between us. *I* used to be the sure one, the main instigator of going our separate ways, although Shaun didn't put up too much of a fight.

Now he's just walked out on me after saying his piece. I feel stung, although I'm not sure I know why.

I sit back down and stare into the ruby depths of my wine, noticing how the glimmer of the overhead lights reflects on its surface, but deeper down, the liquid remains unctuous and dull.

As if nothing could ever burn bright enough to illuminate its murky depths.

CHAPTER 19

Val

Val watched as her granddaughter threaded pink, lilac and yellow beads onto the new bracelet she planned on Wearing to her dance class on Tuesday night.

She jumped when Alexa's voice rang out, reminding Maisie that her favourite television show was due to start in fifteen minutes.

Emma and Shaun had bought her the Amazon Echo contraption last Christmas and Maisie loved it, used it for lots of important tasks, such as remembering her homework and television schedule. She'd even brought it over with her to Val's. The kids of today. Honestly!

'Alexa's my friend, Gran,' Maisie had insisted when Val expressed reservations after reading an article about how the new electronic personal assistants listened to everything being said around them and reported back to the big corporations.

'You don't really need another one, darling.' Val rolled her eyes. 'One thing you're not short on is friends.'

The child had so many that she categorised them into 'school', 'dancing' and 'celebrity' friends, and used Alexa for keeping track of all their birthdays.

The slightly worrying thing for Val was that Maisie seemed to spend an inordinate amount of time following all her favourite celebrities online.

'Seeing their real-life photographs really makes you feel like you know them,' she told her grandmother one day when Val queried the amount of time Maisie spent online.

Maisie's favourite, Ariana Grande, would put all sorts of pictures on there. Family snaps, photos of her as a child, recording in the studio, on holiday… Maisie felt as if she knew everything about her.

Val thought about her own crushes as a ten-year-old girl in the late sixties: you might get a fleeting glimpse on television or in a magazine, and very occasionally the chance to attend a concert, but that was it. Buying their records was the only way to feel like you were closer to them.

Her concern was that this social media thing was all false. From what she could see, mainly over Maisie's shoulder, it consisted of people cutting and pasting all the best bits from their lives and leaving out the ordinary stuff.

Maisie purred like a cat when she perused Katy Perry's fairy-tale existence and Val would smile tightly, not wanting to lecture her granddaughter and spoil her fun, but feeling concerned that Maisie bought into this skewed version of reality so readily.

Everyone knew it was vital that young people needed to learn that life was all about the highs *and* the lows, the triumphs *and* the failures – and understand that you could survive through all of it.

Nobody's life resembled a fairy tale, no matter how much money they had in the bank, yet Maisie and millions of other young girls were growing up thinking it could be achieved at the drop of a hat.

When it was Ariana's birthday last year, Maisie told Val that she had posted a message on the pop star's page and Ariana had LIKED IT!

Maisie's face was a picture; she was so validated by it.

'When I told everyone at ballet class, they all cheered and even Miss Diane looked impressed,' she said happily, her face shining.

'That's nice,' Val said, hoping to acknowledge Maisie's enthusiasm without overly encouraging it.

'You should have seen Piper Dent's face, Gran.' Maisie grinned. 'It crumpled up like someone had shoved dog poo under her nose.'

Maisie knew her gran didn't like to hear her being unkind about people, and Val suspected that was why she hadn't said much more about it. But Maisie's mood was upbeat and bouncy, as if a sweet warmth had spread in her chest and stayed there all day.

Maisie loved dancing, TV programmes and listening to music, and she even liked school, most of the time. She enjoyed reading and writing stories, but she wasn't keen on maths.

The one thing she would really adore, but hadn't got, was a dog. Val was pleased that Emma had said it wouldn't be fair on the animal because there was nobody home all day, which Maisie had grudgingly agreed with.

Val noticed her granddaughter sigh as she began to pack the beads away so she could command the big flat-screen television.

'What's wrong, love?' she said softly. 'Is everything OK... at home, I mean?'

'You mean the weird stuff happening between Mum and Dad?' Maisie said, her bluntness startling Val for a moment. 'They think I'm a little kid, like I'm still five years old.'

'I'm sure they don't,' Val said gently.

It was difficult as a grandparent, being in the middle of it all. Val often wished she'd made a better job of mothering Emma all those years ago, but... well, you did the best you could at the time, didn't you? Life had been far from easy back then.

Privately, Val knew that Emma and Shaun were having problems. But even if Emma hadn't said as much, Val wasn't stupid. She'd seen the secret looks that flashed between them like sparks. It was clear to anyone that trouble brewed under the surface. 'What do you mean by weird stuff?'

'I dunno.' Maisie shrugged. 'Dad is sleeping in the spare room, but when I asked about it, Mum's eyes blinked really fast, like she was trying to think of something to say.'

'I think the central heating makes your dad snore,' Val said, repeating what Emma had told her to say. But Maisie would not be dissuaded from her theory.

'Andrew Carpenter in my class, his mum and dad split up in the new year. He cried in front of everyone but wouldn't go to the office, and Miss Lambert had to stop the lesson until someone came to fetch him.'

'That's sad,' Val said.

Maisie nodded. 'Before he went home, he told the whole class he knew something bad was going to happen because his parents had started sleeping in separate rooms.'

Maisie's parents thought they were being clever hiding stuff from her, but behind their smiles and the extra time she now got to spend on her own with her dad, the child knew something had changed.

Val had tried to speak to Emma about it, suggested they sit Maisie down and tell her the truth. But Emma waved her away.

'She doesn't need to know, Mum,' she said. 'She's too young to realise what's happening.'

But Val knew she was wrong about that.

Maisie was very aware of all of it.

CHAPTER 20

Emma

I sit there for a long time, in the kitchen where we used to gather and talk about our day, until I'm rattled out of my uneasy trance by a key in the front door.

'Only us,' Mum's voice sings out as I hear Maisie barrel down the hallway. The kitchen door flies open and bangs against the wall.

'Hi, Mum, where's Dad?'

'He's had to pop out,' I say, standing up. 'Did you have a good time at Gran's?'

'Of course she did. We always have a great time, don't we, poppet?' Mum appears in the doorway, weighed down by Maisie's school coat and bag.

'Mum, you shouldn't cart that stuff around for her; she's perfectly capable of carrying her school things inside.'

Mum had an operation for a slipped disc last year and it still gives her problems at times.

I rush forward to relieve her of the burden as Maisie flops down on the sofa and turns on the television.

'Homework first, missy,' I say. 'Television off until then.'

'I did my homework at Gran's,' Maisie says, grinning and twisting her head back on the sofa to look pleadingly at Mum.

'Good try.' I take the remote control and turn the TV off again.

'When's Dad going to be back?' Maisie scowls and stomps over to the fridge, taking out a carton of orange juice. 'He said he'd watch *The Simpsons* with me later.'

'You'll have to sort that out with him when he comes home,' I say lightly, putting her school bag on the floor.

Mum catches my eye but I pretend not to notice.

'I'm going upstairs then, to do my stinking science worksheet,' Maisie sighs, slouching out of the kitchen.

'Cuppa?' I ask Mum as I whisk by her towards the kettle.

'Yes. I think a cuppa and a chat would be useful,' she says pointedly.

When we sit down with our drinks, she clears her throat.

'Tell me to mind my own business if you want to. I won't be offended,' she says, although we both know that's not true. 'I can't help noticing that you and Shaun don't seem to be in the best place at the moment.'

'We're fine,' I say, wondering when I'm going to tell her.

I stare out at the hedge at the bottom of the garden. The bony branches are just visible through its shimmering copper leaves. In the winter, we can see through to next door's garden, but once the spring months arrive, with the new growth, our garden becomes much more private.

'I don't want to pry, Emmeline, I just want us to be open about it. Maisie tells me Shaun's hardly been around in the evenings and that you've seemed a bit quiet and sad.'

I'm astonished. I honestly didn't know Maisie had taken any of it in. When she's not watching television, she's lounging around with earbuds in, listening to her music or swiping through her Instagram account on my iPad. Giving the impression that to all intents and purposes she's not aware of much of the adult stuff going on around her.

Mum registers my surprise. 'Oh yes, she's noticed that things aren't as they should be at home.'

'I told you about our new arrangement, living together but *not* together?'

Mum purses her lips and gives me a curt nod.

I didn't go into all the gory details of our decision to call time on our marriage, just relayed the bare bones of it. As I'd expected, Mum was utterly baffled.

'Splitting up but *staying together*?' She looked devastated, even though she'd known for some time that we'd had relationship problems. 'Who ever heard of such a thing?'

'People often look for other solutions now, Mum,' I explained gently. 'We've tailored the new arrangement to our own needs, all three of us. And we think it can work. It *is* working.'

She didn't make much comment after that. Mum's of the old school; believes in sticking it out until the kids are older, no matter how miserable life becomes.

Failing that, you cut ties and separate, keeping it nice and clean and simple.

'It worked well for a while,' I tell her now, picking at a thread on my trousers. 'Until two or three weeks ago, in fact.'

'Well, I'm surprised it worked at all,' Mum sighs, taking a sip of her tea. 'It all sounds terribly messy to me.'

I pause to take a breath. There's no sense in getting on the wrong side of Mum; I need her more now than ever. 'Every Sunday night we'd agree a rota so someone was home for Maisie each day, but so we both had our own time. So it was fair.'

Mum rolls her eyes.

I know she still considers the primary caregiver should be the mother. She could barely contain her disapproval when, eighteen months ago, I explained I would be studying to become a qualified paralegal in order to facilitate my climb up the legal career ladder.

Still, there's no easy way to do this. I just need to come out with it.

'Shaun's been seeing someone else,' I say simply. 'My boss, in fact.'

Mum's mouth drops open.

'And just before you got here, he told me he's moving in with her.'

'But... how on earth has it come to this?' Her face darkens. 'This stupid arrangement you dreamed up, that's what it is!'

'Mum, please. I really can't go through—'

'You're your own worst enemy, Emmeline, always have been. You'd better look sharp and stop this nonsense before it gets out of hand. You're going to find yourself alone with a child... You'll be a single mother!'

Her expression registers sheer horror at the mere thought of it. It would be funny if everything didn't feel so fucking hopeless.

'Thanks for having Maisie,' I say, standing up and gathering up our cups. 'I'd best get on now, I've got some work to catch up on.'

Mum stands too and picks up her handbag. 'Work, work, work. That's all you ever talk about, and therein lies the problem, if you ask me.'

She walks to the hallway and calls goodbye to Maisie upstairs. At the door, she turns back.

'You know, I really do hope it's not too late to work things out between the two of you,' she says flatly. 'I'd hate to see you having to fend for yourself and your daughter alone without her father being present.'

'Plenty of women do,' I retort.

But my words are lost in the opening and closing of the door as Mum leaves the house.

CHAPTER 21

By the time I've dropped Maisie off at school, to my shame, I've managed to swear at one driver who pulled out in front of me, forcing me to stamp on the brakes, and sound my horn continuously at another who cut me up on the approach into town.

I feel fury and confusion burning inside me like hot coals. It was a miracle I was able to get Maisie to school without snapping her head off when she asked me twice more where her dad had been last night.

'I told you, he must be delayed on a job,' I explained yet again, waving Maisie's concern away.

I felt bad dropping her off without giving her an explanation, but why should I let Shaun off the unpleasantness of explaining that he's decided to move out? He deserves to go through that emotional process, see the devastation he's causing first-hand.

I drive to work, the thoughts whirring around in my head without respite.

I miss having someone to talk to. I miss my friends, didn't even realise how badly I was neglecting them and distancing myself. I was always too busy with work when they called to invite me out for lunch or suggested coffee and cake at the small independent café in town we once favoured.

I didn't even notice when they stopped calling, so embroiled was I in the pressures of life.

As my marriage slowly disintegrated, I tried to keep up a dogged determination, to the exclusion of everything else, to enable me to complete my qualification and cement my career prospects at Walker, Dent and Scott.

I found it was so much easier to just stay away from people, away from their claims on my time. More importantly, it enabled me to avoid their probing questions about me and Shaun, even though they were well meant.

At the time, I just didn't feel strong enough to talk about it. I found it preferable to simply turn the other way.

So when I found myself confiding in Joanne about the breakdown of my marriage, it felt like a release of pent-up steam. It was a relief.

Now, of course, I only feel regret that I trusted her.

When I arrive at the office, I dump my bag and files on my desk and, avoiding the curious stares that I can feel boring into the back of my head, head back out and up the stairwell.

I stride across the air-conditioned, carpeted second floor, my heels muted as I pass office doors on my way to the glass offices of the glitterati, who sit at desks with their backs to the sprawling views across the city.

I can see that Joanne is poring over a spread of documents on her desk. As I approach her door, Anya pops her head out of her own office.

'Can I help you, Emma?' she asks pleasantly.

'I just wanted a quick word with Joanne,' I say. 'I need to give her an update on my meeting with a client yesterday.'

'I see.' Anya clasps her hands together in front of her. 'Well, she's asked me to ensure she's not disturbed this morning.'

'Ah.' I glance at Joanne through the glass, but she still appears to be absorbed in the papers on her desk. 'No problem. I'll catch up with her later.'

I turn and walk back down the carpeted length of the offices, suddenly furious with myself for being so easy to get rid of. I'm two or three steps down the stairs when I realise that Anya keeps Joanne's diary. If my boss really is busy, I'd be better off making an appointment to see her later on today, or possibly tomorrow morning. There are things that need saying. Important things.

I head back up to the second floor. As soon as I enter the office space, I see that Joanne is out of her room and talking to Anya in the carpeted area.

'Joanne!' I call brightly, and she visibly jumps, shrinking back towards her door when she turns and spots me.

'Oh, Emma. It's you.'

Anya quickly interjects. 'I did explain to Emma that you're busy and don't want to be disturbed, Joanne.'

'It's fine,' I say, sounding breezier than I feel. 'I just came back to make an appointment to see you – later, perhaps, or tomorrow. There are some important things I need to discuss... about one of the cases.'

Judging by Joanne's slightly jumpy demeanour, she knows exactly what I mean.

'Actually, as Anya has already said, I'm really pushed at the moment, Emma,' she tells me. 'Could you feed back to the lead paralegal on the case? I think that's going to be the best strategy here as I've got new clients coming out of my ears right now. Not complaining, of course, it's just how things are at the moment.'

She smiles at me, showing whitened teeth, her lips stretching so wide it almost looks like a grimace.

Her phone rings and she glances down at the lit screen in her hand.

'I... I have to go. Sorry.' She backs into her office and pushes the still-ringing phone into the side of her thigh, screen down.

A few seconds later, her door closes and she turns around, pressing the phone to her ear.

I wait in the corridor, staring at Joanne through the glass, ignoring Anya's requests for us to look at the diary together. When Joanne has finished her call, I tap on the door.

She glares at me, her jaw set. I open the door.

'I only need a few minutes. I'm sure you're aware there's something I need to talk to you about.'

My knees feel a bit shaky, but my anger bolsters me and I stand firm.

She hesitates for a moment or two, tips her head to one side. I can't identify the expression on her face, but it seems to be laced with dread.

'You'd better take a seat.'

While I walk across the office and sit down, she bends her head, scribbling on a typed document. Expensive gold and beige highlights glittering prettily under the light above her remind me I'm well overdue for a colour and cut myself.

She's purposely making me wait. It seems so childlike.

I look away, around the office. It's dim in here; Joanne always keeps the blinds half closed, as if she's hiding away from something.

The room is very minimalist in its design. Stark white walls, limed oak furniture and filing cabinets that look like tall, glossy taupe sideboards. It's got a rather cold feel; the only concession to softness is a handful of potted cacti dotted here and there.

I wonder if her house interior is similar. Shaun likes simple, clean lines; he always complained about the clutter lying around at home. Clutter that won't offend his eyes any more.

Joanne herself matches the environment. She is a very attractive woman with lightly tanned skin and an enviable ability to wear minimal make-up and still look fully groomed.

She doesn't go for high heels; prefers black Gucci sliders paired with exquisitely tailored dark trouser suits and simple, well-cut silk blouses in various colours that flatter her boyish figure.

I get the feeling her reserved and slightly masculine style is a lot about her job. Once, in a meeting, she slid a bare foot out of her shoe to reveal orange glittery toenails. That told me she has a fun side out of the office. I'm sure Shaun sees lots of that side of her personality.

I don't know her exact age, but she once told me in a meeting that she's in her mid-thirties. I'm guessing the framed photograph on her desk I can only see the back of is of Piper.

Inferiority curls at the bottom of my spine, as it is prone to do when I meet someone who's around my age and has achieved so much more in their career than I have.

As I sit here with Joanne, I'm woefully aware of my own shortcomings.

'Emma?'

'Sorry!' I shake my head. 'I was lost in thought.'

She taps the end of her slimline silver pen on the desk.

'You seem pretty adamant you need to speak to me about something.'

She's playing a game. She must know full well why I'm here.

'Shaun told me he's moving in with you, but you probably know what was said.' She doesn't react. 'I just wanted you to know that I might not be able to get as much extra work done on the new cases as I'd hoped. As you can imagine, having a ten-year-old yourself, it's not easy to wear all the hats all of the time.'

'It's not easy at all,' Joanne says curtly. 'It's tough. I've done it for a long time myself, Emma.'

Her face remains impassive, but that doesn't stop me. The words are rushing out now, and with them comes a sense of relief.

'It's marvellous, isn't it?' I continue. 'All these years of Shaun having no confidence in himself, and now he suddenly turns into Mr Charisma, but I suppose, having just met, you won't have seen the other side of him yet.'

I laugh, but it sounds harsh and out of place.

'I agreed to speak with you this morning to clear the air, but I've no intention of getting involved in a slanging match, now or indeed ever.' Joanne glares at me. 'Say what you need to say, Emma, and then let's agree to draw a line. Otherwise…'

'Otherwise what?'

'Otherwise it's obviously going to be very difficult for us to work together.' *And I'm not going anywhere, so watch your step* is the passive-aggressive subtext I receive.

'Does Piper see her dad?'

Joanne stiffens in her chair. 'Sorry, what do you mean?'

'Does Piper also visit her father, like Maisie will have to do, to see Shaun?'

'I'd rather leave conversations about Piper's dad out of this.' Joanne bristles.

'I… I didn't mean to intrude. I just wondered if—'

'Emma.' Joanne hesitates, pressing her hands down on the top of her desk. 'Just calm down a little.' Then, unexpectedly, she asks, 'Would you like a cup of tea?'

'Thanks,' I say, tears suddenly choking the words that want to keep coming.

She makes some sort of signal through the glass wall of the office, and as if by magic, a minute or two later Anya brings in a tray bearing two cups of tea. She regards me warily as she places one in front of me.

'Thanks, Anya,' I say, subdued.

I pick it up and take a sip, and catch a look that shoots at lightning speed between Joanne and Anya. I don't know what it means, but I can guess. *If she's not gone in five minutes, interrupt with an urgent phone call.*

When Anya has left the office, Joanne sits back in her chair.

'Look, Emma. I'm only too aware of how the pressures of one's personal life can seep into the working day. I understand that, I really do.'

My fingers grip the handle of my cup too hard as I wait for the 'but'.

'But I think it's best we avoid talking about our private lives here. I totally get that things are very difficult for all of us. I'm sure that once everything's resolved, you'll soon feel your old self again.'

I should leave it there. She's trying to be reasonable and nice. But in that moment, I feel like I hate her and I can't let it go.

'I don't think you appreciate the effect this is going to have on my daughter. You two have literally just met. Surely you have reservations about him moving in so quickly?'

'That's none of your business, Emma. This is totally inappropriate.'

I laugh. 'Yes, it is. You two are being totally inappropriate and unprofessional, acting like a couple of teenagers who—'

'Stop right there.' She looks furious and glances through to Anya's empty office, obviously desperate to get rid of me now.

'Look, I'm sorry,' I say, trying to backtrack. 'It's just so hard, trying to work and sorting out care for Maisie. I'm worried how all this will affect her.'

'It's my belief that children are very resilient.'

'Yes, but it's not your daughter who's going to suffer, is it?'

'Leave Piper out of this.' Her expression is grim, and I sense I've crossed a line, mentioning the untouchable, perfect Piper. 'As far as work goes, which is all I'm prepared to discuss in this office, I'm willing to give you a bit of breathing space. You only had to ask.'

Such empathy when she's the cause of the upheaval in my life, I think bitterly.

'I just want Maisie to be happy.' My voice breaks slightly. 'It's going to be a big change for her.'

'Maisie will be fine. I'll look after her as if she's my own. You've no worries at all on that score.' Joanne smiles and tips her head slightly to one side. 'Now, Emma. If you don't mind, I really need to get on.'

CHAPTER 22

Joanne

Joanne was often the first partner to arrive at the office in the morning.

Although she was more than happy to give her daughter breakfast at home, Piper actually preferred to attend the breakfast club at school.

The principal had invited parents in when it first started up, showed them the vast buffet laid out in the light, airy eatery, with its glass walls, gentle water feature and plants, that looked out over the impressive school fields.

It cost a fortune to send Piper to the Nottingham Girls' High School, but its achievement record was second to none and Joanne could rest assured her daughter was receiving the very best education and opportunities there.

It was a pleasure to drop Piper off at the school gates each morning and see her bounding over to the large group of friends who always waited for her by the entrance to the dining room.

She was a popular girl; Joanne must be doing something right in raising her, she thought to herself as she climbed out of the low sports car with a tiny wince.

She was naturally slim and had never had an enormous appetite, so the fact that she'd rather neglected her gym membership the past few weeks because of her workload hadn't made that much of a difference to her appearance.

But she'd stopped her weekly yoga class too and that decision had certainly made a difference to her joints and flexibility. She added it to the ever-growing to-do list in her head.

Standing up straight at last, she turned, surprised to hear car tyres crunching on the gravel behind her.

Expecting the vehicle to belong to Roy or Dan, one of the other partners, her heart missed a beat when she recognised the small red Toyota as Emma Barton's car.

Joanne closed her car door behind her and locked it, and began walking towards the office building.

Shaun had told her he'd had the conversation with Emma.

Piper was on a sleepover at a school friend's house, and despite the fact that Joanne had heaps of work to get through, they'd sat on the balcony last night with the gas patio heater on and a candle lit, sharing a bottle of red wine.

She'd wrapped a light mohair blanket around her shoulders and curled up next to him on the outdoor sofa, relishing the comfort of the sumptuous deep cream cushions where she usually sat alone when Piper had gone to bed.

Shaun poured the wine, and after they'd clinked glasses, Joanne took a deep gulp, savouring the rich berry tang.

'Tell me,' she said softly.

'Well, it wasn't the best feeling in the world,' Shaun admitted, ignoring his wine and staring at the flickering flame in front of him. 'Even though we're not together any more, I feel a bit of an arse for finding happiness so quickly.'

She liked how he showed her his vulnerable side so readily.

'You deserve to be happy, Shaun. You shouldn't feel bad about that.'

'I know.' He lifted his hand and touched her cheek gently with the backs of his fingers.

'You told her you were moving in here?' Joanne swallowed hard.

'I did,' he sighed. 'And then she asked me to leave and so I can't really gauge her reaction. She ranted and raved a bit, but that was no surprise.'

Joanne raised her eyebrows. 'Why, is that her usual behaviour?'

'Can be.' Shaun shrugged, taking his first sip of wine. 'She's quite volatile at times.'

'That surprises me. She always seems fairly calm and together at work. Although, like I told you, she has mentioned she's had difficulties at home.'

'Hmm. Well, me moving out will hopefully improve matters,' he said.

'Piper isn't back until tomorrow evening.' Joanne smiled. 'We've still got some time to ourselves.'

'Sounds great. Although I bet you miss her when she's not around, with there only being the two of you.'

'I do.' She loved how he just understood her. She swirled her glass gently, watching as the deep ruby liquid sparked in the candlelight. 'I'm so pleased you two have already been able to meet a couple of times. You're going to miss Maisie. It's going to be tough.'

He pursed his lips and stared out from the softly lit balcony into the velvety dark space beyond.

'I'm expecting it to be very tough,' he said. 'Maisie and I are close, especially over the last two or three months, when I've been spending more time with her. I think she's going to really miss me too, and I hope Emma doesn't use her to get back at me in some way.'

Joanne widened her eyes. 'Do you really think she'd do that?'

'I don't know. I hope not.' Shaun sighed, turning from the darkness outside to look at her. 'I'm probably being unfair to Emma. She's always wanted Maisie and me to have a strong, healthy relationship, so there's every chance she'll be reasonable about my contact with her.'

'I know we've seen each other's kids at the dance school, but tell me about Maisie.' Joanne shuffled closer, turned to fully face him. 'What's she like?'

Shaun grinned, the deep lines between his eyebrows softening.

'Maisie? Well, that's easy. She's bright, beautiful, clever... full of laughter and life.' He laughed. 'I sound such a geeky dad, I know. But she is just wonderful, Jo. I can't wait for you to meet her.'

'Likewise, I want you to get to know Piper properly. Now you're moving in, we have to sit down and explain things to her. But she really likes you.'

'I understand it's more of a rush than we wanted.' Shaun nodded. 'And easier for me with Maisie living with Emma, so why don't we focus on your side of things for now?'

Joanne's face lit up at his obvious enthusiasm to get to know her daughter.

'I've been thinking how I'm going to tell her you're moving in and that you'll be sleeping in my room.'

'Wow, you're a fast mover,' Shaun teased her.

'This whole thing is crazy fast, don't you think?'

'Absolutely, but I feel so at ease with you, like we've been dating for months. It's mad.'

'We're hardly love-struck teenagers,' Joanne pointed out. 'We've seen enough of life to know we have something special.'

She thought for a moment before continuing.

'I know you said we can focus on my side of things, but I have an idea how to get our girls together...'

'I'm all ears.' He nudged her. 'I like a woman who uses her initiative.'

CHAPTER 23

Emma

Shaun hasn't given me Joanne's full address yet.

'There's no need. I'm always available on my phone,' he says when I tackle him for the second time. Despite my initial threat that he has to take all his stuff in one go, I've accepted his popping backwards and forwards, like the pushover I am.

'That's fine.' I turn away, busying myself with taking paperwork out of my work bag. 'I'll have the school remove you from Maisie's contact details then.'

He looks at me. 'Can't you just leave things as they are for now? They have my mobile number and they don't need to know the ins and outs of our personal circumstances.'

'There are no ins and outs. You're moving out. Period.'

'You know what I mean, Em.' He opens his hands, shows me his long, slim fingers. The same ones that once used to skilfully trace from the nape of my neck down the length of my spine, leaving a trail of goosebumps in their wake.

'I'd rather have everything out in the open,' I say firmly. 'We tried keeping our arrangement hush-hush and look where that got us. We're best just being honest with people.'

'And' – he hesitates, marks out inverted commas in the air with hooked fingers – 'what does "being honest" entail?'

'Ooh, I don't know.' I pause for effect. 'I suppose it means telling everyone you've found someone else and left us. That's the truth, isn't it?'

'I thought that might be your plan.' The muscle in his jaw clenches. 'And yet the real truth is that *you* initiated us splitting up three months ago.'

I hold up my index finger. 'With the proviso that it didn't affect Maisie.'

'Oh yes, your infamous arrangement.'

'*Our* arrangement.'

'Whatever,' he says dismissively. 'Regardless of who suggested it, I'd now like a new agreement for when I get to see Maisie.'

'That's the least of my worries right now.'

It's really important to me that Maisie has a healthy, close connection with her dad, particularly after my own dysfunctional father–daughter relationship. But I won't let him know my thoughts. Let him suffer a bit. He can't have it all his way.

'Least of *your* worries perhaps, but definitely my priority,' he says. 'I'd like to see her at weekends. Joanne and I plan to take the girls out for the day on Saturday, so I'd appreciate it if you'll be flexible about me moving my stuff out. I need to tell Maisie I'm moving out before Saturday. I hope you'll agree it's the best thing for her to do it this way.'

I flick through a stack of case papers and rearrange them. It's a meaningless task and I'm blind to the words on the page, but it conveys the right impression to Shaun. I know he's right about prioritising Maisie in the middle of all this, but it sticks in my throat to say so.

'You lost your right to pick and choose when you decided to walk out on us,' I say levelly, looking up. 'I'll think about it and let you know.'

'Emma. This is not just your call, you know that, right?' His tone is cold. 'Maisie has two parents and I have as much right as you to see her.'

'Try telling that to a family court judge,' I say, enjoying the shock that registers on his face. 'See how your ridiculously short relationship and antisocial working hours fare in a legal judgement.'

His nostrils flare and his lips curl into a sneer.

'You might think you hold all the cards when it comes to our daughter, but you're mistaken.'

'What's that supposed to mean?'

'You'll see,' he says.

CHAPTER 24

The house somehow feels bigger, emptier in the fifteen minutes since Shaun left. The silence crouches around me, but it doesn't feel comforting. It's as though it's waiting for me to fall.

I sit staring out into the fading light, cradling a glass of white wine from an open bottle I found in the pantry. It's not remotely cold enough to drink and the aftertaste lies bitter on my tongue.

I asked Shaun to leave the house, to give me a bit of space. Things seem to be changing so fast, I'm feeling distinctly unanchored.

I know I said some spiteful things. He thinks I'm jealous, but it's not the fact that my husband is in a relationship with Joanne Dent that bothers me.

If I'm completely honest, he could definitely have chosen worse. Joanne doesn't flap, nor display jealousy or waste her time on petty gripes. She is a successful, level-headed woman who has her own young daughter.

And *that's* what worries me.

On the surface, Joanne looks like the perfect role model for my daughter. But her daughter, Piper, is another matter altogether.

Joanne might be a formidable businesswoman, but she has a lot to learn as a mother. Piper literally runs rings around her at the dance school. I don't want that behaviour rubbing off on Maisie, although part of me feels guilty at not giving my daughter more credit in resisting the other girl's influence.

Also, there's the small detail that Maisie can't stand Piper. Along with lots of the other girls and their mothers, she has noticed Piper's behaviour. And the unfortunate way she seems to resent attention falling on anyone but herself.

I sigh, trying to look for the silver lining. Piper has her own circle of friends, so perhaps it might be a good thing after all. Maisie is a sociable girl, and even if she still finds Piper irritating, she might widen her horizons in other ways.

I take a sip of the lukewarm wine and feel the sting of its sourness at the back of my throat.

There's a new sadness; I can sense the weight of it lying on my chest like a warm cat, bedding itself in for the long haul.

I think it's probably natural to feel this way. When two people part and one of them meets someone new, there's bound to be a sense of being left behind in life's journey. As though happiness is smiling on them and leaving you behind.

But this isn't a board game with winners and losers. Shaun and I didn't want to be together any more. Instead of acting like bickering children, allowing Maisie to witness our discontent, we acted like grown-ups. Made adult decisions.

I'm proud of what we tried to do, even if it only lasted a short time.

Through the glass, the garden offers glimmers of its gathering winter sparkle. Now, as I fill the kettle each morning and gaze out of the window, it's frost that glimmers on the grass, not sunlight.

Damp, tangled leaves in earthy shades clog the lawn and borders, but for a few moments, I'm standing by the open French doors, smiling. I can almost hear the echo of Maisie's tinkling laughter as she stomps around in glossy red wellies, shadowing her dad's autumn leaf-raking duties.

How the years march on, whilst we busy ourselves living our best life.

Parenting, relationship, career, health, appearance... we run ourselves ragged ticking all the important boxes, whilst fleeting joyful moments slip so easily through the cracks.

I finish the wine and stand up, walking over to the draining board to set down the glass.

My stomach feels sore, as if it's blistering on the inside.

I can only describe it as the physicality of letting go, of accepting that my husband has veered off onto another path, one that Maisie will tread with him. One that I cannot follow them on.

Up until now, we two have been the sole influencers on our daughter, together. At home, anyhow. Now, she's going to play a part in this new blended family that will no doubt pose its own challenges. Another home where things will be done differently, and not always better.

I tell myself Shaun could have met anyone – a woman I didn't know, someone younger who might resent our daughter and want him all for herself. Keen to start a new family together. It could have been much worse, so I don't want to catastrophise too much.

But I'll need to speak to him, warn him about Piper's public tantrums and open disrespect to her mother. It will be his responsibility to keep an eye on Maisie and to ensure she doesn't get drawn into that behaviour.

Joanne Dent is my boss. It's a bit weird, granted, but personal complications aside, I have always admired her, coveted her confidence and professional abilities.

Before things got so tangled, we'd actually chatted in her office on occasion, like friends. But now... now things aren't as comfortable.

A heat creeps into my neck, inches up towards my face as I recall the things I told her just a few weeks ago – about our marriage, our circumstances.

Personal details I would never have divulged, had I realised.

There's a sharp crack, a searing pain in my hand, and I cry out, dropping the glass with his snapped stem into the stainless-steel sink.

I turn on the tap and hold my punctured palm under the icy-cold stream. The pink water swirls around in a bloody maelstrom before draining away down the plughole.

I grab a clean tea towel and hold it against my hand, leaning back against the worktop.

My chest is tight, my hands shaky. I've been telling myself Shaun's news is no big deal and yet annoyingly, my body seems to be reacting on a physical level that I have little control over.

I tell myself it *will* be OK. Everything will be fine. There's no reason why it shouldn't all work out for the best.

Providing Maisie takes the news well.

CHAPTER 25

After work, at my request, Shaun and I meet in Costa for a quick coffee.

I only have half an hour to spare before Maisie's after-school class finishes, but that should be plenty of time for what I want to talk about.

I park up on the road near the Ropewalk and cut down the side roads, heading for the coffee shop in the Old Market Square.

I texted Shaun that morning. Asked if he'd like us to tell Maisie together about the big changes that were taking place in all our lives.

Overnight, I'd calmed down a little and thought about Maisie, instead of myself. I had a duty to make breaking the news as gentle and effective as possible.

Shaun texted right back, agreeing it was a great idea, and so we arranged to meet here.

I feel a bit sick as I open the door to the bustling coffee shop. I'm not eating much and I feel jumpy and anxious, never quite sure what development is coming next.

I step aside as two young mums reach the door at the same time as I do, their little ones strapped in pushchairs.

It doesn't seem two minutes since that was me: going for a coffee with my friend and her little boy, who I haven't seen for a couple of years now but who is the same age as Maisie.

I arrive just a few minutes before our scheduled meeting time, and so I'm not expecting to see Shaun when I scan the place looking for a free table.

My eyes gravitate to a handsome, broad-shouldered man over on the far side who's smiling at me, and I realise with a start that it is the new well-dressed, confident version of Shaun.

Seeing him unexpectedly like that helps me remember the instant attraction I felt when we first set eyes on each other all those years ago.

The spike of desire I once felt slumps into a tiny pool of sadness and regret that hovers in my throat for a few seconds before I swallow it down.

He raises his hand.

I pick my way through the packed tables, trying to avoid stepping on tiny feet and bulging shopping bags.

'Hi.' He smiles and I notice tiny lines etched around his mouth that I've never spotted before. Maybe it isn't all fun and games for him after all; maybe Shaun is suffering too.

'Hi.' I pull out a chair and put my bag on it, taking out my purse. 'I'll get the drinks.'

I'm in luck; there are only three people ahead of me in the queue, I must have caught a little lull. I didn't need to ask what he wanted to drink; he's a regular latte man, no fancy flavours or additions for him.

I keep my back to him. I have on a new navy and white fitted jacket and a pair of well-cut black trousers that I haven't been able to fit into for a while. I've paired the outfit with a pair of plain black stilettos, but I think I probably look quite slim from the back and the clothes fit me well.

I've lost weight without trying, even though I've been careful to eat regularly and cook myself and Maisie a meal each evening. The appetite just isn't there.

It's surprising the effect four or five pounds can have on the fit of your clothes when it just melts away without effort.

I find myself hoping Shaun has noticed, and then I remember Joanne's svelte body and designer labels. I probably don't look very impressive to him at all.

'You look well,' he says when I return with two lattes.

'Thanks,' I say, sitting down.

I don't return the compliment, even though I've noticed he's wearing a Hugo Boss navy sports jacket I haven't seen before, and I recognise that fresh citrus scent again. It certainly makes a startling change from the dull, woody aftershave he's worn since the first day I met him.

'So, Joanne and I were talking about the girls last night.' He jumps straight in. 'They already know each other from dancing, but as Joanne says, they have different sets of friends. So she's come up with a great idea to arrange a day together, all four of us, to give them a chance to get to know each other properly.'

'OK,' I say, a little disarmed. 'It's important we discuss telling Maisie about you moving out first, though.'

'I agree. Totally. But I think Jo's suggestion could tie in with that quite nicely.'

Jo?! Last month I heard her tear a strip off an intern for calling her that.

'I'm all ears,' I say drily.

'Jo's daughter, Piper, is a sweet girl. I think she and Maisie will get on brilliantly.'

This is my chance to voice my concerns.

'While we're on the subject of Piper, are you aware she's a bit of a madam? If you picked Maisie up from dancing a bit more regularly, you'd see her kicking off at her mother in front of everyone. It's embarrassing.'

'Oh!' Shaun looks nonplussed. 'I don't know about that, but I'm sure Joanne has it under control.'

'That's just it, though; she doesn't seem to have any control over Piper's behaviour, which worries me if Maisie is going to be spending time in her company. And Piper sometimes wears clothes that are way too old for her, in my opinion.'

Shaun discounts my concerns with a flick of his wrist.

'Joanne has suggested we all go to the Superbowl in town. It's a good way for the girls to meet in a nice, informal way, and then we'll go back to Jo's place for food.'

'And how does that fit with telling Maisie you're moving out?' I ask. 'At the moment, she thinks you're just working away.'

'I was intending to tell her on Saturday. Just casually, sort of play it down.'

'I don't think that's acceptable at all, Shaun.' I push my coffee away. The thought of all that rich, creamy milk makes me feel sick. 'Maisie is an intelligent girl, as you know. She's old enough now that she's bound to have questions, and she might well get upset. I think she needs to be in a safe environment like home when you tell her. Not in the middle of Superbowl.'

'Oh, that's disappointing.' He deflates a little. 'But I see your point, I suppose.'

'I think bowling is a good place for her to get to know Joanne and Piper, but we need to tell her about us and about you moving out first.' I tap my fingernail on the tabletop. 'Perhaps Saturday is a bit of a rush. It's a lot for her to take in; she gets the news that her dad is moving out and then within two days she meets his new girlfriend and her daughter.'

He shifts in his seat.

'Like Jo says, kids are resilient. I think this stuff is best out in the open.'

'I agree, but really, what's the rush? Can't you just wait another week or two?'

A couple of people at nearby tables turn to look at us, and I stare back, annoyed and confused as to why they're taking an interest in our conversation.

'No, I'm not prepared to wait just because *you* can't handle it.'
He stands up, his coffee also untouched. 'I was hoping you'd be
reasonable about this, Emma, but I can see you're intent on being
as awkward as ever.'

'Hang on!' My mouth drops open. 'Sit down, please, Shaun. I'm
not being awkward; I'm thinking about our daughter, that's all.'

'Are you?' He steps aside and pushes his chair under the table.
'Are you *really* thinking about Maisie's best interests here, or is it
a case of being more interested in putting obstacles in my path?'

'Shaun, you're being unreasonable. I—'

'If you want to see who the unreasonable one is here,' he says
snidely as he walks away, 'then I suggest you take a look in the mirror.'

CHAPTER 26

Shaun texts me ten minutes after walking out of the café to say he'll be at the house at 6.30 so we can tell Maisie together.

It angers me how he arrogantly picks the time and expects me to be free at his convenience. But I force myself to send a simple text back to say it's fine.

I'm treading on eggshells with him at the moment. He's displaying personality traits that are the polar opposite to the ones I've lived with during our marriage. There is no sign of the dithering and self-doubt that plagued him and irritated me for years. Any such weaknesses seem to have melted away overnight.

Sadly, as I know only too well, those old insecurities have a habit of popping right up again just when you think you're rid of them for good.

For now, though, Shaun is flying high and seems to be giving himself full credit.

I'm due to pick Maisie up from her dance class at six o'clock, so that will give me time to feed and water her before Shaun arrives for our chat.

I get out of the car and walk around it to the front door, stopping dead as I pass the corner of the house. The small opaque side window, the downstairs loo, is broken. When I inspect it, I see it's still in one piece but fractured, cracks radiating out from a central puncture. There's no glass on the floor and no sign of a rock or stone. In fact, it looks just as if someone has punched the glass in temper.

I shiver and rush around the front of the house to open the door. Inside, I peer at the glass from the inside. The middle of the window bows in slightly where contact has been made.

I feel sure the window is too small for anyone to climb through, but still. Tendrils of dread begin to stir in my stomach and I leave the tiny room and close the door behind me.

There's probably a perfectly simple explanation that evades me at the moment. I make a real effort to push the troubling thoughts away. I can't go back to that place. I just can't.

I throw myself into making Maisie's favourite chocolate spread sandwiches for tea. I'm making an exception tonight and skipping our usual hot meal – I have no appetite and I'm certain food will be the last thing on Maisie's mind once her dad gets here.

I can't second-guess how she will react to the news. It makes it more difficult as Shaun and I haven't actually discussed how we'll approach it.

I feel fairly confident that, if it's done in the right way, Maisie is happy and confident enough that she'll take it all in her stride and cope admirably. That's been my experience of her attitude to change so far, at any rate.

I take a sharp knife from the block and cut the sandwich into four dainty triangles, the way Maisie likes them.

But I pull the knife away too sharply and it nicks the edge of my left index finger, drawing blood.

I curse and suck the tiny wound while I open the kitchen drawer and pull out a packet of plasters, awkwardly wrapping a small one round my finger.

I place her sandwich on a plate and wrap the whole thing in cling film before putting it in the fridge. I'm so clumsy lately. I broke the wine glass and yesterday I dropped a plate, which bounced painfully off my foot before breaking in two on the kitchen floor.

Distraction, that's what it is. I shouldn't be dreading this conversation with Shaun and Maisie; I ought to welcome the chance to get things out in the open so we can start to work towards a new routine for our lives.

I hate all this turmoil and unfamiliar territory; I'm exasperated by the broken window I just discovered. I need more stability and less confusion.

Otherwise, I'll start to feel weird again.

Maisie bounces out of class, over to the car.

'We had to do jumping jacks for ages and Miss Diane chose the best three – and I was one of them!'

'Brilliant! Well done.' I lean over and kiss her on the forehead. Her shiny dark curls bounce at the side of her beaming face and her cheeks are ruddy and round, bunching up either side of her nose.

The relative peace and calm of the car interior is zinging with energy and I can't help but smile.

'What's for tea?' Always her first question when she's told me how the class went.

'Well, you might be surprised to hear that you've got chocolate spread sarnies and a bag of crisps.'

'Seriously?' She throws me a sideways glance to check if I'm joking.

'Seriously,' I confirm. 'Relaxed tea tonight because your dad is coming over.'

'Over from where?' She takes a sip of water from the cooler flask I have waiting for her after class. She's thoughtful for a moment before her face lights up. 'Can we all watch a film together?'

I swallow. 'I'm not sure there'll be time for that. I mean, he'll be home for just a little while before he has to go off to work again.'

Her smile dims. 'He's always working. He's hardly ever home now.'

I start the car, check the mirror and pull out into a gap in the traffic. As we gather speed, I notice Joanne Dent's Mercedes parked in its usual spot on double yellows outside the dance studio's door.

I crane my neck to look as we pass and see she isn't at the wheel.

'Well, he'll be home for a while tonight, so that'll be nice.'

Maisie doesn't reply, and I'm reminded of how awkward it's going to be if she doesn't get an explanation soon about why Shaun is always absent.

Our daughter is a smart cookie. She deserves to know the truth and she's obviously already noticed things are changing.

I can only fob her off for so long. I should feel relieved, not anxious, that we're speaking to her tonight.

'So, who were the other two students Miss Diane picked out?'

Her bouncy energy has dissipated, and from the way she stares straight ahead at the road before answering, I guess she's less than satisfied with my answers about Shaun's brief visit tonight.

'Carly and Piper,' she says flatly.

My heartbeat races a little at the mention of Piper's name.

'That's nice,' I remark.

'Piper wasn't the best, though,' Maisie says bluntly. 'Pia was much better, but Piper always gets picked for stuff because of who her mum is.'

It does surprise me that Joanne obviously expects special treatment for her daughter, just because she owns the premises. She's quite low-key at work but seems to have a blind spot when it comes to anything to do with Piper.

'That's a bit unfair,' I say gently as I slow the car and join a queue of traffic at the lights. 'I'm sure Piper is a good dancer and I wouldn't think Miss Diane would pick her if—'

'Miss Diane picks her because of who her mum is and also because Piper sulks like anything if she isn't chosen,' Maisie complains. 'She's already telling people she's going to get the role of Dorothy in the Christmas show.'

The Wizard of Oz is the annual dance show this year. It's a big event for the school and, thanks to ongoing sponsorship from Walker, Dent and Scott, is usually quite a glitzy affair with a generous budget.

'I'm sure the roles will be fairly chosen,' I say mildly. 'After all, Piper was Annie last year so it's only fair for someone else to have a turn in the spotlight.'

'I bet I end up being a boring Munchkin,' Maisie says crossly.

This is not the best way for our conversation to go, I reflect as I turn the car into our road. Maisie was bright and in a good mood when I picked her up, and somehow I've succeeded in turning that around so she's now moody and quiet.

She sits up straight and leans forward, straining against her seat belt.

'Dad's already here!' She instantly brightens.

Shaun's outsized Audi fills the driveway and I feel a snag of irritation that he's acting as if he still lives here. I always parked on the road in front of the drive, in line with Shaun's theory that any car thieves in the area would be interested in his car rather than mine. But now, it's most definitely *my* spot.

On top of this, a good few days ago I asked him, and then when that didn't work, I told him, in no uncertain terms, *not* to use his door key and to text in advance if he was coming to the house instead of just turning up.

As soon as the car stops, Maisie's door flies open and she jumps out and races up the drive. The front door opens and Shaun holds out his arms for her to run into. I feel relieved she hasn't noticed the broken window. I don't want her worrying about it.

I reach into the back seat to retrieve my handbag and also to grab Maisie's dance bag that she left there in her rushed exit.

I trudge up the drive and Shaun, still locked in Maisie's embrace, looks over her head. 'Hi. What's the long face for?'

'That conversation we had about your key?' I say cryptically so Maisie won't pick up on it. 'Remember?'

'You couldn't let me in because you weren't here,' he says simply.

'You knew where I was, though. You could have waited in the car for a few minutes,' I say, looking pointedly at the driveway. 'I'll have to move into my spot once you've gone.'

He kisses Maisie on the top of her head. 'Oh, we're in for a fun evening, aren't we, poppet? Sounds like Mum has got dragon breath again.'

Maisie laughs heartily and takes his hand, and they both disappear into the house, leaving me on the path, loaded down like a donkey.

CHAPTER 27

Inside the house, I dump the bags near the door, slip off my shoes and walk into the kitchen, ignoring the mail that Shaun has obviously picked up from the floor and placed on the side table.

I swallow down my annoyance at his arrogant attitude and instead resolve to make our talk with Maisie a success. *She* is what's important here.

Maisie dashes past me, up to her room, to grab something to show her dad and I seize the opportunity to tell Shaun about the broken window.

He walks into the hallway and I follow as he opens the door to look at the fractured glass.

'Luckily it's not broken,' he says mildly. 'Probably a bird flew into it or something.'

'A bird? It must've been going at speed to do that damage, and I'd have expected to have seen it dead or injured on the path.' I hesitate. 'It looks to me like someone has punched the glass,' I whisper, to avoid Maisie hearing. 'But who would want to do that?'

'Exactly. You answered your own question, Em. Maybe time to knock off reading those crime novels of yours, eh?' He laughs. 'I'll sort out a repair, don't worry.'

Maisie bounces back into the room with her English exercise book and the silver star that Mrs Tetley gave her for her story about a rabbit with a misshapen foot who dreams of becoming a dancer. I confess it brought a lump to my throat when I read it.

'Wow!' Shaun's mouth falls open. 'This is amazing, and you know what, I know two people who would love you to read it to them.'

'You do?'

'Yes, a good friend of mine, a lovely lady called Joanne, and her daughter Piper – you know them from dancing, I think?'

Maisie stares.

'Piper *Dent*, you mean?' she says incredulously.

Shaun's eyes dart my way but he doesn't look directly at me.

'That's her! I happen to know that Joanne and Piper love stories and I reckon they'd adore this one.'

I stand in the doorway, hands on hips. Is he intending to tell her all on his own?

'How do you even know what *they* like?' Maisie demands.

This might be a key moment, but I'm not going to let him cut me out of the conversation. We agreed to tell Maisie together.

I walk to the fridge and pull out the sandwiches I prepared earlier.

'Hello. Mind if I join you?' Predictably, Shaun misses my sarcastic intent. 'Coffee?'

'Sure,' he says, looking back at Maisie, relieved, I think, by the interruption. 'Thanks.'

I hand Maisie the plate.

'Thought you said I can have crisps, too?'

'I think you mean, *Thank you for the sandwiches*.' I frown. 'I'll get your crisps now.'

'Thanks,' she mutters as I walk to the cupboard, but not before I turn and catch her rolling her eyes at Shaun behind my back. I really don't like the way this is going.

I fill the kettle, flick the switch on and carry Maisie's crisps over to the seating area.

'There you go, pumpkin.' I hand her the packet. 'Dad's come over so we can all have a chat together.'

'Dad thinks Piper Dent would like to read my story,' Maisie says mutinously, opening the crisps.

'I'm certain she would,' he says.

'Yeah, right. She's not interested in anyone but herself.'

Shaun sits up straighter amongst the soft cushions, but his shoulders slump a little and I spot that he is chewing the inside of his top lip.

Maisie takes a small bite of a neat triangle of bread, her eyes never leaving her dad's face.

'The thing is,' he begins. 'You know I've got lots of work on now, right, Maisie?'

She nods.

'Well, me and Mum decided it might be easier if—'

No way. I'm not letting him pull this dirty trick.

'*Your dad* has made a decision, Maisie.'

'Yes, I made a decision… partly because of work.' He glares at me and then softens his face when he realises Maisie is still watching him. 'I thought it would be much easier for me to live over the other side of town… to make getting to work easier.'

Maisie frowns. 'But will this still be your home?' She turns to me. 'Dad still lives here, doesn't he, Mum?'

I look at him and raise an eyebrow.

'Well… no, I don't live here any more, not exactly. But I'm not too far from here, and I want you to come and—'

'Why do you need to live somewhere else if it's not far from here anyway?'

I study Maisie's side profile, fascinated. Her still childlike podgy cheeks and upturned nose. All the features of who she'll become are there now and she's changing. Growing up by the day.

Her reasoning in questioning Shaun has stunned me. She's challenging his banal, simplified explanation, interrogating him on what he wants to portray as a simple decision.

In some ways she's not a child any more. She's not easily misled and has logical questions that she expects answers to. I feel proud of her and, if I'm honest, a modicum of satisfaction at seeing my husband wriggling on the hook when he thought it would be so easy to tell his nice cosy story and leave the house unscathed.

'It's not that far but it's nearer the motorway, poppet, so it's far more convenient for work, you see.'

'But you're hardly ever here on weekends either,' she presses him.

Shaun sighs and rubs the heels of his palms on his jeans. He looks at me, but I turn back to Maisie. Reach for her hand.

'Well, it's probably not quite as simple as it sounds,' he says hesitantly. 'You see, me and Mum, we're... we've been going through a bit of a rough time and we thought the space would do us good.'

'Are you splitting up?' Maisie's clear voice cuts through Shaun's waffle. She looks at her father and then turns to look at me. 'Are you?'

'Yes,' I say. 'We are, my love.'

'Emma!' Shaun's nostrils flare.

'We need to tell her the *truth*,' I snap back. 'She's not a little kid any more, Shaun. She can handle it.'

'Yes, but you make it sound so... so final.' He presses his lips together.

'Sorry, am I missing something?' I let out a bitter laugh. 'I thought you'd made your mind up that you're moving out. Aren't you sure?'

'Of course I am. Why do you always have to—'

He stops talking and we both look at our daughter, who is sitting there silently, sandwiches abandoned, staring vacantly into space.

I look meaningfully at Shaun, hoping he'll join me in rescuing the situation for Maisie's sake.

'It sounds horrible, I know that, sweetie,' I say, squeezing her hand. 'But trust me, it will be better for all of us.'

'I'll see more of you, Maize,' Shaun adds. 'I'll still be around loads.'

I don't like the way he puts that. I can't let him think he can just come and go whenever he wants, like he still lives here.

'You'll have set days when Dad will come and pick you up, and I'm sure he'll have lots of great things planned for the two of you.'

'You bet.' Shaun sits down on the other side of Maisie and holds her other hand. 'It sounds a big deal, but life will be better. Trust me.'

Maisie turns to him. Speaks quietly.

'Piper's mum, Joanne Dent… Is she your new girlfriend?'

If it wasn't such a sad, dire situation, I would have laughed out loud at the way Shaun's jaw drops.

'I… No, not really. Not yet. I…' He looks at me pleadingly.

'She's your dad's *friend*,' I say simply, and he nods gratefully.

'That's right, pumpkin. Joanne is my friend and she wants us all to go out for the day on Saturday. I know she really likes you and I bet you and Piper could be really good friends too.'

Maisie shifts in her seat and a sandwich falls off her plate onto the floor.

'I don't think we can ever be friends,' she says. 'I don't think she likes me… and I can't stand *her*.'

CHAPTER 28

That night, for the first time in a long time, I dream I'm back at Clayton and McCarthy again.

I worked there for two years. I enjoyed my job and my colleagues were all pleasant and easy to get along with. Except for one paralegal, Damian Murphy.

He made no secret of his burning ambition to become a fully qualified solicitor, and separated himself from us lowly minions in the admin department, acting as if he was a cut above the rest of us.

In the dream, I'm in the staff car park at the start of the day. Except it isn't the staff car park, it's suddenly a very busy supermarket car park, in that way dreams have of lurching from one reality to another.

My heart is racing and I'm anxious because every time I go for a space, someone else beats me to it.

Then I'm teleported somehow into the office building to find I'm one of the last ones in. The others are all scurrying around like soldier ants, following orders barked at them by Damian.

'Afternoon, Emma.' He glances pointedly at the wall clock. 'The boss has asked me to check the court report you compiled yesterday. Shall we say...' He looks at his wrist watch. 'Ten minutes at my desk?'

When I look down at the floor, the report is scattered in torn pages all around my feet.

'I don't know what silly game you're trying to play here, Emma, but some of us are serious about this case. Some of us are serious about our careers.'

The pages at my feet turn into hissing snakes, squirming and sliming over and around my shoes.

'Emma?' I look up at the curt tone and see Damian tapping his watch. 'Where are your notes?' Again and again he repeats it: 'Where are your notes? Where are your notes?' And each time he speaks, his voice gets slower and lower, like an old record slowing right down, and when I look up at him, his eyes glow red and his skin is burned and his teeth are…

Suddenly, there is a line of vehicles in front of me. My recollection of the dream clicks off like a light and I'm very firmly back in the present.

'Shit!' I jump on the brakes and stop about an inch from the car in front as it slows for the lights.

I open the windows and drag in some air, feeling sick at the near-miss. It was just a nonsensical dream, that's all, and I need to treat it as such. No sense in trawling through it all again.

What happened at Clayton and McCarthy is in the past and it needs to stay there. Sorting my life out *now* is where my energy needs to go.

I force myself to focus on my driving, and when I arrive at the office, I don't go to my desk as usual. Instead, I keep climbing the stairs to the second floor.

There have been times in the past, when I was wrestling with the realisation that things were going wrong in my marriage, when I'd lie awake for hours with Shaun fast asleep beside me.

They were long, lonely nights, when I'd turn everything over in my mind relentlessly, never arriving at any conclusions, just taking a kind of masochistic pleasure in reliving the harsh words and heated arguments, reviewing the promises we'd both broken.

There was never a constructive outcome, just the abject tiredness that followed, dragging myself through the day-to-day work and the stresses of family life that would not abate.

I feel just as exhausted now, but I can't shirk from doing what needs to be done.

I walk down the carpeted corridor and head for Joanne's office. I see her look up through the glass wall, see her expression darken when she spots me.

She has her phone in her hand, and she puts it down and bends her head to the paperwork strewn on her desk, feigning absorption in her work.

I tap on the door and she looks up again. The dark expression has gone and has been replaced with a look of faint irritation. She is wearing her usual natural make-up, but her face is drained of colour.

'Emma,' she says as I push the door open a little way.

'Sorry to bother you so early, Joanne,' I say. 'I just wanted a quick word… if possible.'

'Again?' she says pointedly. 'I'm sorry, Emma, but as you can see' – she waves a hand at the copious paperwork in front of her – 'I'm up to my eyes in case files.'

I don't know why, but I find myself ignoring her obvious rebuttal. I step inside the office, closing the door behind me. Her eyes widen.

I clear my throat. 'I just wanted to say that Shaun and I told Maisie last night. About you and him, about him moving out of the house.'

Her hands, about to sort through the papers yet again, freeze above them instead.

'You really don't need to update me on every conversation you two have. Shaun keeps me up to date with all the salient details.'

Her eyes dart next door to her PA's office, but Anya has her back turned to the glass dividing wall and is currently absorbed in an animated telephone conversation.

'Can I sit down a moment, Joanne?'

'I think I said last time you were here, I'd rather not discuss personal business whilst at work.'

She pushes her phone a little further away from her, and I can see on the large lit screen that she's been looking at Facebook.

She taps the end of her pen on the table. 'But just so you know, Shaun did tell me you'd all had a chat.'

Of course he did.

'He said Maisie took it well. I'm very much hoping the girls will get on.'

Maisie's comment about the girls disliking each other echoes in my head, and I push it aside. 'We told Maisie about your trip out at the weekend. Obviously she was a little shocked, but she knows you and Piper from dancing, so you won't be complete strangers. I just…'

'Yes?'

'I just want to reiterate that Maisie is a sensitive child…'

'We've been through this before, Emma.'

'… and Piper, she seems used to getting her own way. Maisie is used to boundaries and—'

'I don't want to listen to this.' She stands up and stalks over to the door, holding it open. 'Your daughter isn't extra special, Emma, or, according to Shaun, extra sensitive. It will do her good, I'm sure, to get away from… to get out a bit more.'

I burn with fury as I imagine Shaun telling Joanne that I'm paranoid and that Maisie will be better off away from me.

'Now, if you don't mind, I have work to do.' Joanne turns back to her desk. 'As I'm sure *you* have too,' she adds.

Back at my desk, and buoyed by the intimacy of our recent conversations, I pick up my phone and open Facebook.

In the search bar at the top, I type in her name.

Three small profile pictures for people called Joanne Dent load underneath my search and I immediately spot that the top one is her.

The cover photo is blank and the profile picture can't be expanded. Disappointingly, I see there is no visible detail on her profile page. Her information is locked down pretty solid.

In some ways, it's not at all surprising; I've always known Joanne is a very private person. I wouldn't have dreamed of contacting her on Facebook previously, but that was before she struck up a relationship with my ex-husband and my daughter.

We are now bound together in ways I couldn't have envisaged, and for obvious reasons, Joanne's private life is of paramount interest to me.

My finger moves to the top of her page, and before I've really given it any thought, I find myself clicking on the *Add Friend* button.

CHAPTER 29

Val

'You look really lovely, darling.' Val sat on the edge of the bed, watching Maisie study herself in the mirror.

'I don't like these jeans.' Maisie pulled at the denim. 'I've had them for ages now, Gran. I bet Piper is wearing something brand new.'

Val didn't like the sound of this other girl very much, child or not. Three pets in the last year, all sent to new homes now, apparently. A little fashion horse at the age of ten and, according to Emma, a bit of a diva at the dance studio, too.

'Never mind what she has or hasn't got. You don't need new clothes to look perfectly lovely.'

Maisie stepped away from the mirror and gave a heavy sigh.

'I feel a bit sick. I wish I didn't have to go out with them today.'

'Nobody's said you have to go, you know that. You're *choosing* to go because it will be nice to spend the day with your dad and to meet his new friend and her daughter, who'll hopefully become one of your friends in time, too.'

'Joanne is Dad's *girlfriend*,' Maisie corrected. 'He's saying they're just friends because he thinks I'm stupid.'

'Whatever, it doesn't really matter.' Val found she couldn't quite acknowledge her son-in-law getting involved in another relationship so soon. 'I'm sure Joanne and… Piper, is it? I'm sure the two of them will be feeling equally nervous about making a good impression on you.'

Maisie pulled a face. 'You don't know her, Gran. Piper doesn't get nervous about *anything*.'

Val stood up and drew Maisie into her arms. Her little granddaughter was becoming more grown up every day, but sometimes *everyone* needed a cuddle.

'I think I've heard quite enough about Miss Piper. I'm far more interested in the very clever, very beautiful Miss Maisie.'

She planted a kiss on the top of her granddaughter's head and Maisie looked up gratefully. 'Thanks, Gran.'

'Now,' Val said, checking her watch. 'You've got a few minutes to pack any bits you might need in your bag. And don't forget your inhaler.'

Maisie nodded and began to gather her things together, while Val went back downstairs and stood in the lounge, looking out onto the road.

It was a shame Emma couldn't be here to see Maisie off. She'd agreed to work on Saturday morning, apparently, to compile stuff for an urgent case that had just come in.

If Val didn't know better, she'd think that Emma's only priority was her career. That was where she seemed to focus all her efforts and time these days.

Val knew her daughter thought the world of Maisie, but just lately, she seemed to have developed the dubious strategy of pushing away thoughts of her broken marriage by throwing herself into her job.

Val had tried to broach the subject with her several times recently, but it seemed that Emma always conveniently remembered something pressing she had to do before scurrying off.

Today wasn't simply a trip out to the bowling alley. It was a very big deal for Maisie.

It was going to be hard for the child: a whole day stretching in front of her, knowing she'd be seeing her father in the company of a new woman and her daughter. It would be all too easy for her to feel as if she'd been replaced in her father's affections by this girl Piper.

Val prayed that wasn't the case.

Shaun had seemingly planned a day where they could have fun with little pressure. Sometimes Val felt that he seemed far more level-headed and mindful of their daughter's well-being than Emma herself was.

At that moment, his oversized Audi drew up outside the front hedge.

Val could see there was someone in the passenger seat – Joanne, she presumed – and also a small face pressed up against the back window. Piper.

'Maisie,' she called, waving at Shaun through the window. 'They're here!'

CHAPTER 30

Maisie

When her gran called up that it was time to go, Maisie sat down on the end of her bed, closed her eyes and swallowed down the lump of sick in her throat.

She really didn't want to spend the day with Piper Dent and her mum. She'd much prefer to be going out with just her dad. They'd have so much more fun.

Since he'd left home, stuff that used to be ordinary suddenly felt very different; awkward, even.

When she thought back to life only a few months earlier, it seemed so relaxed and easy. Why did everything have to change?

'Maisie, they're waiting!' her gran called again. 'Come on.'

Maisie sighed, hooked her small pink rucksack over one arm and made her way down.

At the bottom of the stairs, Gran was waiting with a smile. She produced a large bag of Haribo Starmix, Maisie's favourite, and tucked it into the top of her rucksack.

'A little treat for you and your new friend.' She smiled, and kissed her on the cheek. 'Have a lovely time, my darling.'

'Thanks, Gran,' Maisie murmured.

Her throat felt dry and scratchy. Perhaps she was coming down with something. That was the phrase her mum always used when she felt a bit off-colour.

If she got ill whilst they were out, her dad would have to bring her back home. That would surely spoil the day for everyone, and Maisie thought it might be better just not to go in the first place.

'Chop chop, off you go then.' Gran opened the front door wide. 'Give my love to your dad, sweetie.'

Maisie walked out of the house and down the path towards the car as her dad jumped out of the driver's side, smiling, and waited at the gate to greet her.

She didn't have a clear view of Joanne from here, but she could see Piper's pert little nose pressed up against the window. Her breath had misted up the glass and settled like a little ring of fog around her mouth.

Maisie gave her a grin as she reached the gate and hugged her dad, but Piper didn't smile back.

It took about twenty minutes to get to the bowling alley. It was located on a retail park with a large parking area. Maisie was the first to get out of the car.

She drew in a big breath of clean fresh air.

She'd felt trapped during the journey. Joanne had persisted in asking her lots of questions about all sorts of things: school, dancing and what Maisie's hobbies were.

'She loves reading, don't you, Maize?' Shaun said in a jolly voice.

'I do like reading,' she said tentatively.

'That's nice.' Joanne seemed distracted as she swiped through her phone. 'So who's your favourite author?'

'I like David Walliams,' Maisie said right away, wishing she was immersed in one of his books in a quiet corner at home right this very minute.

'I've read all his books,' Piper said. 'He's not a *proper* author, though, like Michael Morpurgo.'

'Everyone has their own favourite, Piper,' Joanne remarked. 'There's no right or wrong choices when it comes to enjoying books.'

'That's what my teacher says,' Maisie agreed.

Piper glared and prodded Maisie's rucksack until it toppled back over her side of the large rear seat.

'I like listening to music, too,' Maisie volunteered, ignoring Piper. 'My favourite singer is Ariana Grande.'

Piper let out a loud wail and covered her eyes with her hands.

Joanne twisted around in her seat and squeezed her daughter's knee.

'Are you OK, sweetie?' She looked at Maisie and dropped her voice. 'Piper's friend was there that day at Manchester. Her friend was OK, but Piper still gets upset if the attack is mentioned.'

Maisie hooked her fingers through the handle of her rucksack and chafed the strap against her skin.

'I like Katy Perry best, anyway,' Piper said, letting her hands drop away from her face. 'She's the best singer *and* the prettiest.'

'Oh yes, you like Katy too, don't you, Maize?' her dad said.

'I'm a member of her fan club,' Piper went on. 'I have an autographed photograph and a programme from one of her concerts.'

'That's nice,' Maisie said quietly.

'You'll have to show Maisie when we get back to ours later, Piper darling,' Joanne said.

Maisie felt sick and hot. She seemed to be squashed up against the door as if she hadn't got enough space, which was silly because her dad's car was enormous.

Then the vehicle lurched to take a left turn and parked up outside the bowling alley. Maisie jumped out.

'Maisie's keen.' Joanne nudged her dad and spoke loudly for dramatic effect. 'I think you and I should play against the girls. What do you say, Shaun?'

'I want to play with *you*, Mum,' Piper said sulkily. She slammed the car door behind her far too hard, but Maisie noticed her dad didn't scold her for doing so.

Joanne looked at Shaun. 'OK with you if Piper and I team up?'

'That's fine, but be warned, Maisie and I make a formidable team,' Shaun joked. 'Right, Maize?'

'Right,' Maisie said, gnawing on her thumbnail.

Inside, they queued to pay, then queued again for their bowling shoes. Maisie tried to stand next to her dad, but Joanne held his hand one side, and Piper stood the other side of him.

'OK, poppet?' He turned back and winked at her. She nodded, and when it was her turn, took her shoes from the lady behind the counter.

Suddenly Piper appeared right next to her.

'OH MY GOD, Maisie is a four and a half in shoes!' Piper declared loudly.

'Piper…' Joanne said gently.

'That's massive! I'm only a three,' she added.

Maisie busied herself untying the knotted laces, a flood of heat rushing to her face.

'Big feet, big heart, they say.' Shaun ruffled her hair as he walked by.

'She must take after you, Shaun,' Joanne grinned. 'You've got big feet too!'

'You're not Maisie any more; your new name is *Bigfoot*!' Piper giggled with delight, dancing around in front of her. 'Bigfoot! Bigfoot!'

'Piper, you are a monkey!' Joanne pressed her fingers to her lips to suppress a giggle.

Shaun glanced at Maisie. 'What do you reckon to this cheeky pair, Maize? All the more reason for us to hammer them with our extraordinary bowling skills, right?'

Maisie nodded and smiled. The skin around her mouth felt tightly stretched, like it might split in the corners. As they headed to their bowling lane, she blinked to clear her stupid stingy eyes.

Piper skipped ahead, light and graceful on her tiptoes.

When Maisie looked down, she saw how the shoes looked like ugly big boats stuck on the ends of her clumsy legs.

CHAPTER 31

Joanne

Back at the apartment, she lined the peaches up on the baking tray, admiring how, when she'd finished, it looked like a picture from one of the glossy food magazines she bought each month but rarely read.

She'd taken time to correctly skin the plump fresh fruits, halve and stone them and then drizzle them with honey. She planned to serve them for dessert with vanilla ice cream.

It was Piper's favourite pudding and Joanne was anxious to keep Piper happy. She'd learned long ago that if Piper was happy, then everyone was happy.

Joanne was very aware that most people thought her daughter was terribly spoiled. They didn't dare voice it in front of her, of course, but the truth of what they thought revealed itself in the swiftly exchanged glances after dance classes, when Piper seemed prone to the odd tantrum.

She saw some of the other mums giving their daughters a warning look or even publicly scolding them in front of their friends. Joanne would never do that to Piper. She felt guilty enough as it was about the short amount of time she got to spend with her daughter.

People could criticise her all they liked; they had no idea what it took to manage a high-flying legal career as well as function effectively as a single mum.

With no family living close enough to help her, Joanne had no choice but to employ various people.

Audrey, a registered childminder, collected Piper from her after-school club each day.

Then there was Bahni, a middle-aged Indian lady who acted as a sort of housekeeper/cleaner. She'd been with Joanne for the last three years. Bahni worked thirty hours a week, carrying out a variety of quite simple but essential tasks, from packing up Piper's lunch box during the week to taking care of the laundry and food shopping.

On top of that, there were a couple of non-working mums at school with whom Joanne was on good terms. Piper was friendly with their daughters, girls who also attended Miss Diane's dance academy.

The friends regularly took turns having sleepovers at each other's houses, and the other mums never minded if Joanne needed to drop Piper off for an hour or two on the odd occasion she needed to pop back into the office outside of the working day.

Joanne kept her small army of helpers discreetly in the background. She always felt a little inadequate that she couldn't do it all on her own, without any help.

She winced. There it was again: the perfectionism that had propelled her to success and simultaneously plagued her her whole life.

It was exhausting at times. But it wouldn't be forever.

At some point in the near future, if she was lucky and things worked out between her and Shaun, Joanne wouldn't be facing life alone any more. She could relax a little, let go.

She opened the French doors that led out to the balcony. It was quite cool outside, but with the apartment being on the top floor, with a pitched roof, it got very warm unless it was freezing out.

She could hear laughter and shouting from the grassed area below.

Shaun had taken the girls down there with a couple of racquets and a shuttlecock to get them out from under her feet while she prepared tea. It sounded like they were having fun. He was so good with kids, seemed to know instinctively what they liked to do. Unlike her.

The last time she'd taken time off so she and Piper could have a girlie day, Joanne had bought expensive tickets to a contemporary dance performance at the Playhouse, and Piper had been bored senseless.

Maisie was so lucky, having a dad like Shaun. It was yet another thing poor Piper had missed out on, but if everything went well, maybe that could change in time.

Joanne set the timer for the baked peaches and emptied a large tub of extra-thick double cream into a metal mixing bowl. She added a little vanilla essence and some caster sugar before whipping it.

Having a playful dad hadn't stopped Maisie from being a bit uptight. Piper had made several harmless jokes throughout the day that Maisie had reacted to with a sour face. Particularly the 'Bigfoot' nickname, which privately Joanne thought had been quite apt, though the child didn't seem to see the funny side of things at all.

Maisie was a sturdy girl, tall and broad with strong facial features and curly dark hair. Joanne had caught her studying Piper's petite frame as she skipped around at the bowling alley.

Maisie would never be petite, but it would certainly help if she lost a few pounds. Same went for her mother; Joanne had noticed that Emma had a good bit of padding around her middle where her waistband always looked a little tight.

Women like Emma thought they were doing their daughters a favour, feeding them up, but they were just encouraging poor nutrition, and it was always the children who suffered. You couldn't blame a child like Maisie for feeling sour when she compared herself to a dainty girl like Piper.

Joanne lifted out the electric whisk and covered the bowl in cling film before popping it into her oversized American-style fridge.

Next she checked on the enormous lasagne that Bahni had made earlier. The cheese topping bubbled in the heat and she was gratified to see it had crisped and browned perfectly in its blue earthenware dish.

She turned off the oven and walked out onto the large balcony.

'Tea's ready!' she called down, amused to see Shaun acting as umpire to the two girls.

He looked up, waved and grinned. She gave an involuntary little shudder, thinking about how his strong, muscular arms would feel wrapped around her later in bed.

CHAPTER 32

Maisie

Maisie curled up in the foetal position and pulled the quilt over her head.

Finally she was back home in bed, in her pyjamas with the door closed. Alone. For the first time that day, she felt like she could actually breathe.

She decided she'd rather have a day at school filled with maths, science and religious studies lessons than go out with Piper and her mum again.

They hated her, and the worst thing was, Dad just couldn't see it.

'I don't like Piper calling me Bigfoot,' she'd managed to whisper to him as they threw a few practice balls down the alley.

'She's only joking, poppet,' he'd laughed. 'Try and relax a bit.'

But Piper *wasn't* joking. When their parents were busy whispering or staring at each other creepily like they were the only two people in the place, Piper trained her stare on Maisie. When those pretty cornflower-blue eyes narrowed, they looked as sly as a snake's.

'You're going to lose at bowling, clumsy clod Bigfoot,' she'd hissed. Maisie had almost expected to see a forked tongue flick out of her mouth.

At school, Maisie wasn't a pushover. If someone upset her, she could give back as good as she got. But it was different being out with them all like this.

She could tell her dad wanted it to go really well. He kept asking if everyone was all right, and his voice sounded like when he spoke to the newspaper editors on the phone. His nice, friendly home voice seemed to have disappeared.

To get her back for the Bigfoot comments, she thought about asking Piper if she'd had her feet bound like the girls had done in China a long time ago. Maisie had learned about it in a history lesson at school and it had played on her mind for ages afterwards.

It would've served her right for calling Maisie's feet big. But just as she was about to say it, Joanne came up fussing around Piper, asking if she was OK.

Somehow Piper was really good at choosing to be nasty when nobody was around to hear her.

Halfway through the game, Maisie remembered the bag of Haribo that Gran had slipped into her bag. She took them out and offered them around.

'Yuck, no thanks.' Piper wrinkled her nose. 'They're full of E numbers.'

Maisie offered the bag to Joanne.

'No thanks, sweetie.' Joanne shook her head. 'We try not to eat stuff like that. No good for your teeth… or your thighs, for that matter.' She winked at Shaun and they had a little laugh together.

Her dad had taken a handful, but Maisie put the bag back without having any herself.

Later on, back at Joanne's posh apartment, they'd played badminton on the lawn. It was a rubbish game because there was a bit too much breeze and it kept blowing the shuttlecock everywhere.

But Piper and Shaun had loved it. They collapsed in giggles when Piper was forced to clamber into the circles of bedding plants dotted around the grass to get the shuttlecock back. It wasn't even funny.

Then, when her dad made another silly umpiring decision, Maisie heard Piper say, 'Do it properly, Shaun. Like you did when we played last time!'

Maisie stuck stock still, like a sheet of ice had formed around her limbs.

She'd assumed that this was the first time Piper had met her dad, but it seemed that wasn't the case. They all already knew each other and that was why Maisie felt like a stranger.

Joanne had made a nice tea, at least. Maisie was starving; she was used to having a few snacks throughout the day.

'You're an amazing cook, Jo,' her dad said, helping himself to more lasagne with gusto. 'I could definitely get used to eating like this.'

'Oh, just a little something I rustled up earlier,' Joanne said, and smiled to herself like she'd told a joke.

'Can I have a bit more, please?' Maisie asked.

Joanne and Piper looked up from their own food and watched as her dad placed another big scoop on her plate.

'Goodness, someone must be hungry,' Joanne remarked.

Maisie wasn't sure her mum could make meals like this. It felt sort of disloyal to show she was enjoying it, and for that reason, she left a bit on her plate.

Even she had to admit dessert was delicious, though. Peaches and a very sweet cream to go with it.

She reached for the spoon to take a little more cream.

'Here's a teaspoon.' Joanne took the larger spoon from her and gave her the small one. 'It's very rich, sweetie. Best not to overindulge.'

Piper coughed, and when Maisie looked over at her, she puffed air into her cheeks so her face looked fat.

Maisie glanced at her dad for support, but he didn't seem to notice.

Maisie curled up tighter now, under the covers, and grasped her knees closer to her.

It didn't sound much to tell someone, all the bits of the day that were playing on her mind. And it wasn't really what had been said. It was more the horrible feeling that filled her stomach that she was unsure how to deal with.

It was a feeling she hadn't really felt before. Not a pain, not a sadness... something else.

Something that made her just want to stay home with her mum and her gran and all the things around her that felt familiar and safe.

CHAPTER 33

Emma

I totally expected Maisie to be buzzing with excitement when she got home from her day out.

Looking forward to having her back home, I laid a few snacks out on the coffee table in the kitchen area: crisps, cheese straws, her usual favourites. I envisaged that we'd sit and talk through the day together.

I had a full roster of work scheduled to keep me busy while she was out. The thought of having time to catch up on admin tasks and also finally read through last month's legal updates bulletin was a luxury I'd been looking forward to.

But in the event, I was unable to tick anything off my to-do list. My mind simply refused to focus, choosing instead to play scenes of what Maisie might be up to, on loop in my head.

Every hour that ticked by, I asked myself, was she happy? Was Shaun looking after her properly? Was Piper behaving?

It was silly. Even as I was doing it, I knew I had to learn to trust Shaun and trust that Maisie would be OK. She had new people in her life now who she'd forge relationships with.

I had no control over it.

After I'd given myself a bit of a talking-to, the afternoon was slightly more productive, although I did notice I had to keep rereading passages in the legal updates bulletin.

But now Maisie is back home, her face glum and her energy low, and the panic returns.

'Is she OK?' I ask Shaun as Maisie slinks past me into the house.

'Of course she's OK!' Shaun says. 'Probably a bit tired; we've packed lots in. I think she's really enjoyed it.'

'And Piper…'

'Piper and Maisie got on brilliantly. You're worrying again about things that aren't a problem, Emma. I think it will be good for her to spend time with other people.'

'Apart from me and my mother, you mean?'

His face darkens and he sighs.

'I didn't mean that, but never mind.' He leans forward. 'Bye, Maisie, see you soon!' he calls.

I hear Maisie call goodbye from the kitchen, but she doesn't come out to wave Shaun off.

I close the door and walk into the kitchen.

'So, how was it?'

She's lying on the sofa, staring at the ceiling.

'It was… OK,' she says without looking at me.

'What does *OK* mean?' I grin and nudge her foot. 'Details, please.'

'We went bowling, then went back to Joanne's apartment for tea.' Her voice is flat, disinterested.

'And how was Piper?'

'She was just her normal Piper self. Irritating.'

Maisie suddenly sits up.

'I'm really tired, Mum. I think I'll just go up to my room a while.'

'Oh!' I lay my hand on her shoulder as she walks by me. 'Sure you're OK, poppet? We can talk about anything you like.'

'I'm fine,' she says. 'Just tired.'

She disappears up the stairs and I'm left standing there, wondering what it is I'm not being told.

CHAPTER 34

The next day I wonder if, in my own mind, I exaggerated Maisie's awkwardness and Shaun's reluctance to discuss their outing yesterday.

Yes, Maisie is quiet during the morning, but she's engrossed in some kind of celebrity site online. We have breakfast together and I refrain from asking anything about her outing yesterday. She doesn't volunteer any more information but slowly becomes chattier, showing me glitzy short skirts and make-up on the website.

'I think that stuff's a little old for you yet, sweetie,' I say gently, scrolling through my laptop trying to find a case reference that I need.

'Piper gets loads of stuff from here and she's only ten.' She pulls a face. 'She says all her friends at school do too.'

I look at my daughter, keen to appear reasonable.

'Tell you what, give me half an hour and then we can take a look together. OK?'

She nods, obviously pleased with my compromise.

A few minutes later, my phone dings. Maisie grabs it and slides it across the worktop.

'You've got a text from Dad.'

I tap the screen and the message content loads.

OK if I take Maisie to the cinema this afternoon? Just the two of us.

'Yessss!' Maisie dances around the breakfast bar after snatching the phone back and reading the message. 'Just me and Dad… that's awesome!'

I text back saying that it's fine and that Maisie is very excited. When he collects her just after lunch, he comes to the door.

'She's so pleased it's just the two of you,' I say in a low voice while Maisie is getting her coat.

'Well, I figured it's going to take some time for everyone to feel comfortable together,' he says sensibly. 'It's important I spend time alone with Maisie, too.'

I could hug him, but I don't. In a way, it's an admission that perhaps things didn't quite go to plan yesterday, but I know instinctively that it's best I don't question either him or Maisie any further, for the time being.

There's something else that's piqued my interest, anyway.

'Does Piper see her father?'

Shaun shrugs. 'No. I mean, she can't. Sadly, he died a few years ago.'

I feel a squeeze on my heart when I think about the casual way I asked Joanne about it. No wonder she changed the subject so quickly.

'I didn't know that. What happened?'

He stiffens slightly. Coughs.

'Joanne is a private person, she wouldn't want me discussing stuff like that.'

'I see. Sorry I asked, then.'

It must have been pretty traumatic.

'No worries,' he says, brightening again.

I have to admit Shaun looks well. He's lost a few pounds, and with his obviously new, sleek designer wardrobe, he cuts a stylish figure. It's a long way from the well-worn tracksuits he favoured just a few weeks ago. He's not a man who'd be intimidated by being with a woman who is far wealthier than him. He's just not made that way.

When they've gone, I carry on working for a while longer. After that, I flick on the TV and, seeing there's nothing interesting to watch, decide to pick up on the crime thriller I discarded when all the upheaval started.

As I reach over to close the lid of my laptop, a message pops up on the screen.

Joanne Dent has accepted your friend request.

I'd forgotten about Facebook! I feel a frisson of embarrassment that it's taken Joanne this long to accept it. Perhaps she would rather *not* be friends online.

My logic at the time was that perhaps she might post some photographs from their day out at the bowling centre. I thought it might put my mind at rest if I could see that Maisie was relaxed and enjoying herself.

I click on the notification and the screen loads with her profile page, once sparse but now populated with a grid of photographs. Joanne smiling in selfies, Joanne with Piper at home and at various other places, and the most recent one, which makes me draw in a sharp breath, Joanne, Shaun, Maisie and Piper together.

I tap on the picture and it fills my phone screen. Shaun obviously took the selfie in front of the bowling alley before they went inside.

I stare at the four faces. Three of them happy, one… not so much.

Maisie said the outing was just 'OK'. To anyone else, she is smiling just like the others, but I'm not fooled. Her eyes look troubled and I'd say she's simply showing her teeth, rather than actually smiling.

But it does strike me that they look like a proper family: two sisters with their parents. Maisie is dark-haired compared to Piper's silvery-blonde locks, but then Shaun and Joanne have opposite hair colourings too.

The four of them look like they belong together. A brand-new family, just starting out.

The photograph seems to grip me in a sort of trance. I want to close Facebook, to un-see the picture, but it's too late for that.

My fingers tremble slightly and the bottom of my back feels damp. It's silly I should feel so unsettled.

There's a sharp rap at the door and I freeze. I'm not expecting anyone.

I could just ignore whoever it is. I'm not in the mood to face anyone right now.

Then I hear a key rattle in the lock and the door begins to slowly open.

CHAPTER 35

Twenty-four years earlier

The problem is that you never quite know what is and isn't acceptable on any given day.

Yesterday, leaving food on your plate went unnoticed. Last week, it earned you a bedroom lock-in so long that when you vomited with fear, nothing came up at all. Your stomach was completely empty.

Today's punishment has been given because your father found mud on the bottom of your shoes. But who is to blame? You know the rule about dirty shoes and you flouted it.

There is hardly any light left at all in the sky now. You squeeze your eyes shut and try to breathe normally, but you can't seem to get enough air into your lungs.

And then you hear your mother's footsteps on the stairs.

One... two... three and pause.

Please, no, you pray silently. Please don't let it be that.

But when she opens the door, smiling and holding the tray, you know that it is no use praying any longer.

CHAPTER 36

Val

When she called round unannounced to drop off a few laundered items of Maisie's school uniform that had been left at her house, it was a shock to find Emma in a bit of a state.

Emma tried to put a brave face on it, but Val was her mother, for goodness' sake. She immediately spotted her daughter's red-rimmed eyes and tear-stained cheeks, despite Emma's hasty attempts to wipe away the evidence.

'Whatever's wrong?' Val laid her granddaughter's folded skirt and blouse on the stairs and embraced Emma. 'Is everything all right?'

She scanned the kitchen over Emma's shoulder and saw there was no sign of Maisie.

'I'm fine, Mum.' Emma sniffed. 'Come through and have a drink with me.'

Emma stood at the counter while Val filled the kettle. She let the water run for a couple of seconds, noticing a half-finished glass of wine on the kitchen top.

'Shaun has taken Maisie to the cinema.'

'So you've got some time to yourself. That's nice,' Val said cautiously, glancing around the kitchen, which seemed to be in more disarray than usual.

Now that her life was busier, Val mostly picked Maisie up and looked after her at her own small bungalow in Ruddington.

She had a very slow Internet connection there that made online browsing unreliable. That was useful in that Val sometimes managed to get Maisie out in the garden in the warmer months, walking around the local park or even popping to the local tea rooms for a slice of cake. In the cooler weather, they'd complete jigsaws together, bake or watch a nature programme on television.

Anything was better than Maisie sitting constantly glued to her computer, coveting the lives of strangers, like she did at home.

Consequently, Val hadn't seen as much of Emma's house recently. It seemed to have deteriorated quite rapidly.

Emma followed Val's line of vision.

'I know it's a bit of a mess in here, Mum. I'm going to get it sorted this weekend.'

Val avoided pointing out that it was already Sunday afternoon and there wasn't much of the weekend left.

'If you're struggling, then you've only got to say,' she said gently. 'I can bring my rubber gloves and we'll get it done together in no time.'

'I know. Thanks.' Emma sniffed. 'I've just got a lot on at the moment, that's all.'

She glanced down at her phone and Val spotted the photograph.

'Oh, that's… Maisie.' Her voice faltered. 'And Shaun.'

'And his perfect new girlfriend and her daughter,' Emma added somewhat sourly. 'Shaun's new family.'

'I wouldn't look at it like that.' Val spooned coffee into two mugs and poured hot water in. 'Maisie has you and she has her dad. It's too soon for any new families to be formed, love.'

Emma looked at the photograph wistfully. 'They look happy, though, don't they?'

'I'm not sure Maisie looks that impressed.' Val wrinkled her nose. 'Did she enjoy herself yesterday?'

They took their drinks over to the comfy seats.

'I don't think so, not really. But she wouldn't say much about it. Neither would Shaun.'

'I see.' Val sipped her coffee thoughtfully. 'I could try asking her about it, just a gentle nudge.'

'I don't want her to be upset, Mum. She'll speak when she's ready.'

Val looked at Emma and tipped her head to one side. Her daughter's skin looked dry and grey. Her eyes were constantly darting around the room. Anywhere but settling on Val's face.

'Are you sleeping, Emmeline?'

'On and off.' She shrugged.

Val's eyes fluttered around Emma's face and hands.

'You're not… going down *that* road again, are you?' Her tone was fearful. 'It's just you look—'

'No! Of course I'm not.'

'Promise me that if things get that bad again you'll tell me.'

'I will.' Emma stood up and walked over to the breakfast bar. 'I'm sorry, Mum. I have to get this work done.'

Val pulled away from the kerb and drove down the road.

A few years ago, Emma had become hooked on prescription sleeping pills and was secretly popping them during the day when Shaun was at work. Val had spotted the awful condition of her skin, and that was when Emma had confessed to the problem.

Val knew Emmeline wouldn't thank her, but if things didn't improve, she'd have to ring Shaun. It was important he was aware of any warning signs.

Lord knew, he was probably very distracted at the present time.

Val had been shocked at how attractive his new woman, Joanne, was. She wasn't really sure what she'd expected her to look like, but she seemed confident and very sorted. Emma, on the other hand, seemed like she was in danger of beginning to fade away, just like last time.

Both Val and Shaun knew how quickly it could happen, and how utterly devastating it would be for everyone involved if Emma lapsed.

For Maisie's sake, it had to be avoided at any cost.

CHAPTER 37

Maisie

Maisie squealed and ran ahead of her dad out of the cinema.

He was pretending to be a giant robot again and people were staring. She wanted to *die* with embarrassment, but at the same time, it was so funny!

She yelped with pleasure as he caught up with her and captured her in his arms from behind. He started talking in that weird robot voice he did, and he was so loud, everyone could hear!

'NOW YOU MUST BE TICKLED TO DEATH!'

'Dad, please,' she gasped, struggling for breath now. 'Stop.'

'Sorry, poppet.' His arms quickly fell away and he produced her inhaler from his pocket. 'I'm an idiot. I shouldn't have tickled you.'

She pressed and breathed in deeply a couple of times.

'I'm fine now.' She grinned, handing the inhaler back to him. 'And before you ask… I won't tell Mum.'

'Phew.' He wiped his forehead dramatically. 'I reckon I'm in enough bother with her as it is.'

They'd had a great time watching the film. They had laughed, Maisie had cried at a sad bit, and her dad had laughed at that too. They'd eaten too much popcorn and drunk too much fizzy pop. It had been brilliant.

'Next stop: the milkshake parlour.'

'Really?' Maisie's heart soared. She'd assumed her dad would drive her straight back home after the film because it was a school day tomorrow.

'Another hour out won't hurt, and besides, I have a surprise for you.'

'What is it?' She stuffed her knuckles in her mouth with the pure anticipation.

'You'll see.' He pushed open the door to the parlour and let Maisie walk in first. 'Ta-dah! Well, look who's here.'

'Hello, Maisie, how nice to see you again,' Joanne said.

She and Piper were sitting at a table for four next to the window.

'Hello,' Maisie said, looking up at her dad.

'I thought it would be nice for us all to meet up for a milkshake after we had such a lovely day yesterday.' Her dad winked at her.

Maisie nodded and forced a smile. Piper had her head down, tapping away on a mini iPad, playing some sort of game.

'Piper. Say hi to Maisie.' Joanne nudged her.

'Hi,' Piper mumbled without looking away from her game.

Joanne stood up. 'We'll get the shakes in while you girls catch up here. Strawberry or banana, Maisie?'

'Strawberry, please,' Maisie said in a small voice.

There was a short queue at the counter and Maisie watched as her dad and Joanne joined it. He slid his arm around her waist and she turned her face up to kiss him. Just like her Mum used to do, a long time ago now.

She glanced across at Piper's game. Remembered what Miss Diane always told them about making conversation with new students at the dance school to make them feel welcome.

'I like Candy Crush,' she said. 'What level have you got to?'

'Don't speak to me while I'm playing!' Piper snapped, and then groaned. She tossed the iPad down on the table and covered her face. 'You made me go wrong. *Idiot.*'

'Sorry I spoke,' Maisie snapped, her face reddening.

'Have *you* got an iPad?' Piper asked spitefully.

'No, but I'm allowed to use my mum's.'

'That's rubbish. I have an iPad mini *and* a big iPad Pro, too. They belong to *me*; I don't have to share them with anyone at all.'

'Lucky you,' Maisie mumbled.

'Do you have horse-riding lessons?'

'No, but I'd like to.'

'I have my own pony at the stables in Papplewick. His name is Chester and I have a whole shelf of trophies and rosettes in my bedroom at home that we've won together.'

'Cool! Can I see Chester when I come over?' Maisie asked, suddenly excited. 'I'd like to see your trophies too, Piper.'

'You can *see* him, but you can't ride on him.'

'Why not?' Maisie frowned.

Piper glanced at their parents, still standing in the queue. 'Because you're too *fat*, silly. You'd completely flatten poor Chester.' She laughed loudly, like she was on stage.

Joanne turned round and smiled over at them.

'Stop being mean, or I'll tell on you.' Maisie felt her eyes prickle, so she stuck her fingernails into her palms to make it go away.

Piper smirked. 'Tell on me for telling the truth?'

There were a few moments of silence. Maisie thought about joining her dad and Joanne at the counter.

'Have you got any real precious stones in your jewellery box?' Piper asked, turning to stare at Maisie.

Maisie hesitated. Maybe Piper wanted to be friends after all.

'I've got a pretty cubic zirconia necklace my gran bought me for my birthday,' she said with a little smile. 'The stone is set into a real silver heart.'

'That's just a *fake* gem; it isn't worth anything, silly. I've got a real diamond necklace *and* a solid gold bracelet with a real ruby in it.' Piper chewed the inside of her cheek and rolled her eyes up, thinking for a moment. 'Let's see. Have you got a—'

'It's my turn now,' Maisie said smartly. She was fed up of being the one who answered all the time.

'Ha! You haven't got *anything* I haven't got.' Piper stuck out her tongue.

'I might have.'

'Go on then.' Piper sniffed smugly. 'Try me!'

Maisie sat up a bit straighter and said clearly, 'Have you got a dad?'

Piper suddenly looked exactly like Casper the ghost. She dropped her head back, opened her mouth and let out a massively loud howl.

The whole parlour came to a standstill as everyone – staff and customers – turned to stare.

Suddenly Joanne was pushing past Maisie to reach Piper, who started to sob.

'Sweetie, what's wrong?' She looked at Maisie. 'What happened?'

'We were just playing a game.' Maisie shrugged. 'Then Piper started howling like a wolf.'

'She… she said I haven't got a dad,' Piper wailed, burying her face in Joanne's side.

'Maisie, is this true?' Her dad's face was one big frown as he put a tray of tall glasses on the table.

He never got angry with Maisie, but she thought he looked pretty close to it right now.

'Th-that's what she said,' Piper stammered between sobs. 'Sh-she said she has a d-dad and I don't.'

'My poor baby,' crooned Joanne, cradling Piper in her arms.

'I never.' Maisie raised her voice. 'I asked her *if* she had a dad. That's all.'

'That's not really a question you should be asking people.' Joanne sounded like adults did when they were biting down a shout. 'It's really none of your business, Maisie.'

'It was Piper who started the game,' Maisie offered.

'Maisie, that's enough,' her dad said, his voice dangerously low. 'I think you should say you're sorry to Piper for upsetting her.'

'She started the horrid game, though! Asking me all sorts of questions, being nasty about what she's got and what I haven't. She said the necklace Gran bought me was rubbish.' Maisie looked at her dad for support, but he just shook his head sadly.

She clamped her mouth shut. It was no good trying to make them understand how horrible Piper had been to her; she couldn't explain it properly, couldn't find the words to say how it made her feel inside. Like she would never be good enough.

What was so bad about asking if Piper had a dad, anyway? Everyone had a dad, didn't they?

While everyone fussed around Piper, Maisie reached over and helped herself to a bright pink milkshake. There was heaps of whipped cream on the top with coloured sprinkles and a real strawberry that had been split and perched on the rim of the glass.

She drew the thick, sweet liquid up through the straw, closing her eyes to savour the taste.

When she opened them again, she saw that Joanne was staring at her with the strangest look on her face that made Maisie shiver even though she still had her coat on.

CHAPTER 38

Emma

While Maisie is out with her dad at the cinema, I put an easy-listening playlist on Spotify, pour a glass of wine and allow myself the pure luxury of simply drifting, eyes closed, on the couch.

But it's in that halfway house between wakefulness and sleep that the past seeps into my thoughts like wisps of poisonous gas…

It was an unusual day at Clayton and McCarthy, as the office was quiet. Quite a few of the more senior staff were attending a conference in Birmingham.

Damian announced authoritatively to the admin office that he had been left in charge for the day. 'Mr McCarthy has asked me to allocate some case tasks that need to take precedence over anything else you might be doing.'

He picked up a piece of paper from his desk and read aloud from it.

'OK, Andy, you'll work with me today on witness statements; Candice, you're to visit the court to pick up some papers. And Emma… I'll need you to be on photocopying duties, please.'

The others glanced over at me and I felt my face ignite. This was exactly the kind of task the clerks should be dealing with. I was a legal secretary.

'Surely one of the admin staff can do the photocopying,' I said lightly. 'I was hoping for something a bit more substantial.'

'There's no room for delusions of grandeur here, I'm afraid,' Damian replied smugly. 'We all have to muck in and get the job done.'

'But nobody else is *mucking in*, are they?' I struggled to keep my voice level. 'Everyone else has been given something interesting to get their teeth into.'

A couple of the others glanced pointedly at each other and moved away to commence their own tasks.

Damian held his palms high to shut me up. 'Just carrying out the bosses' orders, that's all. Barbara has all the files you'll need upstairs. Thank you, Emma.'

With that, he turned his back and bent forward, busying himself shuffling paperwork on his desk.

I stalked back to my own desk and took my phone out of my drawer before heading upstairs.

As most people were at the conference, it was super quiet up there. I leaned against the wall for a moment in the corridor, reluctant to commence the mind-numbing job I'd been allocated.

Eventually I tapped on Barbara's office door.

'Morning, Emma!' She appeared, small and mouse-like, in front of me. 'Apparently you need some files from me.'

I nodded, forced a smile.

'There we go.' She plonked an armful of brown folders into my outstretched hands. Each one was stuffed with paperwork. 'And that's just for starters, I'm afraid.'

Glumly I trudged back downstairs and headed for the photocopier room. It was small and stuffy, but at least I didn't have to work under the glare of Damian all morning.

At first I tried to scan each page to get an overview of the case, but after only ten minutes or so, the boring nature of the job took over and I became blind to the print on the pages.

After about an hour, I took a break to make coffee in the kitchenette downstairs.

I nodded at the receptionist, Janine, and took the short corridor on the right of her desk, slowing down when I heard Damian's voice. He was speaking quietly, but I had good hearing and there was no mistaking his pompous tone.

'The medical paperwork is being copied as we speak. Once the files are collated, that's it, you're in the clear. I have the original and there'll be no trace of the change. Trust me.'

I tiptoed back down the corridor and out into reception again. I passed a couple of waiting clients and headed back upstairs to the photocopier room. There, I leafed through the files I'd already processed.

There were no medical papers in there. I started the next set of papers collating on the machine and began to methodically check the remaining folders.

My heartbeat raced when I opened one to find a clipped section of paperwork marked *AlchoBio Metrics Ltd.*

I rifled quickly through and soon established that this was a private breathalyser test that was admissible in court as evidence if requested. The detailed report concluded that although the client had alcohol in his bloodstream, it was well below the legal limit at the time of the accident.

The door opened and I quickly closed the folder and looked up.

'How's it going?' Damian asked, eyeing the files.

'Good. Everything is fine,' I said quickly, busying myself with checking the collated paperwork.

'I know you think I'm having a go, Emma, allocating you this task, but I gave it to you because I knew you'd get the job done with minimum fuss.' He threw me a wolfish grin. 'In its own way, this is probably the most important job of all.'

I nodded without commenting and turned back to the machine.

'I'll leave you to it, then,' he said, closing the door behind him.

I made myself an extra copy of the medical information, and when I'd copied the rest of the folders, I carried the pile out into the main office.

It was deserted.

I realised it was lunchtime. Nobody had bothered to ask if I wanted anything from the shop or fancied a walk to the café, as we often did.

I swallowed hard. I hadn't worked there that long, but maybe it was time to make a fresh start somewhere else. As usual, Dad's face floated into my mind's eye, along with his critical words.

You'll never amount to anything.

And then I had a light-bulb moment.

I remembered I'd seen Damian locking away some files earlier and dropping the tiny drawer key into the pot that held his pens.

After checking at the office door that nobody was yet on their way back from lunch, I walked across the office and peered into the red plastic pen holder on his desk.

I fished out the key and opened the drawer. There were three folders in there, the second one marked exactly like the one I had copied earlier.

I scanned through the paperwork inside and found the original medical results. When I perused the figures, I saw immediately what it was I was looking for.

My heart pumped with adrenalin; I was unsure whether I felt pleased or terrified by the information I had inadvertently uncovered.

I took a photograph of the original results with my phone, then replaced the file in Damian's desk drawer and ensured the folders were back in exactly the order I'd found them.

Finally I locked the drawer again and dropped the key back into the pot.

Back at my own desk, I folded up my copy of the medical report and pushed it to the bottom of my handbag.

And then I waited.

*

When Shaun brings Maisie back home later than we agreed, it's clear they aren't speaking to each other.

'What on earth's the matter with her?' I ask him as she storms into the house without even saying hello to me.

'I'm afraid she's been a bit of a madam, Em. I can't explain now…' He looks back at the road. The car engine is running and I notice for the first time that he has a passenger. 'Joanne's waiting and Piper's fast asleep on the back seat. She's exhausted, poor thing.'

'I thought you and Maisie had gone out on your own, just the two of you.'

'We met up with them later. Maisie really upset Piper, Em, she wasn't nice. But look' – he takes a step back on the path – 'I'll explain another time. I'll call Maisie tomorrow and have a proper chat with her. In the meantime, maybe you can speak to her about how she might think about other people's feelings.'

'Hang on, you can't just leave it like this. What happened?'

'I'll call,' he says firmly before turning abruptly and walking back to the car. I raise my hand to acknowledge Joanne, but she must be looking the other way.

I close the door and call out to Maisie. She doesn't answer, but I can hear music up in her bedroom.

I climb the stairs and tap on her door.

'Only me,' I say. 'Turn the music off a moment, poppet. I want to talk to you.'

She presses a button and the music stops.

'What happened with Dad today?'

'I don't want to talk about it.' Maisie buries her face in her pillow.

I'm getting heartily sick of my daughter coming home in a terrible mood and nobody wanting to enlighten me as to what has been happening.

'Did you upset Piper… or Joanne?'

'No! *She* upset *me* but nobody cares about that!' Her voice sounds muffled, but she won't move her face from the pillow.

'Come on, Maisie. I can't help you if you won't share stuff with me. What happened?'

She turns her face towards me and sits up in bed, clasping her hands together in front of her.

They hate me,' she whispers, her eyes widening. 'They both hate me.'

'Don't be silly! Nobody hates you. What happened?'

Her eyes are unfocused and her face is pale. I watch two small red spots appear on her cheeks and she swallows hard.

And then she lurches forward and a fountain of bright pink vomit shoots out of her mouth and drenches the bedding.

CHAPTER 39

About a week later, I'm in the kitchen having a quiet coffee before I wake Maisie when I hear a shriek followed by feet thundering down the stairs.

I plonk my cup down, spilling coffee on the counter top.

'Maisie? What is it?'

'Our herb garden!' Her face is horror-struck when she runs into the kitchen barefoot, in her pyjamas. 'Someone pulled up all our plants… all of them.'

'What?' I rush to the window and raise the blind. Maisie's bedroom window overlooks the back garden at a more convenient angle than the kitchen, but I can see scattered plants on the edge of the lawn.

Maisie and I planted the small herb garden together in the spring. We'd planned it out on paper and separated each herb section with small white decorative stones. Maisie kept a diary cataloguing the growth of the plants and was in awe when we used the herbs in cooking. She loved to pick them fresh and present them triumphantly to whoever was cooking that day.

I pull my dressing gown tighter around me and slide my bare feet into the pair of flip-flops I keep by the French doors. 'Wait here,' I say, unlocking the doors and stepping out into the dewy freshness of the morning.

I walk across the crisp, frosted lawn to the border, shivering as an icy breeze blasts my lower legs and toes. Immediately I see that Maisie is right. Not a single plant remains in our garden. They all lie on the soil or the grass, dying.

'Do I have to go?' Maisie frowns as she stuffs a foot into her lace-up pumps. 'I'd rather just spend the day with Dad.'

I'm still not clear what happened to cause so much upset after her trip to the cinema with Shaun. According to Maisie, it all began with some silly game that Piper started in the first place, and ended with Joanne's daughter screaming the milkshake parlour down.

Maisie has been quiet all week. My mum looked after her when she stayed off school for a couple of days after the vomiting incident, and she hasn't been to her dance classes.

She's had next to no appetite and has actually taken herself off up to bed without me having to scream, threaten and beg as per our usual routine. It's all very odd, but I put it down to her having some kind of tummy bug that manifested itself so colourfully on Sunday evening.

This morning, when she tore downstairs to tell me about the herb garden, is the most energy she's had for a while.

Shaun hasn't called as he promised to explain why Maisie was so upset, and to be honest, I haven't overly chased him. I sent him a text but he dodged the subject, saying it's all been forgotten now. Joanne has been out of the office this week working at home, apparently, so I can't ask her anything about it.

But on Friday afternoon, Shaun texted again to say he'd pick Maisie up at ten the next morning for a special day out.

When I told Maisie, she wasn't at all pleased.

'I'm sure you'll enjoy it,' I say now, trying to keep my tone light. 'I think Joanne has some nice things planned for you all to do.'

'It's weird.' Maisie reaches for her other shoe. 'The way you know her.'

'It's not weird.' I throw her denim jacket over the back of the chair. 'I work with her, I told you.'

'Piper says she's your boss,' Maisie remarks. 'She says that you work *for* her.'

I'm not surprised at these repeated bitchy comments. Sadly, it's what I expect from Miss Piper Dent. I guess she has to release her vitriol somewhere, and it looks like this time, I won the jackpot.

'Joanne is my boss. Regardless of what's happened, I know she'll look after you while you're with her.'

Maisie says nothing, but she takes her time putting on her shoe. After a few moments, she begins to snipe again.

'You don't even care Dad isn't living here any more.'

'I have no choice but to accept it, Maisie. We both have to.'

'But you don't care he has a new girlfriend.'

I walk over and stand behind her. Press my hands down onto her shoulders.

'Can we just stop this?' I say softly, bending close to her ear. 'Can you and I not argue? Especially not today.'

'Sorry,' she says petulantly. 'It's just that… I'd rather stay here with you.'

'I know.' I walk around the couch and sit down next to her. 'But it's important you go today because you're going to be seeing a lot of Joanne and Piper. It will be nice for you all to get to know each other, and besides, I'm going to replant our herbs while you're gone, so you'll have something to look forward to when you get back.'

On the back foot, and not wanting to frighten Maisie, I told her that an animal must have dug the plants up during the night. But there was a clear footprint in the soil; it looked like it was from a training shoe.

I felt as if I might be sick, but Maisie watching anxiously from the door gave me the strength to put on an act.

At 10 o'clock prompt, Shaun knocks on the front door. Finally, I seem to have got through to him about not treating the house as if he still lives here.

He tells me briefly what they have planned for the girls but to keep it a secret so he can surprise Maisie.

A few seconds later, she appears behind me. I kiss her at the door and she slips her hand into Shaun's.

'Have a great time.' I smile widely at her. 'Can't wait to hear about what you've been up to.'

'She'll have the time of her life.' Shaun grins. 'Trust me.'

I glance at the clock. It's after seven, and Shaun said he'd have Maisie back for six.

I tell myself it's no big deal; they've probably just lost track of time.

I'd got a whole host of things I wanted to get through today. I had a chunk of case files to reference-tab, ready for bundles to be prepared on Monday for counsel. Shaun had already cleared all his drawers and bedside table, as well as half his wardrobe, so I planned to take the opportunity to conduct a bit of a spring-clean on my own belongings. It might be an opportunity to get more organised, especially after Mum's gripe about the messy house.

I'd also put some time aside to pop into town to make a start on the new wardrobe that I'd promised myself to take advantage of the storage space I have now. Since being a teenager, I've fantasised about building a collection of expensive shoes and keeping them in labelled boxes, all stacked and ready to wear.

Now I have the chance, I think about the prohibitive cost involved and where I would even wear such pieces.

But somehow, the day has slipped away from me. I did manage to tab the case files, but all my other plans seemed to fly out of the window.

I went out to replant the herbs, but on closer inspection I saw that lots of the roots had been completely torn off them. As if someone was determined they would not be saved.

I'm ashamed to say I've lounged around, turning the television on and then off again. Picking up my Kindle and putting it back down, unable to get into any of my selected reads. Uninterrupted, I have sometimes finished a good book in a day, but there's no chance of that happening for the foreseeable.

In the end, I simply gave up and just vegged out on the sofa, various recent conversations with Shaun and Joanne replaying constantly in my head, together with musings about what the broken window and the plant incident might mean. But there are no conclusions drawn; I've just succeeded in working myself up, and ended up wishing my daughter was here, just to have someone I love close by.

I've honestly felt perfectly OK with Maisie visiting Joanne's house and with the four of them acting like some sort of new, improved patched-together family.

But now, reflecting in my quieter moments, I'm not sure I feel quite as good about it, especially since Maisie always seems upset in some way when she gets back home.

Before Maisie came downstairs this morning to leave with her dad, Shaun whispered that Joanne had arranged a visit to an animal petting centre in Farnsfield. Apparently it's one of the most popular tourist attractions in the whole of the East Midlands, booked up for weeks in advance.

'Groups of kids pet the animals on a strict rota,' he said. 'But Jo knows the owners, so Maisie and Piper are being treated to their own VIP session. They get to pick the best animals to have all to themselves. How good is that?'

'Sounds wonderful.'

'We won't have to queue to get in either. Like our table at Mario's the other night. Jo always seems to find a way to get round such inconveniences!'

I nodded mutely, wondering how our kids were supposed to learn to share and take their turn if they were allowed to just walk straight in and get the run of a place meant for everyone to enjoy.

I've checked Joanne's Facebook account several times today, but she hasn't posted anything online. Shame, I would've liked to have seen Maisie happy and relaxed for a change.

Right on cue, a text pings through.

Sorry we're late… Back for 8! S

I feel a niggle of irritation and don't reply. Instead, I pour myself a glass of red wine.

It does the trick. A few minutes later, I'm feeling more relaxed about Shaun returning Maisie later than planned. It's not as if anything is spoiling. There's no school tomorrow and I've nothing exciting waiting for her to do.

I wonder if it will seem dull for Maisie, coming back home after being entertained and treated as a VIP all day.

They eventually get back at 8.30. I happen to check out of the window and see Shaun's car pull up, so before Maisie even gets out, I have the door wide open and stand waving.

Shaun waves back but doesn't get out of the car. He waits until Maisie reaches the door and then drives away.

I'm irked. I wanted to tell him about the herb garden and remind him that he hasn't arranged for the downstairs loo window to be fixed yet.

'I don't want to go out with them again,' Maisie says when I close the door.

'Why, poppet? What's wrong?'

'I just don't.'

'OK, well look. Let's talk about it tomorrow. In the meantime, I'll put Dad off if he suggests an outing. Until things get sorted out. Fancy a cocoa?'

'I'm really tired, Mum,' she says, and she disappears upstairs, back to her bedroom.

CHAPTER 40

The next morning, I get up early and sit at the breakfast bar, surrounded by my scattered paperwork.

My laptop displays numerous tabs indicating all the additional documents that I need to read and digest ready for an important meeting after the weekend with our client, a weight-loss company who are dealing with a civil law suit over misleading advertising.

Head down, I scan through the paperwork first, making notes. Through the fog of my absorption in work, I'm vaguely aware of Maisie padding into the kitchen and walking over to the sink.

Just as I get to the end of the page I'm reading, I'm startled out of my focus by a glass shattering on the floor.

Maisie screams and jumps back.

I jump up, shove my feet into my flip-flops and rush over to her. 'Are you OK? Have you cut yourself?'

'Sorry… I just wanted a glass of water,' she whispers as I slide my arm gently around her shoulders and guide her backwards, away from the broken glass.

My fingers connect with what feels like pure bone on her shoulder, no padding of flesh.

I look at her and swallow hard. When was the last time I really looked at my daughter? She is gaunt. Her skin is pale, emphasised by dark circles under both eyes, through lack of sleep, I'd guess.

She's wearing a big baggy sweatshirt, one of Shaun's old ones she sometimes used to throw on at night, instead of fussing with a blanket, while we watched television.

She raises a hand to push back a strand of hair that's escaped its bobble, and I see that it's shaking. Then I notice her nails are bitten to the quick.

'Come and sit down.' I lead her to the comfy seats near the television and sit next to her. 'You haven't had any breakfast. How about a slice of toast and a nice glass of fresh juice?'

Her beautiful blue eyes stare back at me just the same as they've always done, but it's as if Maisie isn't behind them this time. They look dull and lifeless.

'I'm not hungry,' she whispers, and stares out of the window into the garden.

It's a windy day, strong enough that the bare branches of the blossom tree and the skeletal hedge wave in the blustery air.

'You know you can talk to me, sweetie?' I cup my fingers under her chin and turn her face to look at me. 'You can tell me anything that's worrying you.'

'I know, Mum,' she says, her voice rising an octave with irritation. 'Nothing's wrong.' She turns away again and her fingers pinch and pull at the sweatshirt.

It's hard to tell how much weight she's lost in her nightwear and the baggy clothes she's taken to wearing. I don't know why I've not noticed how her dress sense has changed recently, the way she wears oversized sweatshirts and cardigans over her school uniform.

I glance at the pile of paperwork on the kitchen top and bite my lip. My focus has been elsewhere for a while now. Work has become a refuge.

Feeling sorry for myself after Shaun's desertion, and with my dad's critical voice constantly echoing in my ears, somehow I've allowed my concern for my daughter to slip down the list.

'Let me get you some food.' I make to stand up and she glares at me, eyes flashing.

'I told you, I'm not hungry,' she snaps.

I'm seized with a sudden fearful feeling.

'If someone is upsetting you, Maisie, I want to know about it.'

'What?' She looks at me, eyes wide. 'What do you mean?'

She must know I mean Joanne and Piper, but I'm not going to put words into her mouth.

'Look, I know it's been difficult for you, going to see your dad and trying to fit in with a different family, but—'

'I told you,' she says, standing up. Her cheeks flush pink. 'Nothing is wrong!'

Then she turns on her heel and stomps back upstairs. I feel instinctively that it's best not to follow and bombard her with questions. I think I'll speak to Mum about it, see what she thinks.

The house is quiet for a couple of hours. I work and Maisie stays in her bedroom.

Later, I hear the rumble of the boiler kicking in. I stand at the bottom of the stairs and listen.

Maisie is in the shower.

Upstairs on the landing, I pull out a warm, fluffy bath sheet from the airing cupboard and stand outside the bathroom door.

For once, I'm thankful that Shaun never got around to putting a lock on it, despite my repeated requests when we first moved in. It's not really been that much of an issue. We've always respected each other's privacy and knocked first to see if the room is free.

I crook my index finger and tap the knuckle on the wood, so lightly even I can barely hear it. Just to satisfy myself that I did it.

Then I open the door and walk into the bathroom.

The small window is closed, the extractor fan hasn't been turned on and the room is full of steam. The shower curtain is pulled across the full width of the bath, a plethora of brightly coloured fish and sparkles bobbing around inside it, affording my daughter an almost opaque screen.

'Only me,' I call, striding across the room. 'I brought you a fresh towel.'

I hear a sharp intake of breath, and her hand shoots out to grab the shower curtain to cover her at the open end of the bath.

But she's too late. I'm already there, peering around the waterproof fabric to catch a glimpse of her, and what I see makes me catch my breath.

'I'll just leave the towel here,' I say, fighting to keep my voice level. I fold it double and place it on the small wooden stool at the end of the bath that I use for my glass of wine and my current paperback.

Then I rush out of the room and close the door behind me.

Back on the landing, I allow myself to sink against the wall to draw in breath and squeeze my eyes against the shocking vision.

I can't believe the change in her is happening as quickly. To lose weight this fast she must literally be starving herself.

The shower is off now and I imagine Maisie drying her newly thin body and bony shoulders.

It's all I can do not to rush up and gather her into my arms, tell her everything will be OK and that I'm sorry that me and her dad did this to her, wrapped up in our petty squabbles and desperate to make our own lives perfect again.

But I don't rush back in. I know it will do more harm than good at this point because Maisie is closed to any suggestion that something is wrong. For some reason, she won't talk about what happens when she visits her father.

I pad quietly back downstairs.

First thing tomorrow morning, I have to get Maisie an urgent doctor's appointment. I could kick myself I haven't done so before now.

I also know I need a long, frank conversation soon with Shaun, whether Maisie approves or not.

CHAPTER 41

At eight a.m. the next morning, while Maisie is getting ready for school upstairs, I call the surgery.

When I finally get through, I have the good fortune to speak to a receptionist who I know very slightly from a local conveyancing issue a while ago, I manage to get Maisie the first appointment with Dr Yesufu on Tuesday morning.

I'm sure Joanne isn't going to be impressed that I won't be at the office first thing to brief her on my findings for the client meeting later that day, but that's just tough luck. I feel like someone just gave me a good shake, and my focus and concern is definitely now off the job and back where it should be, with my daughter.

For now, I decide not to mention the appointment to Maisie. No sense in causing further tension.

As I end the call to the surgery, I hear mail dropping through the letter box.

I walk into the hallway and pause at the bottom of the stairs.

I pick up the small stack of mail and take it back into the kitchen. Flicking on the kettle, I discard the circulars and brightly coloured pizza delivery flyers and open the one remaining letter.

I don't hear the kettle click, I forget about Maisie upstairs. It's all I can do to keep standing.

I manage to get myself over to the seating area, where I sink down into the soft cushions and steel myself.

I read the note for the third time as the thin, cheap lined notepaper quivers in my shaking fingers.

The envelope is smaller than the regular office size, and my name and address are printed neatly and clearly in blue ink in the same hand as the note.

I'm no handwriting expert, but the print is even and the lines straight. I'd say the person who wrote this took time and care to get things right. They wanted to ensure that the note reached me safely, and that I – and only I – fully understand the short, loaded message within it.

They succeeded. In the last couple of minutes, my heart rate has doubled and my chest feels tight as a drum.

I sit down and allow the note and envelope to fall to the floor, but the words play on repeat in my mind.

> *I'm so enjoying being in touch again – more to come soon!*
> *Remember. I'm always watching… and waiting* ☺

The words drip with threat and a dark intention that chills my blood, but I instinctively know that if I take this note to the police, they'll laugh in my face. Who could blame them? Take the note apart and there's nothing there at all.

But it's what happened *before* I received the note that drives the creeping sense of dread invading me.

The two unexplained flat tyres within a month that appeared to have been punctured without any obvious cause. Shaun had insisted at the time it was just bad luck and after a while, I'd forgotten about it. But now I'm beginning to reconsider…

There's also the fractured opaque window of the downstairs bathroom that greeted me when I returned to the house two weeks ago. The glass wasn't broken, just cracked, as if someone had banged their fist against it in temper.

And only yesterday, the decimating of our little rectangular herb garden, the young plants callously unearthed and scattered around the lawn.

I believe these are the 'being in touch' events the writer of the note refers to.

I could anticipate a police officer's response without suffering the humiliation of seeking it: 'The car tyres are probably just very bad luck, madam. An animal could have dug up the plants, and there's no evidence of a brick or boulder to show that someone intended damaging your window.'

Something is off, though. I can feel disruption in the air, like the wind subtly changing direction. I just can't lose the feeling that bad things are around the corner.

You see, I can never forget the threat that was issued to me two years ago.

If it's the last thing I do, I'll repay you for what you've done to me, the way you've ruined my career, my life. Keep looking over your shoulder, you utter cow, because you'll never know when it's coming.

But more importantly, I can never forget that the person who said it is dead because of me.

CHAPTER 42

Maisie doesn't want to go to her dance lesson, but I insist.

As far as I'm concerned, part of the problem is that her world has somehow become far too narrow. Me and Mum, Shaun, Joanne and Piper are the only people she sees regularly.

Besides, I have an idea, if I can get her there.

With tremendous effort, I push the anonymous letter I just received from my mind. Maisie is what matters most. I might have lost sight of it temporarily, but without doubt my focus is back on track.

'I think it's time to reconnect to your friends, poppet. It's been a few weeks since you had Sandeep over, or when you visited one of your pals' houses. Why do you think that is?'

Maisie shrugs. 'Nobody likes me any more,' she says flatly.

'Oh sweetie, whatever gives you that idea?'

'They all like Piper more than me. I think she's been telling them nasty things about me.'

I feel cold inside. I can still remember what it's like to be the odd one out at school, when you're not in favour for no reason you can understand.

Shaun's reaction to this would be so predictable, if I tried to discuss it. There's no way he'd accept that Piper could be so conniving and heartless. I have no problem at all imagining it, but it's not going to be helpful to agree with Maisie. She'll just feel more isolated than ever.

'You've been friends with those girls for a long time, Maisie, they can't just dislike you for no reason, in the space of a few weeks. You should try and join in with them again. Ignore Piper.'

She pulls a face but stays quiet.

'There are friends at school I never hear you mention any more, too. Friends that don't even go to the dance school or know Piper.'

'Nobody wants to be my friend at school either. I think the dance girls have told the others horrible things about me.'

I feel so helpless. Maisie's usual teacher has been off sick for a while, so I can't just have a quiet word with her.

'If I need to speak to the head teacher, then I will,' I say in a steely tone.

'No!' Maisie stomps past me. 'Just leave it, Mum. You don't know anything about it and you'll just make everything worse. I don't want to talk about it any more.'

Just up the road from the dance studio, Maisie kisses me on the cheek and gets out of the car. I watch as she walks limply to the entrance. Gone are the days of her bounding in, excited to see her friends and get to class.

Groups of mums and girls – most of whom I recognise – stand around talking, but nobody turns to acknowledge Maisie, much less speak to her.

She climbs the steps and disappears inside, and I'm about to pull away when I see Joanne's Mercedes slide into her unofficial double-yellow parking spot directly outside the building.

Piper, sheathed in a bundle of sparkling pink net, skips out onto the pavement, posturing and preening to Sandeep and her mum, Sarita, who have just arrived on foot.

Joanne half gets out of the car and shouts something to Sarita, who laughs and waves.

It's all I can do not to stomp over there and dress Joanne and her daughter down in front of all the other mums. I'd like to ask my boss what she thinks she's playing at, allowing her daughter to demonise Maisie to the other girls.

But I know Maisie will never forgive me, and Shaun will think I'm off my trolley.

No. It's best that I stick to my original plan.

I pop to the small Sainsbury's nearby and pick up some milk and juice to replenish the fridge. The wording of the letter keeps looming large in my mind and I keep pushing it away.

I keep a strict eye on the time, and a full ten minutes before the end of Maisie's class, I'm back waiting in my spot up the road. With two minutes to go, I grab my handbag, lock the car and walk quickly down to the corner of the dance studio.

Cars are beginning to park up, and I can see Sandeep's and Zoe's mums ambling down the road. I'd love to speak to them, invite the girls over to ours, but there's something much more pressing I need to attend to.

As per her usual routine, Miss Diane pushes open the double entrance doors.

I scurry up the steps and she staggers back slightly, clearly surprised.

'Sorry to startle you,' I say, a little breathlessly. 'Could I have a quick word? It's really important.'

'Of course.' She smiles. 'Come through, Emma, and I'll catch up with you as soon as all the girls are safely out.'

I could hug her, I feel so grateful she can give me a few minutes. As I walk past her, I notice her smile dissolve as she spots something outside. When I turn round, I see that Joanne has just pulled up in her car.

I step to the side of the entrance porch and wait.

The girls cluster together on their way out, giggling, hunched over their phones. One of the groups contains a surly-looking Piper and a few of Maisie's friends. Piper looks up and meets my stare as she passes, narrowing her eyes and smirking without any fear of reprisal. The light-hearted mood she came in with seems to have dissipated for some reason.

Inappropriate it may be, but it takes all my resolve not to grab her arm and pull her to one side to reprimand her. It's scary, the powerful wave of emotion that ebbs and flows within me on behalf of my daughter.

I feel like my heart will burst with sadness when Maisie finally appears, dawdling behind everyone else, alone. Her head remains down as she shuffles along with an expression like she has the weight of the world on her thin little shoulders.

'Maisie!'

She looks up almost fearfully, and her eyes widen when she sees it's me.

'Mum, what are you doing here?' She glances at Miss Diane's back as she talks to a parent at the door. 'Please don't cause any trouble. You promised.'

Actually, I did nothing of the sort. I just didn't comment when she asked me not to go down to school.

'I'm not going to cause any trouble.' I ruffle her lank dark curls. 'I need to speak to Miss Diane and I want you to wait here. I won't be long.'

Her expression darkens. 'What are you going to say to her? Why can't I be there?'

'I just need to speak to her about various things. Nothing for you to worry about, poppet.'

'Right. I'm all yours!' Miss Diane turns, beaming. She looks from me to Maisie and back again.

'I wanted a private word, if that's OK,' I tell her. 'Maisie is going to wait here.'

'Perfect. I'll lock the doors and then we know our little dancer will be safe.' Miss Diane smiles at Maisie and she gets a lukewarm response. I'm embarrassed.

We go into a side room and Miss Diane closes the door before we both perch on plastic chairs.

'Thanks for seeing me,' I begin, awkwardly. 'I wanted to ask if you've noticed a change in Maisie? It seems her friends have all but deserted her lately.'

'Oh no, I certainly hope that's not the case.' She frowns for a moment, thinking. 'You see, the girls don't really chat much during lessons, as they're expected to focus on their dancing. But I would have thought Maisie would be full of excitement rather than down in the doldrums.'

I stare at her, not quite sure what she means.

'Hasn't she told you?' Her smile fades a little. 'I announced during the class that I'm giving her the role of Dorothy in the Christmas show.'

'What? No, she hasn't! That's wonderful, thank you so much.' My cheeks colour with pride for Maisie. I haven't had much chance to speak to her but I know that just a few weeks ago, she would've blurted out her news before I even uttered a word.

'In answer to your question, I hadn't noticed anything about her friends, but I'll certainly keep an eye out now.' She hesitates, as if she's not sure whether to say something. 'There are certain mothers who are rather pushy, I'm sure you know that, Emma. One in particular causes a lot of trouble when I give other children the chance to step into the spotlight.'

I know exactly who she's talking about. An unexpected rage sweeps through me like the blast from a furnace door.

I honestly don't know what comes over me. I jump up and storm past Miss Diane, past Maisie in the foyer. I slide the bolts back on the double doors, fly down the steps and collar Joanne Dent in front of all the other dance mums.

CHAPTER 43

Val

When Emma rang, Val was just on her way out to attend an over-sixties keep fit class at the local leisure centre.

She pushed the telephone handset closer to her ear, trying to understand what the problem was. Her daughter babbled on so fast and Val's hearing wasn't what it used to be. But she could hear that Emma was distressed, and that decided it for her.

'I'm on my way over,' she said. 'Put the kettle on, I'll be there in twenty minutes.'

She texted Kath to let her know something important had come up and that she wouldn't be able to make the class after all, and then she drove across town to Emma's house.

The traffic was thankfully still bearable, just on the cusp of rush hour, and Val made good progress. On the way, she thought about some of the things she wanted to say to her daughter; a conversation that was long overdue.

Unbeknown to Emmeline, Shaun had been in touch, concerned about Emma's increasing unpredictable behaviour, he'd said. Val had been pleased to hear from her son-in-law; had always thought of him as a good husband and father. She could hardly blame him for moving on.

'I noticed the house was in disarray when I last visited. I admit I've been worried she's slipping back into the habits of her *difficult time.*' She paused, knowing he would understand exactly what she meant. 'Has Maisie said anything about her mum?'

'No, no, it's just a few things I put together. Maisie seems to have developed a bit of a mean streak with Piper, and Emma has told me that she feels worrying things are happening to her that she can't explain away: a couple of flat tyres a while ago, a broken window… She feels someone has got it in for her.'

'Not *that* again,' Val muttered.

'Exactly. And Joanne – you know she's Emma's boss?'

'Hmm.' Val's loyalty to Emma wouldn't permit her to fully acknowledge or side with this new, attractive woman who seemed so sorted.

'Well, Jo has noticed Emma making mistakes at work – unable to meet her deadlines, that sort of thing – and yet Maisie says all she does at home is work.'

'And you said something about Maisie being mean?'

'Emma says she doesn't want to come over to Joanne's so much, but I think that's Emma's own influence, because she's upset about me and Joanne.' He paused. 'Maisie seems withdrawn lately, and she's been very unpleasant to Piper, who is trying her level best to make her feel welcome.'

Val had noticed that Emma didn't ask her to have Maisie much lately; she just used her as a pick-up, drop-off service for school and dancing. Val had also been called upon when Maisie had been off school with a tummy bug.

'Leave it with me,' she told Shaun. 'I'll try and talk to Emma, but you of all people know she can be quite stubborn.'

'Oh yes,' Shaun agreed. 'That I certainly do know. Thanks, Val.'

So after that conversation, Emma's phone call asking Val to go over there had, in the event, been quite opportune.

When she arrived at the house, Emma was already waiting for her at the door, looking rather dishevelled.

'What's wrong, love? Where's Maisie?'

'She's upstairs, Mum. She's fine.' Emma swallowed, running a hand through her tousled hair. 'Actually, she's not fine at all, but she's not in any actual danger at the moment.'

'Danger?' Val repeated faintly, stepping into the hallway and walking directly into the kitchen while Emma closed and locked the front door behind her.

It all sounded rather worrying. Val defaulted to her first port of call in a crisis and made some tea.

The two women sat in silence for a moment or two before Emma began to speak.

'Mum, have you noticed that Maisie has lost quite a lot of weight recently?'

Val thought for a moment. 'It's hard to tell, love. She's started wearing all these baggy garments. I thought it must be some kind of hip-hop trend.'

Emma gave a tiny smile despite her obvious distress. 'No, it isn't that, Mum.'

'Well as you know, she doesn't come over as often as she used to, but when she does, she always eats her meals. She didn't last week because she felt poorly, of course.'

'She normally eats, though?' Emma brightened a touch. 'At home, she never seems to be hungry, so I find that encouraging.'

'Her plate is always clean, never much food left,' Val confirmed.

'That makes me feel better. Only I walked in on her in the shower and I was shocked at how thin she's become.'

'Oh.' Val's face dropped. 'I don't like the sound of that. Have you spoken to her about it?'

'Every time I ask her what's wrong, she insists she's fine. But her body doesn't lie, and besides, it's more than that. She's got no energy, she spends hours upstairs. I barely see her when we're home.'

Emma grimaced and took a deep breath.

'I'm afraid I got rather carried away after Maisie's dance class today, Mum. I tore a strip off Joanne Dent in front of the other mums. I accused her of things that I absolutely suspect are true, but haven't got any actual proof of.'

'Oh dear.' Val clasped her fingers together.

'She's my bloody boss when all's said and done. I should've kept my big mouth shut.'

'What exactly did you say to her?' Val imagined Shaun might well be calling her again later that evening.

'It was just a red mist,' Emma confessed. 'I remember saying something about her own jealousy and that brattish daughter of hers, but I can't recall my exact words. I can just remember the look of horror on the faces of the other mums.'

'Oh Lord.' Val glanced behind her at the copious paperwork covering the worktop. 'Looks like you're snowed under as usual, Emmeline. Have you discussed your concerns about Maisie with Shaun?'

Emma's face darkened. 'No, he isn't interested, Mum. He's too busy with his new family; with Joanne and Piper. It's so hurtful for Maisie and I think they're quite mean to her behind Shaun's back. Between you and me, I think that's part of the problem.'

Val shifted uneasily in her seat. After Shaun's phone call and then Emma's assertions, she felt she was a very difficult position. 'Do you want me to talk to Maisie, love?'

'I think that might be a good idea, but first, I've made a doctor's appointment for her first thing Tuesday morning. I haven't told her yet. She's going to kick against it but she's going. It's not up for negotiation.'

'Very sensible, I think, under the circumstances.'

'Maybe the doctor showing concern might shock her out of this rut she seems to be in.'

'Let's hope so.' Val put down her mug. 'Perhaps you could speak to Joanne. Apologise?'

'Whatever I said, I feel justified. Miss Diane virtually admitted that Joanne is forcing her always to favour her daughter at the detriment of the other girls. She owns the dance school property, you see. Joanne is such a bitch and nobody ever challenges—'

Val coughed, interrupting her daughter. She had to calm her down somehow.

'And how are you, Emmeline? How are you bearing up with all this change?'

She watched as her daughter's eyes darted nervously around the room.

'I'm OK.' She hesitated. 'I feel a little unnerved, if I'm honest, Mum. Things keep happening. Small things that seem to have perfectly good explanations, but I just have this bad feeling that something terrible is going to take place.'

'Sounds like textbook anxiety to me,' Val said gently. 'You've had enough experience of it by now to recognise it. Don't neglect yourself, love. You can only care for Maisie if you're in a healthy place yourself.'

'I got this in the mail today.' Emma pulled out an envelope from the back pocket of her jeans. She extracted a single sheet of notepaper and handed it to Val.

Val reached into her handbag for her reading glasses and read the short letter.

'This looks like your handwriting, Emmeline.'

She watched as her daughter's face flushed. 'I know, but I can assure you it isn't. I wouldn't send it to myself, would I?'

'Of course not. But it sounds a bit cryptic. What does it mean?'

Emma explained quickly about the other things that had happened recently.

'Don't you see, Mum? Someone is trying to frighten me. To someone else, the note doesn't sound threatening at all. At first I was convinced it was something to do with what happened... you know, back then.'

Val nodded; how could she forget? It had been an ordeal for the whole family.

'But while I was waiting for you to come over just now, I realised I've distracted myself with the past, and now I have a far more plausible explanation.'

'You do?' Val took another sip of tea, hoping Emma had come up with a sensible theory.

Emma looked over her shoulder to check they were still alone.

'I think Joanne Dent wrote it,' she whispered. 'I think Shaun told her about what happened to me, about how ill I became because of it, and I think she's trying to push me over the edge so she can get me out of this house and have my husband and daughter all to herself.'

'Heavens above,' Val said, trying not to show her growing concern about Emma's very obvious paranoia. 'All this worrying is going to do you no good whatsoever. I think, at Maisie's appointment, you should mention to the doctor how you're feeling too.'

'I actually feel fine now I've realised it's her. I just have to decide what to do about it.'

'That's quite a claim, Emmeline. I'd be careful not to start throwing accusations of that nature around, especially when they involve a criminal lawyer.'

'She's clever, Mum, I'll give you that.' Emma stared into the middle distance, a strange smile on her face. 'But she isn't clever enough to fool me. There's something that doesn't quite add up about Joanne Dent, but trust me, I intend to find out what it is. Even if it kills me.'

CHAPTER 44

Emma

After my mother has left the house, I sit and reflect on our conversation. Maisie hasn't spoken to me since the incident at the dance school, and refused to come out of her bedroom even to see Mum off.

I'm certain my mum doesn't believe me about the note, or about Joanne's hidden personality. The way she looks at me, I can see she thinks it's all in my imagination.

Everyone who meets her thinks my mum is such a lovely person, and she is in a lot of ways. She's mellowed a great deal. But I know of a different side to her. An aspect of her personality that was far more prevalent during my childhood.

Unforgiving, critical, and worst of all, supportive of my father's tyranny and cruel words.

I don't want to think back to that time now. We've moved on as people, and I'm sure she did the best she could at the time. For many years it felt normal to me; until I had my own daughter, that is.

That's when I knew with every fibre of my being that I would never allow a man to treat my daughter in that way.

And that's why it will always hurt, even if we never talk about it.

Before she went home, Mum popped upstairs to Maisie's room. She was up there for about ten minutes, and when she came down, she looked concerned.

'I think you're right. She has lost a lot of weight,' she whispered. 'It was easier to see in her pyjamas. They used to pull a little across her tummy and thighs, and now there's oodles of bagging fabric.'

I nodded, relieved she'd seen it for herself.

'I wouldn't worry yourself too much, though. She says she feels well enough and that she just wants a break from going to Joanne's house and dancing, so she can chill out at home for a while.' Mum hesitated. 'I asked her about Joanne and Piper and she shrugged and said they're OK. By that, I take it she means they're not her favourite people but are tolerable.'

'I don't think she tells me everything that happens there,' I said, but Mum didn't comment. 'As for dancing, it's one of the few things that still gets her out of her bedroom.'

I'm shaken from my thoughts by my phone ringing. When I check the screen, I see it's Mum calling. She must have only just got home.

'Emmeline?' She's breathless and she sounds upset.

'Mum, are you OK?'

'Yes, but… I went straight upstairs when I got home, you know, after what you said about Maisie not eating. I just had this strange feeling driving back and then… I found it all, in her bedroom!'

'Mum. Slow down, what are you saying?' I feel sick with dread at hearing what's bothering her, but she's making no sense at all at the moment.

'I checked her bedroom at mine. I looked in her bedside cupboard where she keeps her magazines and there was food. Lots of rotting food, all wrapped in paper towels.' Mum suppresses a sob. 'She hasn't been eating at all. She's been fooling me, hiding the food. Why is she doing this?'

The strangest sense of calmness descends on me.

'It's good you've found out, Mum,' I say slowly. 'Because now we know for sure that someone is hurting Maisie in the most deceitful way.'

'What do you mean?' Mum wails, unnerved. 'Hurting her how?'

'It's clear that someone has got to her. Emotionally. They're trying to destroy Maisie from the inside out.'

I just can't get to sleep tonight.

All afternoon I've ignored texts and phone calls from Shaun. I bolted the doors on the inside in case he tried to gain entry with his key. But remarkably, he didn't come over.

I try to push thoughts of the letter I received to the back of my mind, just like I buried the actual note under the contents of my bedside table drawer once Mum had left.

Maybe it was just someone playing a silly prank and the stuff that's happened recently is exactly as Shaun and Mum have suggested: simply bad luck.

If someone really wanted to scare me, I'm sure they could come up with something a bit more inventive than messing up the herb garden and writing a cryptic note.

Keep looking over your shoulder, you utter cow, because you'll never know when it's coming.

Besides, it doesn't make sense. The person who issued that threat three years ago is dead. And dead people don't damage tyres and windows.

Unless it's nothing to do with what happened back then and this is a person who wants to scare me for other reasons…

Once I've given the past a way in, it is unstoppable, and before I know it, I'm back there at Clayton and McCarthy.

Damian was one of the last people to return from lunch.

I called out to him on his way across the office.

'Damian, when you have a minute, could I have a quick word?'

He laughed and carried on walking as he answered me. 'When I *have a minute*, yes, you can, Emma. Not sure that's going to be today, though.'

'Fine.' He couldn't say I hadn't asked now.

Mid afternoon, Mr McCarthy himself arrived back at the office. I knew I couldn't hold on to what I knew or there would be questions asked of my judgement. So I tapped on Barbara's door and ask if I could have a few minutes with him.

'What's it about?' she asked.

'It's confidential,' I said curtly, and her nostrils flared.

'Take a seat on the chairs and I'll ask him.'

I watched from the client waiting area as she picked up the handset and called through to Mr McCarthy. She looked at me pointedly as she spoke to him.

Then she put down the phone and nodded towards his office, which sat across the corridor from hers.

I knocked on the door and he called for me to enter. I stepped cautiously inside and he regarded me suspiciously from behind his desk.

'Emma, take a seat. What's so urgent it can't wait for an appointment?'

I guessed Peter McCarthy was in his late fifties. He had coarse salt-and-pepper hair and was a hulk of a man: over six feet four tall. He carried his height easily but walked with a slight limp due to a car accident he'd had in his thirties.

Things had moved on a lot in the workplace since Peter first opened the practice, although you wouldn't necessarily know it at times. His nickname downstairs amongst some of the employees was 'dinosaur' because his management style belonged back in the dark ages.

He frowned as I sat down without invitation, obviously irritated by my interruption.

'I'm sorry to have to bring this to you,' I said, genuinely regretful as I unfolded the wedge of paperwork in my hand. 'But I think you'll agree it needs addressing right away.'

His face suddenly became grave as he noted my serious expression. 'What have you got there?'

I stood up and spread the copied pages of the medical report on his desk.

'I was asked to photocopy this for the counsel's court bundles,' I explained.

He scanned the report and nodded. 'OK, so this shows the client was under the legal alcohol limit while he was driving the car. That's a good thing.'

I pulled my phone out of my jacket pocket.

'But this is the original report. I had to take photographs because Damian Murphy locked the physical copy in his office drawer.'

This time Peter looked at the report and his face paled.

I cleared my throat. 'As you can see, it looks very much as though someone has altered the original document.'

'And you say Damian did this?' Peter's brow grew increasingly furrowed as he stared down at the paperwork.

'I'm saying that as far as I'm aware, he's the only one who has handled a copy of the original report,' I said carefully.

'My God,' Peter muttered, looking again between the photos of the original report and the tampered version I'd photocopied. 'If this fake report is used, the whole company could be struck off the SRA register.'

'Exactly.' I nodded. 'Which is why I felt I had to come up and see you right away.'

'Yes. Of course.' He loosened his collar. 'You did the right thing, Emma. Where's Damian now?'

'He's at his desk.'

Peter thanked me and I quickly made myself scarce.

Later, I popped down to the staff kitchenette to make a drink. I was staring thoughtfully out of the tiny side window that looked out onto the brick wall of the neighbouring offices when the door opened quickly behind me and closed again.

I turned round to face Damian, his face a twisted mask of hatred and fury.

'You absolute fucking bitch,' he spat, and I stepped back, my palms in the air. Behind me, I met the edge of the worktop, and I found myself leaning back over it to distance myself from him. 'Why did you have to do that? What couldn't you have spoken to me?' He bit his lip. 'I could've explained.'

'Explained? I had a duty to report it, as well you know.' I took a breath and forced the words out as powerfully as I could manage, even though my knees were shaking. Foolishly, I'd expected Mr McCarthy to protect my identity as whistleblower, at least for a while. 'As you would have done if you'd discovered that someone else in the office had falsified results.'

'Did you know I've just bought a new house? That I'm getting married in December?'

'I didn't, but that's not my problem, Damian.' I softened my tone slightly. 'I did ask to speak to you first. You left me no choice.'

He pushed his face closer to mine and spoke through gritted teeth.

'If it's the last thing I do, I'll repay you for what you've done to me, the way you've ruined my career, my life, in a matter of minutes. Keep looking over your shoulder, you utter cow, because you'll never know when it's coming.'

And with that, he turned on his heel and walked out of the kitchen, slamming the door forcefully behind him.

CHAPTER 45

Maisie

Her mum had been acting totally weird all weekend, and when she had a go at Joanne in front of everyone, Maisie actually wished she herself could drop down dead on the spot.

Maisie had known what her mum's reaction would be if she saw her new slimline body in the shower. Her mum simply didn't understand that she'd been getting fatter. Unbelievably, she seemed to find it cute. 'Puppy fat,' Gran had laughingly called it when she caught Maisie staring into the mirror, pinching at the excess flesh around her middle.

Ariana Grande had no puppy fat, and neither had most of the other girls at her dance classes.

The other girls had started staring at her, and Maisie felt certain it was because she looked revolting in her leotard and tights. And every time she glanced around, Piper would be whispering with the group of girls that used to be Maisie's own best friends.

Why, oh why, did Piper have to join all of Maisie's classes? Before Maisie's dad moved in with Joanne, she only saw Piper at ballet. But now she had access to all Maisie's friends, all of the time, and she had poisoned them against her.

There was something wrong with Maisie, there had to be. That was why *she* was always telling her she was too fat, too lazy, too ugly. She'd even said that that was why her dad had left home, to get away from her.

Unless she tried to make herself more likeable, her friends would be lost forever.

At first Maisie had ignored the nasty comments, but after she had heard the same insults again and again, the vicious words somehow seeped into her skin and she thought about them every time she looked in the mirror and every time a meal was served.

The worst thing of all was that Maisie knew that if she told her mum all the stuff that was wrong with her, and that Dad had left them because he couldn't stand being with her any longer, her mum would end up hating her too.

And if that happened, Maisie thought she might as well just be dead and save herself the heartache.

On Tuesday morning, Maisie dressed in her school uniform as usual.

She hated school like she hated everything else right now. The only good thing about it was that Piper wasn't around, and also she didn't have to listen to the hateful comments she endured at the dance school.

It had got much worse since Miss Diane had made the announcement. Maisie hadn't even told her mum yet. She didn't want to face up to it.

It had happened halfway through class. They usually had a quick break to grab a drink. People used it as an excuse to mess about and chat. Maisie used to be one of them, but now she always stood at the back of the group on her own, hoping nobody would notice she was there.

Miss Diane clapped her hands and the room fell immediately quiet.

'I have a special announcement to make.' She beamed, scanning all the curious faces. 'I've decided who will take the lead role in the Christmas show!'

There was a burst of anticipation, a buzz of voices as everyone tried to guess.

Maisie glanced over at Piper, who stood staring at the dance teacher, a self-satisfied smirk on her perfectly made-up face.

'So this year, our Dorothy is going to be…' Miss Diane hesitated tantalisingly and some of the girls giggled. 'Maisie Barton!'

Maisie staggered slightly, as echoing gasps rose around her. 'What?'

'Her? She looks awful!'

'She'll make a rubbish Dorothy…'

Miss Diane pushed through the rows of girls and led Maisie out to the front.

Please God. Let me just die before I get there, Maisie silently pleaded. But she didn't die. She stood next to Miss Diane, and tried to smile at the sneering faces.

'I know you'll all join me in congratulating Maisie,' Miss Diane said, a hint of warning in her voice.

She began to clap, and the girls all reluctantly joined in with a smattering of applause.

Nobody cheered, nobody rushed up to hug her.

But everyone turned as Piper ran crying out of the hall.

Downstairs, Maisie refused breakfast. She honestly didn't feel in the least bit hungry. She'd lain awake since the early hours with a banging headache and the horrible taunts replaying in her head.

She felt relieved when her mum didn't go on and on about how she wasn't eating enough. Although Maisie could see she had lost weight in the mirror, it wasn't nearly enough to make everyone like her again.

As her mum drove her to school, Maisie suddenly noticed where they were.

'You've come the wrong way again,' she told her. Mum had done it more than once; she called it being on automatic pilot when she had a lot of pressure on with work. 'You should've turned off back there.'

'I'm not taking you straight to school,' her mum said firmly. 'We have to call in somewhere else first.'

'Where? I'll be late!' Maisie's headache pounded harder when she thought about having to walk into the class with all eyes on her and sarcastic comments from people who used to be her friends just a short time ago.

Even though Piper went to a completely different school, the faces that stared at Maisie now in class and during breaks and lunchtimes looked uncannily like Piper's own, with their narrowed eyes and sneering lips.

She didn't know why people had started being nasty to her; it could only be, as *she* kept saying, that Maisie had become truly ugly and unlikeable.

It was true she didn't like joining in silly playground games like she used to. Sometimes she just felt so shaky and unwell, she'd take herself off to a quiet corner. It hadn't taken long for the others to find someone else to replace her on the courtyard benches.

'It's fine. I've called school and left a message for your teacher that you'll be in later.' Her mum glanced across at her. 'I made you an appointment with Dr Yesufu.'

'What?' Maisie's face blazed. 'I don't need to see the doctor, Mum.'

'I think you do. You've lost too much weight, Maisie, and I need to know you're not ill.'

'I'M FINE!' she shouted, and her mum looked shocked. 'I've told you a hundred times, there's nothing wrong with me.'

'Yes, you keep telling me that, but it's clear that something *is* wrong. So I need to ask the doctor to check you're OK.'

'I told you I didn't want to go to dancing any more but you wouldn't listen.' Maisie scowled.

'You need a hobby, otherwise you'll just waste away stuck in your bedroom,' her mother snapped back.

Maisie felt too furious to respond. She could tell when her mother was resolved and couldn't be convinced, and this was definitely one of those times.

They travelled the rest of the way to the surgery in silence.

CHAPTER 46

Dr Yesufu gave Maisie a jolly smile but she didn't return it. She sat moodily in the chair next to her mother and folded her arms.

There was a photograph on the desk of Dr Yesufu's family. His wife wore traditional African dress with a brightly coloured turban, and his children, a boy and a girl, both quite a bit younger than Maisie, wore Western clothes.

She imagined he was a good father who loved his wife and his well-behaved children. She'd bet he would never leave them for a new life with another family.

Her mother began to speak, and although Maisie gave every impression she wasn't bothered, she tuned in with interest.

'I've been concerned because Maisie has lost a lot of weight in a short time, Doctor. When I ask her about it, she denies that she's not eating.'

'Ah, I see. We must begin with first things first.' Dr Yesufu stood up, his ebony skin glowing under the fluorescent strip light. 'Come over here, Maisie. I can take your weight and height measurements so we know what we are dealing with.'

She slipped off her shoes and stood on the antiquated-looking column scales. Then she stood against the wall against a height chart.

Dr Yesufu grunted to himself a couple of times and wrote something down on paper.

'Please, sit down, Maisie. I must now take your blood pressure.' He produced a black cuff and slipped it over her hand until it circled her upper arm. He pressed a button and the cuff inflated, giving Maisie a feeling of pins and needles.

'Ow,' she complained.

'Uncomfortable, I know.' He grinned. 'But necessary. Now, let's see.'

He consulted a digital screen and then wrote another number down.

He considered his notes a moment and then addressed her mother.

'Now. I'm pleased to say that Maisie isn't dangerously under-weight at this point.'

'See!' Maisie told her mother triumphantly.

'However, you are on the borderline of becoming underweight, young lady.' He looked at her. 'You're looking quite pale and tired. This trend of losing weight quickly must not continue, or you could soon become ill. Do you understand?'

Maisie nodded meekly. 'I'm still eating, just not as much.'

'Her gran found food she'd hidden,' her mother blurted out, as if she were telling tales to the teacher.

Dr Yesufu frowned.

'That was just leftover food I'd forgotten to take down,' Maisie objected. 'Gran gets annoyed if I leave food and plates up in my room, I was going to bring it down but then I forgot.'

'Ah, it seems that little mystery is solved!' Dr Yesufu looked pleased, but her mother still wasn't having it.

'All her clothes are baggy on her now, Doctor. And she stays in her room for hours on end.'

Dr Yesufu looked at her. 'Maisie, could I ask you to pop back into the waiting room for a few minutes, just while I finish off the details with your mother here?'

Maisie shrugged and stood up, shooting her mother an annoyed look. She walked out of the office, leaving the door slightly ajar.

She pushed open the double fire doors in the corridor leading to the waiting room and let them sweep closed again. Then she tiptoed back to Dr Yesufu's door and pressed her ear close to the gap.

'I appreciate it is difficult for you, as her mother, not to worry, Mrs Barton, but an obsession with food is often a pre-teen thing and a passing phase. That is all.'

'But she was never like this before her father left home!' Maisie winced at her mother's desperate tone. 'I think she's taken it badly and certain people in her dad's house are making her feel bad.'

'You suspect abuse?' Dr Yesufu's voice turned suddenly grim.

'God, no! But I think Maisie perhaps feels insecure and a little inadequate in the company of her dad's new partner and her daughter. The girl is the same age as Maisie, and I think she's a bit of a bully.'

'The best advice I can give you is to keep the lines of communication open between the two of you. Talk to your daughter, tell her you trust her to be sensible.'

'I've tried talking to her, but she just insists she's fine. She used to be such a happy little girl, smiling and full of energy.'

Maisie frowned at her mother's description. She was ten years old; Year 6 at primary school and starting at the high school next autumn! She was hardly a *little girl*.

'I understand your frustrations, I do,' Dr Yesufu said quietly. 'But my best advice right now is to monitor Maisie while giving her a little space. Don't focus on food in your conversations; that could just make things worse. With any luck, this difficult time will pass and she'll soon be back on track.'

There was a pause in the conversation, and Maisie realised her mother was crying. She recoiled in horror, opened the double doors in the corridor slowly and quietly and slipped out into the waiting room.

She found a seat in the corner, away from crying children and fraught mothers. There were a lot of old people who looked thin and tired. It was a horrible place and she didn't want to become ill.

Inside, she felt a dull ache of shame that she'd caused her mum such worry. At the same time, she didn't know what to do about it.

Nobody liked her and Maisie could hardly blame them. It was true what she'd been told: the only chance she had to make things better was to become a slimmer, prettier and cleverer person. Being herself was just not good enough.

When she saw her body changing in the mirror, it felt like something good was happening. She was getting closer to her goal. Closer to being a girl her parents could love and be proud of. Yet the very thing that was worrying her mum and gran was the only thing she had to hold onto.

Not eating had become all she was good at, and maybe *she* would leave her alone if she did as she was told.

She had to do it for a little while longer. She had no choice.

CHAPTER 47

Emma

I grab my bag and jacket and thunder downstairs and out of the office building, pulling the door closed behind me and pushing against it to make sure it has locked.

The cleaners come in three times a week, but today is not one of their set days, so I know there'll be nobody here in the building until the morning, when one of the partners opens up.

Joanne never seems to be around these days, but I can't say I'm disappointed about that. I thought she might haul me upstairs to discipline me for my outburst at the dance school, but so far I've had little reproof for it even from Shaun. It almost makes me more anxious.

I'm so grateful the work day is finally over and yet I've somehow managed to leave later than I should to pick up my daughter.

After Maisie's doctor's appointment this morning, I've been over-thinking the situation all day long. Do I play down her reluctance to eat, as per Dr Yesufu's advice, or do I tackle it head on?

It's often so easy to see what other people should do in a situation like this, but when emotions are running high, I've discovered that dealing with your own dilemma effectively is another thing entirely.

Driving to Maisie's school this morning after we left the surgery, I said, on a whim, that if she wanted me to, I would speak to her dad about having a break from visiting Joanne's house. Her face lit up at that, so I guess I must've done something right.

I push away thoughts of Shaun's angry face when I confront him with her decision.

I half walk, half run towards the car, fishing blindly in my handbag for the keys. I don't know how I've managed to forget the clock, however absorbed I've been in thinking through my problems.

I should have left fifteen minutes ago to be sure of arriving at the dance studio a few minutes before her class finishes. I know Mum is at her watercolour class tonight, which is held at a college on the outskirts of the city, so she'll not be able to help out.

Soon as I get in the car, I'll shoot a quick text over to Miss Diane to let her know I'll be ten minutes late.

My stomach contracts when I realise this will be the third time this month. I silently swear to myself that it will be the last.

My fingers close on my keys and I press the button to unlock, but as I reach the car, all the urgency drains out of me. My posture deflates like a burst balloon and my jacket slips from the crook of my arm onto the gravel.

'Oh no!' I whisper.

The driver's side back tyre is flat as a pancake. I stand stock still for a few moments, while I wait for a solution to present itself.

I bought the car a little while ago and one of the recurring niggles on my never-ending mental to-do list has been to join a vehicle rescue scheme. Periodically the task has surfaced in my mind, only to be repeatedly dampened down as I promise myself I'll deal with it later. Of course, I never have.

And now this. The flat tyres on Shaun's car a while ago niggle at the back of my mind, but I don't allow my imagination any leeway.

I glance hopefully back at the building, as if someone who knows how to change a tyre might appear. But as I'm fully aware, I'm the last staff member to leave tonight.

Momentarily, I recall with regret that my go-to person for problems of this nature has always been Shaun. One panicky call from me and he'd appear as if by magic, sorting stuff out with the minimum of drama.

I've never learned how to change a tyre, had no reason to. But now, I realise, there are probably a hundred similar jobs I've always relied on him to step in on.

I could call a cab… if I hadn't left my purse on the side this morning, knowing I had a banana and yoghurt in my bag and a fiver in the inside pocket.

There's no time to ask the cab driver to stop by the house first for my purse, and in the meantime, the seconds are ticking by while I continue to dither.

I swallow my pride, grab my phone and call Shaun. Fully expecting the day to get worse and it to go to voicemail, I'm shocked when he actually answers.

'I'm stuck at work with a flat tyre, and Maisie's dance class has just finished,' I bluster, furious at myself for appearing so rubbish in the face of what is probably his now seamlessly organised life. I'm pretty sure Joanne would *never* neglect something like rescue cover. 'And Shaun? Someone has vandalised the garden.'

'What?' He's incredulous.

'It's true. Ask Maisie. She found the plants torn out, and after the window, well, I'm worried someone might have—'

'Calm down, Emma, focus on what's important here. We need to talk, but now's not the time,' he says levelly. 'Joanne is on her way over to the dance school to pick Piper up, I'll ask her to pick Maisie up too.'

'No! Can't you do it?'

'Don't be ridiculous. It doesn't take two of us to pick up the girls and Jo will nearly be there now. Maisie can stay here with us tonight. Doesn't sound as if you'll be home yourself any time soon.'

He ends the call before I can explain that that's not such a great idea. Perhaps Joanne didn't tell Shaun exactly what I'd accused her of: damaging my daughter. Unpleasant bits of conversation are slowly coming back to me. I don't want Maisie going around there any more. Shaun will need to take her out on his own, or come to the house to visit at agreed times. I have to try and get things back on a level, get Maisie into an ordinary routine.

Unless I call Shaun back, he won't know all this, but the last thing I want is to keep Maisie and Miss Diane waiting any longer.

So I just stand there staring at the flat tyre. Feeling the most alone and vulnerable I have for years.

I finally get home about 7.30. By 7.45 I've changed into my comfies and I'm sitting with a coffee in the kitchen. There's nothing I can do for Maisie now she's with Shaun but still, I feel like I've betrayed her in a way.

I press the soles of my feet down onto the tiles and relish the warmth of the under-floor heating that kicks in automatically at four o'clock each day. I don't bother closing the curtains. It's too dark to see outside now, and when I stare at the glass, I see myself reflected back.

I get up and pull the blinds. You never know who might be out there, watching and waiting.

It was a sobering moment earlier, when I finished speaking to Shaun and realised I had nobody to call for help or advice.

People seem to have drifted away, out of my zone of acceptable contact. Friends, acquaintances... there is simply no one to turn to in an emergency.

I ended up googling a local garage who offered a relay rescue service. Within an hour, they came with a tow truck that wasn't required. The mechanic changed my tyre and issued me with a handwritten invoice for eighty pounds for his trouble.

He was a stocky, gruffly spoken man with flecks of silver peppering his sandy hair, and wore a navy boiler suit, its poppers open to accommodate a stout belly sheathed in a T-shirt that looked as if it hadn't been white for some time.

'Don't give credit normally. But seeing as you work here, we can sort something out.' He crouched down to inspect the tyre, pinching at its flat edge. 'Can't see anything obvious; it's maybe a slow puncture.'

'Is it possible someone could have done this deliberately?' I asked him. 'It happened a few weeks ago too.'

He looked up at me and grinned.

'Anything's possible. I see a lot of strange things in this job, the pickles folks get themselves into.' I tried not to look at his rotten teeth. 'Depends if someone's got a grudge against you, love. Anyone come to mind?'

CHAPTER 48

I can't think of a reason to stop Maisie visiting Shaun at Joanne's house.

She wasn't happy when Joanne picked her up from her class last week. I started to explain about my dilemma with the car but she just won't hold a proper conversation with me these days.

'I told you I didn't want to go and you said you'd sort it, Mum,' she says sulkily as she shuffles into the hallway. 'But you haven't sorted it and I'm going there more and more.'

'At least you're getting to see your dad quite a bit,' I offer, but realise it sounds a bit dismissive. What can I do? Shaun won't hear of anything being amiss with the arrangement and somehow, it's become my problem when it's all his doing in the first place.

I swallow down the twisty feeling I have inside, we kiss goodbye and I wave her off as Shaun's car drives away. I don't lie around downstairs, surfing endless crap on the Sky channels, but go upstairs to the study to work.

I have a really productive morning, easily completing the important tasks I'm responsible for on our current cases.

It's one of those gorgeous winter days when it's fine and sunny, and although I can sense the cool backdrop of winter lurking, there's a faint warmth to the day, particularly in the big kitchen living space, flanked as it is by the French doors and their floor-to-ceiling expanse of glass.

At lunchtime, I take the trouble to set a few bits out on a wooden platter... just for one. Italian meats, a few olives, some sun-dried tomatoes and a sliver of Manchego I still had in the fridge. I slice up a small ciabatta roll and sit at the breakfast bar with the doors slightly open to enjoy the sharp freshness of the air which serves to clear my head a little.

It's nice to feel like a grown-up and it makes me realise that I don't really buy much food for me; I buy the stuff Maisie used to love and put an extra portion out for myself.

Why did Shaun and I never make the effort to enjoy a simple lunch like this together at weekends? We became like ships in the night, our only aim to cover care for our daughter. As if we – our relationship – never mattered.

After lunch, I lie on the sofa and read. I actually read! For all of ten minutes before I stop with a jolt and a panic that somehow I've forgotten to do something. But no. I haven't forgotten anything. My case work is done, Maisie is safe with her dad... It's simply a luxury I've never known but which I certainly intend to embrace from now on.

I spend the afternoon catching up on weeks' worth of cleaning and ironing. Not such a luxury, but by late afternoon, as I sit with a cup of tea and a biscuit, the satisfaction is palpable.

It's so true that small tasks can give a sense of achievement far beyond their perceived importance. Little pleasures, like a short nap, time to enjoy a simple lunch without multitasking. Just giving myself some time for *me*, rather than family, home or work.

It sounds silly, and of course I know on an intelligent level that there's more to life than work. But it's only now, at the ripe old age of thirty-four, that I'm finally understanding that simple stuff can enrich my life. Better late than never, I guess.

I jump up at a banging on the front door. Glancing at the wall clock as I dash into the hallway, I see it's only just turned four o'clock.

I agreed with Shaun for Maisie to be back by six so she has time to have her bath and relax a bit before bed, and to be fair, he's kept to our agreed timings since I expressed my annoyance after her late return from their farm visit.

I open the door and jump back in exaggerated surprise.

'Well, I didn't expect you back yet!' I say in jest.

Maisie stumbles into the hallway. Her eyes are dark and haunted, and she doesn't say a word as she slides past me like a shadow.

'Whatever's the matter?' I look behind me, but she's already darted into the depths of the house. Shaun stands there looking blank, his hands stuffed into his jeans pockets. 'What's wrong with her?'

'I don't know,' he says. 'The girls have had a nice afternoon, at a swimming party. One of Piper's school friends whose mum said Maisie was welcome to go too. Apparently Maisie knows her from dancing.'

'But Maisie didn't take her swim stuff to yours.'

'She borrowed one of Piper's swimsuits.' He shrugs.

'OK, so they had a nice time at the party… then what happened?'

'Nothing *happened*. Jo picked them up, and when Maisie got back, she just said she wanted to come home.'

I look back over my shoulder, but the house is quiet. Wherever Maisie is, she's unusually silent.

'Did you ask her why she wanted to come home early… if anything was wrong?'

'Of course I did! I can perform parental duties perfectly well when you're not around, you know.'

I wait for his defensiveness to ebb.

'She said she just felt tired,' he says, his voice dropping back to its usual octave. 'That's all. We wondered if you'd drilled it into her that she had to come home early.'

'No. I haven't.'

'It's bound to affect her, Em. Your paranoia.' He stares at me. 'These outbursts of yours… I feel like I hardly know you any more.'

'I'd better go and see if she's all right.' I start to close the door. 'Bye then.'

Just before it clicks shut, he calls out: 'Emma?'

I open it again and stick my head out.

'Don't do that thing you always do.'

'What thing?'

'Make a big deal out of it with Maisie,' he says, pulling his car keys out of his jacket pocket and jiggling them in his hand. 'She's fine and nothing happened. OK?'

I press my lips together and close the door without answering.

I've seen my daughter virtually every single day for the last ten years, and if there's one thing I know for sure at this moment, it's this:

Maisie is most certainly not fine.

CHAPTER 49

Maisie sits neatly and quietly on the end of the couch, as if she's somehow trying to make herself look smaller.

Her hands are folded in her lap, her rucksack is placed on the floor next to her shoe-clad feet, and she stares vacantly out of the glass doors at the garden beyond.

This is not usual behaviour for the girl who used to be bursting at the seams to tell me about her day. The television would be on within minutes of her arrival and the house filled with her singing and laughter. That seems like a long time ago now. Things have certainly changed, although she still won't talk about it.

'We can watch a film together later if you like.' I sit down at the other end of the couch to give her some space.

She doesn't look at me or answer, so I mirror her posture and we stare out of the window at the blossom tree's bare branches, which wave slightly in the breeze. Just a few months ago they were a riot of pastel pink and green, decorating the lawn with petals.

'Would you like a glass of juice?' I ask after a few minutes.

She turns her head and looks at me with a forlorn expression. 'Water, please,' she croaks.

'Water?' I grin, trying to lighten the situation, although inside I feel a heat burning. 'Are you on a health kick?'

She doesn't answer, and when I take the drink over, I notice she's slid her feet out of her shoes and bent her legs up onto the seat cushion. It's a sign she's relaxing a little, but I'm careful not to interrogate her, in line with Dr Yesufu's advice.

'I've got lots of work done today while you were with your dad,' I volunteer.

'I was hardly *with* Dad,' she says quietly, staring down into her glass.

'Oh, that's right. He said you went to a party with Piper?'

I phrase it as a question to encourage her to elaborate, but she doesn't. Her eyes gravitate to the window again.

'It's getting cooler out there,' I remark. 'No pretty pink petals on the blossom tree now.'

She nods, solemn.

'Has Joanne got a big garden?' I venture. 'With a lawn and trees, I mean?'

'She lives in an apartment at the top of an old house; Linby House, it's called. There are massive gardens around it but they're for everyone to use, not just her.'

'Ah, yes. Communal gardens.'

After a beat of silence, Maisie speaks again. Her voice sounds choked.

'I didn't want to go to the party, but Dad said I had to.'

'He did?' I'm shocked.

'He said I should go because I'd enjoy it, but I didn't want to go because although it was a girl from the dance school, she hadn't invited me. Only Piper.'

'That's probably because she goes to Piper's school,' I suggest. 'It doesn't sound as if she minded you tagging along.'

'I don't think she wanted me to go, but Joanne called her mum and said they were stuck with me for the day and could she bring me along.'

I swallow. 'I'm sure she didn't say she was stuck with you.'

Maisie stays quiet and I feel like I've just discounted her opinion.

'At least you must have known some of the other girls from dancing.'

She nodded. 'There were a few people there from ballet, and Miss Diane came to watch them do a dance they'd practised.' Maisie hesitated. 'I think the other girls hate me because I got lead role in the Christmas show.'

'I'm sure that's not true. They're envious, maybe, but hate is a strong word. Getting the part is something to be proud of and celebrate, and we're not going to let anyone spoil that for you.' She stares stonily at the floor. 'Your dad said you were able to borrow one of Piper's swimming costumes for the party.'

Her pale cheeks flush and she takes a tiny sip of water.

'Did you feel comfortable wearing it?'

'It was too tight,' she says.

'Good job you only had to suffer it for a couple of hours then.' I grin.

Maisie doesn't smile. 'I looked fat.'

'Don't be silly,' I huff. 'I'm sure you looked perfectly lovely.'

'I looked FAT.' She glares at me. '*They* said I did.'

'Who did?' I feel suddenly sick, realising how awful it must have been for her.

'All of them. They made up a song about it and kept singing it when the mums went up to the café.'

'Even Piper?'

'I don't want to talk about it any more,' she says, and with that she stands up and walks out of the kitchen and upstairs. I hear her bedroom door open and then close with a dull thud.

It's obvious that Piper is a slight child with a much smaller frame than Maisie, who is in no way fat but who has quite wide shoulders and is longer in the body.

Surely Joanne would have the sense to select a suitable swimsuit for her to borrow, perhaps one that was too big for her daughter. It doesn't take much to see the difference in the two girls and understand that Maisie is hardly going to feel comfortable in a costume that fits Piper.

I pick up my phone and call Shaun. It puts me straight through to voicemail.

'Just to let you know, Maisie's very upset. The girls were teasing her at the party, saying she looked fat. Did she tell you? They're probably jealous about Miss Diane giving her the lead role in the Christmas show. Apparently Piper heard it all, possibly even joined in. Can you ask Joanne about it?'

I end the call, aware that my message will sound curt when he listens to it, but I won't lose any sleep over that.

I'm angry with Shaun. He must have known Maisie was upset when she asked to come home early, but instead of getting to the bottom of what was bothering her, he just blindly agreed to bring her back and wasn't honest about what happened at the party.

And instead of supervising the girls, it sounds like Joanne just buggered off up to the café with the other mothers for a good gossip.

I felt secure in the knowledge that Joanne understood all about ten-year-old girls and how cruel they can be. Now, I'm not so sure.

I hear a cry from upstairs and I tear up to Maisie's bedroom.

She's sitting on the edge of her bed, bent double over her knees and gasping in air. I know she left her bag downstairs with her inhaler in.

'It's OK, it's fine. Just slow down, slow your breathing down.' I force myself to speak calmly, and sit next to her rubbing the top of her back. 'Breathe, that's it. That's good.'

I snatch up a paper bag from the floor and empty out the new hair bobbles that are in it. Then I open it up and hold it to Maisie's face.

'Breathe in and out, into the bag. That's it, sweetie. Well done.' Her breathing deepens and slows a touch. 'Keep going. Brilliant.'

I help her to sit up straighter.

'Wh-what's wrong with me, Mum?'

Her eyes are wide and dark as she looks pleadingly at me. My heart feels like it's cracking.

'You've had a panic attack, I think. It's not serious, don't worry, poppet.' I play it down while inside I'm burning up with concern. 'Are you worried about something?'

I know exactly what she's worried about, but I have to give her the chance to open up to me. Dr Yesufu said to keep communication open between us as much as possible.

She stares at me, and neither of us speaks for a moment. I feel like she's ready to confide in me, so I wait. And then she breaks her gaze.

'You know you can tell me anything, Maisie. Anything at all.'

I know she doesn't like going to Joanne's house and I know there's been some teasing by the sounds of it. But what I'm seeing in my daughter goes beyond that. It's as if someone is being so mean or frightening, it's actually changing her personality.

A few weeks ago, I knew everything about my Maisie, and now... we hardly seem close at all.

'I'm OK,' she says, turning away from me.

CHAPTER 50

Maisie

I want to tell Mum, I do. But I don't know *what* to tell her.

I just hate being around *her*. The way she looks at me, like I'm disgusting. She's really good at doing it so nobody else sees.

And the way she says stuff out loud sometimes so other people laugh at me when we're at the dance school.

She's always kind and pretends she likes me, but it's just for show. Dad would never understand, either. He just sees the best in everyone.

She says she's telling me stuff so that people will like me, to make me look better, but it just makes me feel sad inside and hate myself.

And every single time, after she's said horrible things, she tells me she's doing it for my own good.

She says nobody would ever believe me against her.

I think she's right.

CHAPTER 51

Joanne

She placed the croissants and preserves on the table, then a jug of orange juice and glasses. Finally she brought over the pot of fresh coffee.

'You're spoiling me.' Shaun smiled, looking at the spread. 'This is wonderful. Thank you.'

'I thought it might tempt you to sit down and relax. Enjoy your breakfast, instead of worrying.'

He sighed, nodding as she offered to pour him a coffee.

He looked as if he had the weight of the world on his shoulders, thanks to that mad mare Emma. Who'd have thought she'd turn out to be such a paranoid, over-defensive parent when she seemed so logical and capable at work?

Joanne had deliberately stayed away from the office until she decided what to do about Emma's outburst at the dance school. Actually, it had been laughable, accusing her of being jealous that Maisie had been chosen for the lead role in the Christmas show. And claiming that Joanne was somehow to blame for Maisie having no friends.

The woman had been furious and almost incoherent. Miss Diane had virtually fainted with embarrassment behind her.

And since Maisie's visit, Emma had been calling and texting Shaun all night. When he'd finally spoken to her, she was almost hysterical with rage, blaming him for the fact that Maisie had had some kind of panic attack after spending time at the apartment with them, and specifically at the swimming party.

'Maisie has never had a panic attack in her life.' Shaun shook his head when he finally got off the phone. 'And all this weight she's losing… I'm beginning to wonder if it's being on her own with her mother that's driving her crazy.'

He wasn't joking.

'Maybe she'd be better off if I had full custody.'

That had stopped Joanne in her tracks. Yet the more she thought about it, the more she realised it could work.

So, when Piper announced she had a sleepover at one of her new dance friends' houses, Joanne decided to use the opportunity to broach the subject of his ex-wife and daughter with Shaun. Hence their leisurely breakfast.

She'd noticed how adept Shaun had become at finding something to do when Emma made yet another ridiculous accusation. She also saw how strained his face looked yesterday, how he went out and sat on one of the benches in the grounds and stared endlessly at the old oak trees that framed the boundary of the communal gardens until she called him in.

Perhaps it was time for her to take control of the situation.

She watched now as Shaun reached for a croissant and began to spread it thickly with butter.

'I thought we might talk about Emma while we're on our own,' she ventured.

'Not much to talk about.' He shrugged. 'Emma is Emma. She'd pick a fight with herself.'

'You must realise we can't just allow her to make these wild accusations, Shaun? Word gets around, and I'm friends with lots of the mothers who were at the swimming party, know them professionally. She's already made a fool of herself in front of the dance mums.'

'And?'

'And you can't just ignore this stuff. It needs dealing with. Surely you can see she's getting worse. You said it yourself, all this nonsense about someone having a grudge and breaking windows, pulling out plants, while I'm in line for the wicked stepmother from hell award… It's madness.'

He took a bite of his pastry and chewed it slowly.

'She's causing trouble everywhere,' Joanne continued. 'Look at what you said happened at her last company.'

'What happened there wasn't really her fault, Jo. She couldn't have known what her colleague would do and she honestly thought she was doing the right thing in reporting him.'

'But my point is, there's a trend there. Making trouble for people.'

'Hmm. She's obviously in a bad place at the moment,' Shaun said. 'I'll have a chat with her.'

Bad place! Now he was making excuses for her. Just like he did all the time with Maisie, who could be quite spoilt and needy, Joanne had noticed. The slightest wrong word from Piper, and Maisie had a complete meltdown when she got home to her mother.

If Emma had some kind of personality defect, then it was quite likely Maisie had inherited the trait. Sometimes, the way she stared at Piper when they were watching TV downstairs… it chilled Joanne.

You read stuff all the time about kids hurting other kids. Maisie was taller and way bigger built than Piper.

Joanne had tried to talk to her several times about her weight, but it was like wading through treacle. The kid just didn't want to listen.

Well, it wasn't her problem, it was Shaun's. If he only recognised it. At the moment, he seemed intent on keeping his head down and hoping Emma would go away.

A ploy that didn't seem to be working.

'Aren't you going to eat?' Shaun's voice cut through her thoughts.

'Course.' She reached for a croissant and spread it thinly with strawberry jam. It felt like cardboard in her mouth as she chewed.

'I'll try and speak to Emma about the swimming party today,' Shaun said. 'I need to talk to her about the house, too.'

Joanne breathed a sigh of relief. She'd fully expected him to procrastinate about raising the prickly subject.

The last thing she wanted was to be saddled with Maisie full-time, but at least she'd be able to exert some proper control over the girl if she came to live with them. She felt confident she'd soon lick her into shape, if she could only get her away from Emma's grasp.

She could see the four of them in a nice big house in its own grounds in a picturesque village setting, somewhere like Colston Bassett which was over twenty miles away from her current apartment in Linby. A beautiful rural setting where she could get some wear out of her Hunter wellies and Barbour jacket, but only twenty minutes from the city centre where she felt at home in her sharp suits and Gucci flats. Perfect.

She'd a little work to do on Shaun, to convince him that Maisie would be better off at the same school as Piper, but she was good at convincing people to follow her advice. It was one of her most effective skills.

Luckily, Shaun wasn't a man who felt intimidated by his partner being the main breadwinner. Conveniently, it also meant that Joanne naturally had a bigger say in any decisions that involved money.

Maybe this time, she could make it work. Bury her own insecurities and embrace the idea of a blended family. The real fly in the ointment was Emma.

Emma might be intent on causing trouble for them at every turn, but it was all just playground stuff. None of it really bothered her, because Emma had no reach.

Her life was all work and pandering to her oversensitive daughter.

Perhaps Maisie would be better off living with them. They could be a proper family then.

CHAPTER 52

Emma

'You might be able to talk Shaun round to believing your twisted little fantasies, but don't try it with me, because I'm telling you now, it won't wash.'

I shrink away from Joanne's wild eyes and bared teeth as she leans across her desk after asking me to pop up to see her. I glance across at Anya's office, but she's not there. Joanne's far too clever to show her true colours when there's anyone else around.

'What are you talking about?' I bite my lip in an effort to stop my eyes stinging. 'How would *you* feel if your daughter was made to feel inferior like that?'

She seems to catch herself acting aggressively and sits back, takes a breath.

'I appreciate you must be worried about Maisie's weight. We've all noticed it. But what you can't do is blame other people for it.'

I'd swear this woman is a completely different person to the one I've worked with. She's always seemed so calm and rational… so together. I wonder if Shaun has seen this other side to her.

Granted, I embarrassed her at the dance school, but I didn't expect this at work. She must've been saving it up.

'Look, Emma, I don't know what's happening in your head. If I'm perfectly honest, I don't care. A few weeks ago, you gave us your blessing, and now it seems you're hell-bent on trying to cause trouble for us.'

'That's not true,' I say. 'But I'll not sit back and let Maisie be pushed into the shadows.'

Joanne laughs. 'She manages that all on her own. I hear Piper asking all the time if she wants to watch something on TV or play a computer game in her bedroom. If you want the awful truth, *your* daughter is jealous of *mine*. She's jealous of how she looks, what she has, and she's jealous because Shaun and Piper get on so well.'

Fury whirls around my chest like a cyclone. I stand up and bang the desk with the flat of my hand.

'Just so long as you and Piper both remember that Shaun is Maisie's father, and legally, right now he's still my husband. So just be careful if you think you've got your feet firmly and permanently under the fucking table, Little Miss Perfect.'

And with that, even though it's only mid morning, I stalk from her office, down the stairs and out of the building.

I jump into my car and drive to a small park quite close to home but off the beaten track.

I park up on the rough gravel at the entrance but I don't get out. It's cold, and I came away without my jacket, so I leave the engine running and the heater blasting.

There's nobody else here at all and the isolation is just what I need to wind down after the unpleasant altercation with Joanne.

The three of us used to come here when Maisie was small. There are a few pieces of play equipment in the fenced-off children's area where Shaun and I used to sit on a bench while Maisie ran around and let off some steam.

We'd often talk about the future, about when Maisie was older, what we'd be doing, where we'd be working. It was all unknown at that point; the only thing we were certain of was that we'd be together.

Joanne has probably already been on the phone ensuring Shaun knows her side of what happened, what was said. Everything carefully constructed to frame me as the unreasonable, desperate ex-wife.

But who have I got to rant to? My mother, and that's about it. And that's not going to happen because I know she still holds me accountable for Shaun and me splitting up in the first place.

Never mind. It's quiet thinking time I need right now, because something is bothering me that I can't quite put my finger on. Something that would be really hard to explain to anyone else.

Joanne seems to me like a person without a past. I know that sounds really weird, but it's as near as I can get to the feeling that everything she does, everything she says, is an act. And that nobody really knows the person who is underneath it all.

I've asked Shaun a couple of innocuous questions over the past few weeks, just the usual: how long was she married before, where is she from.

And he doesn't know the answers. I know my husband well enough to spot when he's being evasive or just doesn't want to discuss his new life with me. I'm pretty certain that's not what is behind his shoulder shrug every time I raise a question about Joanne's past.

He really doesn't know.

'Maybe you should ask her a bit about her background,' I suggested to him recently. 'Show some interest.'

'Joanne is a big believer in drawing a line under what's gone before,' he said easily. 'Piper's father died in a tragedy too bad to speak of, that's all I know. They don't talk about him now because Piper was too young to remember much about him and Joanne doesn't like to bring up what happened.'

A perfectly reasonable answer, some might think. And Shaun himself seems satisfied with it.

But as a mother myself, I find it a little odd.

Most women I know, if they lost their husband and the father of their only child, would keep his memory alive for the child's sake at least. So that they were aware of where they came from.

Unless she had something to hide, that is.

CHAPTER 53

I don't go back into the office. If Joanne wants to fire me, then let her.

I know that's an illogical reaction, but I feel I might burst if I set eyes on her again before I've had a break.

Later, I can see there's something wrong – more so than usual – as soon as Maisie emerges from the dance studio and looks for my car from the top of the steps.

I spot Piper standing directly behind her and it looks as if she's whispering something in Maisie's ear, but as the girls step outside, Piper melts back into her own crowd. I recognise some of the girls in there as one-time good friends of Maisie.

My daughter descends the steps in front of the studio. There are no friends at all around her today, giggling together and showing each other pics of their favourite celebs or funny animal videos on their phones.

Her face looks drawn and pale, as if she's been sitting quietly, not flushed like usual from bopping around.

She spots the car and runs down the steps and along the pavement without looking back.

'Did you leave class on your own again today?' I ask lightly when she opens the door.

She stuffs her dance bag down at her feet and folds her arms in a huff.

I start the car and pull a banana and a small carton of orange juice from the door pocket on my side.

'Piper is now officially friends with all my friends. Every single one.'

'Oh. Well that's all right, isn't it?' I keep my voice light. 'You can have the same friends.'

She shakes her head. 'We had to get into friendship groups for a dance exercise and Piper got all my friends in hers and then said there was no room for me.'

I pass the fruit and drink to Maisie, but she gently pushes my hand away.

'Not hungry.'

I toss the banana and drink onto the back seat, glancing at Maisie's bony wrists protruding from the baggy grey sweatshirt that she never seems to take off these days.

But as Dr Yesufu suggested, I don't comment on her appetite. In the absence of any better advice, I have to listen to him and try a different tactic for a while at least.

'I wish Dad would dump Joanne so I don't have to see her any more.' Maisie scowls.

I'm trying hard to see both sides, I really am.

I suppose it's natural that there's a bit of rivalry between the pair of them. Two little girls with big personalities thrown together. Things are still very new and take some adjusting to.

'You never know, you and Piper might become closer in time.' I smile at her, but her scowl doesn't shift.

It's hard to know what to say for the best. I can understand Maisie being a bit peeved and feeling proprietorial about her dance classes; she's been going for a full year now. But she has to understand that her friends being involved with Piper doesn't mean she has to take a step back.

'Maybe you two can share friends like you do other stuff. You go to Joanne's house now and I bet you play with Piper's stuff while you're there and watch TV in her bedroom.'

'No,' Maisie says firmly. 'She's selfish. Joanne tells her to share but she won't, and Piper said on the first day I went there that I'm not allowed in her bedroom.'

I open my mouth and close it again.

I'm obviously not asking the right questions when Maisie comes back from Joanne's house. I was under the impression that the two girls got on OK; both Shaun and Joanne have led me to believe that.

I stop at traffic lights and lay my hand on my daughter's arm.

'Don't worry about it, poppet. You can make an effort with your friends and everything will come right again, I'm sure.'

'That's just it, though. All my dance friends think she's brilliant. She bought a bag of these glittery pom-pom hair slides for everyone when she started the classes. Now everyone really likes her.'

Clever. No doubt that's Joanne's doing, designed to get Piper in everyone's good books from the off, and it sounds as if it worked.

'She's told everyone she's going to get the part of Dorothy off me. But I don't think Miss Diane will let that happen.'

I glance at my daughter, notice her troubled expression. It would be easy to wave her concerns away as nothing, but this stuff is the most important thing in the world to her right now.

She must feel as if she's battling against Piper's instant popularity with her dance friends, and now with her own dad, too.

'Just remember, everyone there likes you too,' I tell her. 'You've got lots of friends and you've been going a long time, so if you feel pushed out maybe it's just a blip. Let's invite some of them over to the house like we used to do. You've always been popular there and Miss Diane has obviously rewarded your loyalty and hard work.'

Maisie sighs and says nothing. When I look at her, she doesn't seem at all convinced.

After a few moments, she speaks.

'There's something else too.'

'Oh yeah?' I say, dreading what might be coming next. 'What's that?'

'I heard Joanne talking to one of the other mums, telling her that they'll be moving. Once Dad has sold his house.'

When we arrive home, it's a relief to just get inside and take a few deep breaths.

After Maisie's revelation, I had to really focus on my driving and the road. I felt disorientated, a bit dizzy even. At one point I thought I'd have to pull over, but then Maisie opened her window and the fresh air brought me to my senses.

When we get inside the house, I walk into the kitchen, tossing my keys on to the counter and sweep a few errant crumbs with one hand into the other.

I throw them into the bin and when I look up, out of the window, a sharp movement near the hedge catches my eye. I narrow my gaze as I try and focus.

I can't discern an exact shape, but it looks to me like there is someone crouching behind the hedge, watching the house.

I swallow down a knot of panic and rush to the patio doors, unlocking them and flinging them open in one swift movement.

'Who's there?' I call, my voice wavering slightly despite my efforts to sound assertive.

I stand stock still for a few more moments, but the shadowy bulk I could swear I saw there has gone.

I close the doors and lock them. Despite it being daytime, I pull the curtains and lower the kitchen blind.

'Are you OK, Mum?' Maisie asks from the doorway.

'Yes, fine. Come in here, I want to talk to you.'

'I didn't mean to make you sad when I told you about the house,' she says, observant as ever.

'OK, Maisie. I'm going to ask you a few questions and I want you to think really carefully before answering.' Her eyes widen. 'You're not in trouble, it's just very important you tell me exactly what you can remember and that's all. It's fine to say if you *can't* remember. Do you understand?'

She nods and sits next to me when I pat the seat cushion.

'Where was Joanne when she spoke about Dad selling the house?'

'She was over by the main doors, talking to Carly's mum. I'd left my water bottle there and went to fetch it before our barre exercises.'

'That's good. Now, this bit is really important. Can you remember exactly what was said?'

She frowns, thinking for a moment.

'When I walked behind them to get my bottle, Joanne was describing a house.'

'What did she say?'

'She said, "The kitchen is massive, and it's got five bedrooms and a stream running along the bottom of the garden." Then she said, "We've just put an offer in" or something like that.'

I nod.

'Then Carly's mum said, "When are you moving?" and that's when Joanne said, "As soon as Shaun can sell his house."'

I bite down on my back teeth when I imagine those two privileged women, money coming out of their ears, talking nonchalantly about private business that affects Maisie and me. The fact that some random mum at dancing gets to hear that Shaun is trying to sell the house before I do makes the blood in my veins literally boil. And Joanne talking about it like that at the dance studio, in front of people I've known for years...

'Mum! Stop it!'

Maisie pulls at my hand and suddenly I'm aware of a sharp pain where my thumbnail has carved into the skin of my finger, drawing a thin crease of blood to the surface.

'Sorry.' I tuck my hand under my thigh. 'What did you hear after that?'

'Nothing,' Maisie says. 'I had to run back to join the others before the exercises began.'

'OK. Well, you did the right thing in telling me, poppet.'

'Have we got to sell the house, Mum? Where will we live?'

It breaks my heart to see the furrows on her brow. These are not worries any ten-year-old should be grappling with.

'I'm sure there's a perfectly reasonable explanation,' I say. 'She was probably talking about someone else.'

'She definitely said it was Dad and she meant *this house*. Will we have to move out soon?'

'I don't know, Maisie!' I snap without thinking, and her face falls. 'I'm sorry, sweetheart, I'm just tired. I'll make you a sandwich and then I'm going to have a little lie-down while you watch some television.'

'I'm not hungry,' she says, her voice flat. 'I'm going to my room.'

When she's left the kitchen, I snatch up my phone and text Shaun.

I need to speak to you TODAY. If you don't come, I'll drive over to Joanne's.

CHAPTER 54

When Shaun arrives at the house, he takes great interest in the hallway, and generally glancing all around as he walks into the kitchen.

It occurs to me he's calculating what needs to be done in order to get the place fully saleable.

'Just as you left it,' I remark, letting him know I've noticed.

He smiles bashfully. 'Of course. I was just thinking what a big place it is. Anyway, what was it you wanted to talk about? It sounded urgent.'

'I'll get to that in a minute.'

We walk into the kitchen and I realise I've left the curtains and blind drawn.

'Had a migraine and shut all the light out?' he quips.

'No. I thought…'

He stares at me, waiting.

'I thought I saw someone in the garden earlier.'

'Oh for goodness' sake, Em.' He sniffs. 'Some things never change, eh?'

It's a jibe, a slur. He doesn't believe a word I say any more, but I force his comment out of my mind. There are more important things at stake here.

I make two coffees and take them over to the seating area.

'Maisie is upstairs in her room. I can call her down if you like; I didn't know if you wanted to talk first.'

'That would be good.' He nods. 'I wanted to discuss a few things, but firstly, the house.'

'What about it?' I say sharply. 'Surely we both agree that Maisie needs all the stability she can get right now. First you leave, and now... well, I know you wouldn't want to sell up. You wouldn't do that to her.'

'It's a big place, Em,' he sighs. 'Far too big for the two of you, and then there are the bills associated with a large house: council tax, heating. The list goes on.'

'So you want to sell because you're worried about my bills?'

'Well, I am paying half of them,' he states tartly.

'But nobody asked you to leave.'

'Emma!' he snaps, and then gathers himself, softening his voice. 'I don't want this to be a slanging match. I just need to tell you that things are changing, and this is one of them. I want to sell the house.'

'Well. It's nice of you to tell me, but actually, I already knew.'

He blinks at me.

'Maisie overheard Joanne telling one of the other mums at dancing. She was crowing about your new place having five bedrooms and a big garden with a stream running through it.'

'Shit.'

'Shit is right. That's how it made our daughter feel.'

'I can understand that. I'll certainly speak to Maisie about it.'

'Maybe you should speak to your girlfriend, too. Tell her to keep her mouth shut in public places... if she can resist bragging about her wonderful new life.'

I'd like to ask why he even needs money from the sale of this house. Joanne has enough funds to buy it outright, I'm sure. But I know the answer; she wants to see commitment from him, wants to cut me out of his financial responsibilities completely.

'Point taken,' Shaun says quietly. 'Listen, before I pop up and see Maisie, there are a couple of boxes I want up in the loft. Just photographs I took that I need for my new portfolio. Is it OK if I—'

'Take what you want,' I say curtly.

He empties his pockets out on the kitchen worktop and leaves the room. I hear him pad softly upstairs and push the loft trapdoor open, a light rumble as he pulls down the ladder.

I pick up our cups and take them over to the sink.

He'll want my agreement to sell the house, but I won't give it. Not today. Why the hell should I make it easy for them?

Yet deep down, I know selling up is best all round. Although Shaun pays half the bills, in reality, I know before long, I'll struggle on my own. If I could cut my outgoings, and I had a bit of money behind me from the sale of the house, I would perhaps feel less vulnerable financially.

Maisie and I could get one of those new compact eco-houses a few streets away from the embankment. Or even a neat two-bed apartment in the new Trent Basin development.

The idea of a new home feels good. Positive, in a way. Perhaps it's the fresh start Maisie needs to get back on track and find herself again.

But I've no intention telling Shaun my thoughts for a day or two at least.

I load our dirty cups into the dishwasher and walk over to the seats again, pausing to run my fingertip over Shaun's smooth black leather Hugo Boss wallet that I splashed out on for Christmas last year.

It's ludicrous how pleased I feel that he's still using it. It's like I've scored a point over Joanne, somehow.

He's left his car keys here too. A tiny Perspex box full of coloured mints, his late grandad's penknife that, when opened out, has every tool you could ever need, and he's left something else.

Two Yale door keys complete with a little plastic tab. Handwritten on the white label is: *Linby House*.

The keys to Joanne's apartment.

CHAPTER 55

Maisie says she feels too ill to go to her dance lesson. She's been off school all day and Mum kindly came over to the house to look after her.

Later, I leave Maisie in bed with my mum pottering around in the kitchen and drive to the dance studio.

I'm at a loss as to who to speak to for advice. What I need is someone who knows Maisie well. Someone who can give me their opinion about whether my daughter really is ill.

I park a bit further up the road than my usual spot. The last thing I want is for any of the other mums to see me and get chatting. I need to wait until I can catch Miss Diane on her own again, when everyone has left.

Within a few minutes, the students begin to spill out of the doors. There's no ruddy-faced, happy little girl with dark curls and a winning smile. My car door is not wrenched open with a bubbly account of the lesson before she even takes her seat.

My Maisie is in bed, lying listlessly like a wilting flower. A passing phase or not, I can't just leave her there, waiting to see if she recovers. As her mother, I have to do something. I have to listen to the alarm bells that ring in my head all day and all night.

Miss Diane emerges from the studio doors and waves a few of the girls off. I groan as a couple of the more gossipy mothers approach her, praying they don't stand there for long.

My wish is granted. Miss Diane seems to excuse herself and disappears back inside the studio. I wait until the two mothers and their daughters walk away, and then I get out of the car and walk quickly towards the building.

I try the closed external doors and breathe a sigh of relief that she hasn't locked up yet. I slip inside and walk through to the main hall where the classes take place.

Miss Diane is crouched down unplugging equipment from the wall. I'm wearing soft-soled shoes, and she doesn't hear me approach.

'Hi, Miss Diane, could I have a quick word?'

She gasps and stands up quickly, her hand flying to her throat.

'Oh, it's you again, Emma. I thought it might be Joanne...' She smiles nervously and I wonder if she's also living on her nerves because of Joanne Dent. 'Is everything all right? We missed Maisie tonight.'

Unbidden, my eyes prickle and I nod, blinking the emotion away.

'Oh no, what's wrong?' She slides an arm around my shoulders, and to my shame, I feel hot, salty tears roll down my cheeks and drip from my jawline. 'Come and sit down.'

I follow her to a couple of wooden chairs against the wall, sit down and take the tissue she offers me.

'Sorry,' I snivel. 'I don't know what's come over me. I just...'

'Take your time. I'm in no rush to get away. I'll go and lock the main doors so we aren't disturbed.' She glides across the sprung wooden floor, light and graceful in her shell-pink ballet slippers. The exact delicate colour of Maisie's own.

Two minutes later, she's back and hands me a glass of water. 'Now. How is Maisie?'

'She's... not good. She won't get out of bed.'

Miss Diane looks taken aback. 'Is she ill?'

'The doctor says probably not, but I think she is. She isn't eating properly, she's lost all her spirit. It's as if...' It's too awful to say.

'Go on.'

'It's as if she's lost her love for life and just wants to… be left alone.' I dab at my runny nose. 'I came here again because I couldn't think of anyone else who knows Maisie as well as you. Her class teacher at school has been off sick for weeks and they have a supply teacher in, you see, and Maisie has begged me not to involve the head teacher.'

'Of course,' she says softly, sitting down beside me. 'I'm glad you came to see me again. As it happens, since I've been keeping a closer eye on her, I have noticed a change in Maisie's behaviour.'

'You have?' I look at her, my eyes wide. 'In what way?'

'She's always been my little star, first to volunteer to give examples at the barre, full of ideas, a bundle of energy. Just lately, she's seemed lethargic and quite miserable. Lurking at the back of the group on her own. That's why I sent you the note about the Christmas show?'

Note?

She presses her lips together when she sees my puzzled expression.

'She didn't give it to you, did she? I told you I chose her for Dorothy, in the Christmas show. Instead of jumping with excitement when I announced it to the group, she scurried off to the bathroom. When she came back, she wouldn't engage in conversation with me. I asked if we could discuss the role, all three of us.'

'I never got the note,' I say quietly.

Miss Diane sighs. 'I might've known. I should've come out after class and looked for you.'

I realise again how I've cut myself off from more and more people without really even trying.

She touches my arm. 'It's not a criticism, Emma. My intention was to give you a call if you didn't respond to the note.'

I nod. 'Please do that right away in future, if you have even the slightest concern about Maisie. I should have let you know there were problems at home before now.'

Miss Diane nods. 'Please don't think I'm prying, but I overheard some of the other mums talking.' She hesitates, and I nod for her to continue. 'I heard that you and Maisie's father have split up and he's moved in with...'

'Joanne Dent,' I provide. 'Yes, it's true.'

I dread to think what those gossipmongers have been saying, but that's the least of my worries right now.

'I'm sorry.' I hang my head. 'I should have spoken to you, to make you aware.'

'It's often useful to know these things, just in case personal stuff spills over into class, but it's your own business and I'm truly sorry I had to ask.'

I don't know why it never occurred to me to tell her, instead of letting her find out via the local gossip network.

'You have my sympathy,' she says, looking at her hands. 'I know only too well that Joanne can often be... let's say, *difficult*.' She hesitates. 'I need to know that, if I speak frankly, you won't go off in a rage and confront her like last time.'

I nod. 'I promise. You have my word. I'm sorry I embarrassed you like that. I don't really know what came over me.'

'Confidentially, Joanne is furious that Piper didn't get the lead role in the show. She's threatened not to renew the lease on this place in the new year unless I change my mind.'

My mouth falls open. How far will that woman go to give her daughter everything in life? At the expense of Maisie and the entire dance school, too!

'What are you going to do?'

'I'm thinking about it. I can hardly just tell her where to get off; this is my livelihood. I rue the day her daughter started here, if I'm honest. But... well, I can't help but think Maisie doesn't want the part anyway.'

'I'll talk to her,' I say, suddenly desperate for Maisie to keep the role.

'Anyway, that's another conversation, and I digress. You came here to talk to me about Maisie.' She smiles kindly.

'I just don't know what to do. She's lost so much weight recently, and my mum found food she'd hidden. As you've said, she seems completely listless and devoid of energy.'

'And you mentioned your doctor?'

'I took her to the surgery. He weighed her and calculated her BMI and concluded she was borderline underweight. He told me that young girls often go through phases and that a bit of weight loss and being faddy with food is completely normal.'

Miss Diane frowns. 'I'm not sure hiding food should ever be considered normal.'

'My thoughts exactly.' I feel better already, just being validated, rather than have Dr Yesufu patronise me as a panicky mother. 'And she's so young to be worrying about how she looks. Anyway, his professional opinion is that trying to tackle it could be more harmful than letting it run its course.'

'Well, I'm not sure about that either.' Miss Diane sighs. 'I see more and more of it here at the dance school. Young girls acting like teenagers, wearing make-up and worshipping celebrities. It's worrying.'

Piper instantly comes to mind.

Miss Diane continues. 'If you don't mind me saying so though, I'd say she's bound to feel a little insecure given that you and her father have split up. Perhaps it's best we don't put any more pressure on her with a lead role in the show.'

I pause, my fingers toying with Joanne's house keys in my pocket, trying to decide whether I dare say what's really on my mind. She sees my hesitation.

'Go on.' She lowers her voice. 'You can trust me, Emma. If there's anything I can do to help Maisie, you only have to say.'

CHAPTER 56

Since I've been toying with the theory that Joanne may have something to hide, ideas have been coming thick and fast.

I admit I want to be proved right just for the satisfaction of it, but my main concern is Maisie. What if Joanne is poisoning Shaun and Piper's minds against her so they can be one happy family of three, without Maisie?

I've often assumed Joanne might be planning to take Maisie away from me, now she's got Shaun. But perhaps it's the opposite.

I confided my thoughts to Miss Diane, and although she looked a little taken aback, she agreed there could be more to it.

I'm sick to death of feeling like Shaun and Joanne, and even Piper, are doing stuff to me and my daughter. It's such a negative, reactive place to live my life. Maybe it's time I took some action of my own instead of being such a passive victim.

The first thing I need to do is find out a bit more about Piper's biological father. The man who must never be mentioned.

While Maisie is upstairs watching TV in her bedroom, I search how to order a copy of a birth certificate online.

My heart sinks when a list of mandatory information pops up. Father's name is required, along with place of birth, plus other information that I don't have. The narrative states that unless such information is available, it's not possible to order a duplicate certificate in the interests of guarding against identity theft.

Frustrated, I close the laptop just as my phone pings.

Did I leave some house keys at yours? Shaun.

No. I press send and feel the tingle of both anger and fear in my fingers. I don't want to think about the trouble that will ensue if I get caught out.

I tidy around the kitchen and make a pot of fresh coffee, pausing to scan the garden.

My heart starts hammering and I will myself to calm down. But it's no use. Just the thought of someone watching the house has unnerved me and sent me spinning back to the past yet again.

The morning after I acted as whistleblower over Damian's illegal actions, I left the house with a heavy heart.

After a night of questioning my motives and conscience, I'd come to the conclusion that he'd put me in an impossible situation.

He'd insisted I should do the photocopying, despite my initial complaints. What really rankled was the thought that he'd decided I'd be the person least likely to spot his crime, either too unobservant or too meek and mild to cause a fuss.

If that was true, I had certainly set him straight.

When I arrived at work, I immersed myself in the laborious task that lay ahead: sorting through archived files to find salient details from a historical case.

I felt grateful for the routine nature of the work. Unsurprisingly, I found it difficult to keep my mind on the job in hand.

Of course, Damian was absent that day, and for the next couple of days after that. Nobody had said what had officially happened but I could imagine some sort of internal inquiry was underway. Perhaps even police involvement. I felt relieved I didn't have to see Damian, or avoid him.

I quickly realised that nobody said good morning to me any more since I'd shopped him. It was painfully clear that I'd become the office pariah, but that was OK. I knew I'd done the right thing, whatever the others thought.

Reassuring myself that I'd acted correctly was quickly becoming second nature.

Late afternoon, three days after the incident, I was engrossed in making notes at my desk when I suddenly became aware that the office had fallen silent.

When I looked around, Peter McCarthy was standing in the doorway, his face ashen.

'Can I have everyone's attention, please?' he said gravely. 'I'm afraid I have some terrible news.'

We all sat to attention, and for once, nobody glared at me. All eyes were pinned to Peter.

'I'm devastated to have to tell you that Damian took his own life last night.'

A collective gasp filled the room. I felt my hand gripping my throat, and despite being seated, I felt dizzy with shock at Peter's insensitive and sudden announcement. It was obviously too much to ask for him to take me aside first, to warn me.

Peter's voice continued on the edges of my awareness.

'We don't have many details at this early stage, but his fiancée's mother called to tell me personally.' His voice cracked. 'It's so desperately sad, and particularly in the light of him leaving the company so suddenly.'

'He was betrayed,' someone murmured, and all heads turned to look at me.

Peter coughed, gathered himself. 'As I said, that's all we know for now. I will, of course, pass on more information as I receive it. Barbara is going to start a collection for flowers, and once we have a date, we'll close the office so colleagues can attend the funeral.'

He turned and walked out of the office, and a low buzz immediately filled the empty space his words had left.

Damian... *dead*!

His snarling face and final threat filled my mind, and I got up from my chair and ran to the bathroom, past sneering faces and angry words.

After being sick in the loo, I splashed cold water over my face and studied my drawn features in the mirror.

Was the face staring back at me the face of someone who had driven another person to their death? Would Damian have killed himself if he still had his job?

His final words to me echoed in my head:

Keep looking over your shoulder, you utter cow, because you'll never know when it's coming.

CHAPTER 57

Twenty-four years earlier

She places the tray carefully on your bedside table.

When you turn your face into the pillow and begin to weep, she strokes your hair gently, and when she speaks, her voice is soft and kind.

'One day you will thank me for this. Food is the enemy to being loved. You must keep yourself looking beautiful or be alone in this world. The choice is yours.

You hear the clink of cutlery, the softness of a napkin in your hand.

'Purging is a valuable tool you can use all your life.'

You turn your face to look at her, and she smiles lovingly as she helps you sit up straight. She hums a tune as she tears up the bread and drops it into the bowl.

'I'm here to help you, my darling. I'm here to help you be as beautiful and lovable as you can possibly be.'

You nod and try to hide your shaking hands as she begins to spoon the soup and bread into your mouth.

Later, when you vomit it back into the bowl, she holds your hair and soothes you with her loving touch.

'I'm so proud of you, my clever best girl,' she whispers as your stomach heaves and roils. 'I feel so much closer to you now, because this is our secret, my darling. This is just between us.'

CHAPTER 58

Emma

Mum comes to take Maisie to her house for a few hours – supposedly so I can work. I wave them off at the door, noting my daughter's vacant stare and a patch of dry, flaky skin on her forehead.

Five minutes after they leave, I head out to the car, the Linby House keys in my pocket.

Shaun obviously didn't notice the keys were missing when he came back down from the loft and scooped the contents of his pocket back up from the worktop. And now I've told him I haven't seen them, so he must assume he's lost them elsewhere.

After I said I needed time to think about the house sale, he couldn't get away fast enough.

'We're heading to Leicestershire for the afternoon tomorrow,' he said by way of explanation for his haste. 'Joanne has agreed that Piper can have the afternoon off school to look at a pony that's for sale. She's promised her another one when we move.'

He rolled his eyes and smiled, but I looked back at him blankly.

'You'll need to come over again soon,' I said. 'There's something more important than a house sale that we need to talk about.'

He raised his eyebrows.

'Maisie,' I said. 'She's troubled. Someone is upsetting her, I'm sure of it. Surely you can see she's fading away in front of our eyes?'

'Right. If you say so.' He backed away, as if I was exaggerating again. 'See you soon, then.'

He clearly wasn't interested in talking about the possibility that Joanne or Piper – or both – was responsible for systematically destroying Maisie's self-esteem. That didn't fit in with his nice clean break from the two of us.

I felt like shouting at him until he came to his senses, but I let him go.

I have other plans that may well prove to help my daughter.

By 3.20, I'm heading up the long, leafy driveway of Linby House. It's impressive, I can't deny that.

As the car reaches the top of the driveway, a large red-brick house looms in front of me. There's a turret on either side, and a large glass balcony spans the top floor, overlooking fields and the neighbouring village of Papplewick.

I park up outside in a marked visitor spot. Judging by the numbered parking bays, the house looks to be divided into six apartments. I don't know the number of Joanne's apartment, but Maisie told me it's at the top of the building.

I get out of the car and glance down at the keys in my hand. A sturdy-looking entrance door has a keypad and also a lock, so I would think one of the keys will be for that. The other should be for the front door of the apartment.

I walk around a decorative fountain, its water half frozen and trickling through. I'm just about to slide the key into the lock when the main door opens.

My heart feels like it has jumped into my mouth. What if I misheard the time and Shaun and actually he and Joanne were only just leaving now? But I needn't worry. A young woman bustles out holding a baby and struggling with a large padded bag that I assume holds all the necessary paraphernalia one has to carry everywhere with a very young one.

'Lifesaver, thanks!' She beams as I hold the door open.

I allow it to click softly behind me and stand for a moment in the airy, calm entrance hall. The wooden flooring and high ceiling give the impression of space, although the area itself is not enormous.

I climb to the first floor and look down, out onto my parked car, from the large stained-glass windows. Up on the second floor, there are three doors and a final staircase. No lift here, no wonder Joanne is so slim.

I'm puffing a bit by the time I reach the top, but I'm gratified to see just one door. Number 6.

I raise the key to the lock and then, just to be safe, I knock. If they're still home – which is unlikely, as there's no car outside – I can say I found the keys on the floor at home and came over to return them.

No answer, so I slide the key in and turn it.

Inside, another short flight of carpeted stairs greets me. This takes me into the apartment proper. A very tasteful space decorated in neutral colours, with smooth wooden floors and lots of mirrors and pale textured fabrics.

There's no time to delay. I know what I'm looking for, so I get straight to it.

All the doors are open, and I can see at once which one is Joanne's bedroom. Simply decorated with an antique oak sleigh bed and built-in wardrobes, the view is mesmerising. Large picture windows look out over the grounds of the house and the fields beyond, the whole scene framed with beautiful mature oak trees.

Briefly I think about our own little patch of garden. Shaun and I loved it when we first bought the house. We regarded it as sizeable, a step up from the postage stamp we had at our first place.

He must stand and laugh about that now, as he soaks this view in each morning.

I look at the bed and look away again. It's too close to home. I really don't want to think about Shaun and Joanne entwined on here.

Turning my attention to the task at hand, I systematically search the drawers, but it's soon apparent there is nothing that can help me here.

I leave the bedroom and glance into the room to my right, which is the main bathroom. Next to it is a small, neat office.

I pull at the top drawer of a small black filing cabinet and groan when I find it locked. I peer into a pen tub on the desk and smile. The so-called security systems people have are generally laughable. No wonder burglars have a field day in posh areas like this.

I open the drawer and feel obliged to Joanne for her immaculate organisation. Each suspended file pocket is neatly labelled: *House*, *Car*, *Bank* and *Personal*.

Sliding my hand into *Personal*, I retrieve a folder. I place it on the desk and slip my phone out of my pocket.

Inside the folder, I find a paperwork gold mine that answers a lot of questions and my suspicions feel validated at last.

Leafing quickly through, my fingers close on the last item in there: a small photograph. I stare at the image, trying to make sense of it, but there's no time to ponder.

I take the required snapshots quickly and efficiently, then replace the folder exactly where I found it and make sure I close the drawer properly.

I leave the apartment exactly as I found it, and after listening at the door for a moment, and satisfied that nobody is out there, I step out and pull it closed behind me.

A couple of minutes later, I'm driving back through the leafy gravelled corridor that leads to the main road.

My mouth might be dry and my breathing is definitely erratic, but my mission is accomplished.

I now have what I need to find out a little more about my husband's lover and her nasty little daughter. Between them I am certain they are destroying Maisie in the most calculated way.

The information I have gleaned here today might just help to prove that.

CHAPTER 59

'How has she been since you took her to see the doctor?' Mum is whispering in case Maisie is skulking around listening in. 'Do you think we've done the right thing, not mentioning the food waste I found?'

'I honestly don't know, but there's no way she's eating enough, Mum,' I sigh, sitting down in the comfy seats. 'If you hadn't fed her when she got in from school yesterday, I don't think she'd have had anything all evening, and she used to graze constantly before going to bed.'

'But I didn't feed her.' Mum frowns. 'She said you'd bought her a McDonald's on the way home from school.'

'What? She told me you'd made her a sandwich. You know what my thoughts are on fast food, and it's nutritious food she's badly in need of.'

'I know, I did think that. But I thought you'd been lenient to get her to eat something. You're in such a mad rush these days, what with work and worrying about that Joanne woman, I thought you might've weakened for once, especially since you've been so worried about her lack of appetite.'

I shake my head, feeling a shiver all the way down my arms.

'Maisie,' I call upstairs later. 'We have to leave in five or we're going to be late.'

There's no response, but I can hear her moving around in her bedroom.

I pick up my handbag and check I have my wallet and phone. I can't help but contrast her muted reaction to the last time we had one of our cinema and tea outings, just a couple of months ago.

'Girls only,' we liked to taunt Shaun when we arranged to go out, usually once a month or so, although it had been less frequent recently.

'Charming,' he snorted, playing the game. 'Everyday sexism, that's what it is.'

Last time, we saw the latest Disney Pixar offering at the Cornerhouse in Nottingham and then enjoyed tea at an Italian chain restaurant in the same complex.

Maisie had been inordinately excited all week and couldn't wait to get her performance class out of the way on Saturday morning.

We laughed so much during the film we both got stomach ache. In the restaurant, Maisie predictably ordered her favourite choices: dough balls to start, pepperoni pizza, and finally, the *pièce de résistance*, ice cream with three toppings and chocolate sprinkles.

I scroll through the photos on my phone now, finding the one that's seared into my mind. Maisie is sitting with the long silver spoon poised high above the glass sundae dish piled high with ice-cream delight.

A lump presses against my throat and I swallow.

When Maisie begged me to let her miss tonight's dance class as she had a headache, I used it to my advantage, insisting we go out together. I didn't buy her headache excuse and felt sure that getting her out of the house and spending time together might just be what we both need.

My finger begins scrolling again and I tap on the snap of the photograph I found in Joanne's folder, squinting with the effort of trying to work it out. A much younger Piper is there, sat on the knee of a man who has identical bright blue eyes. It's got to be her father, Joanne's husband, who tragically died.

But there is a fourth person in the photograph, too. A child who looks to be around Maisie's age now. The girl is smiling, but unless it's my imagination, her eyes look sad. Haunted, even.

It could just be a family friend, but I just know something's not right. I can feel it in my bones.

I hear Maisie's bedroom door open upstairs, so I put away my phone, slip on my shoes in the hallway and check my watch. Two more minutes and we really need to leave the house.

Maisie appears at the top of the stairs dressed in what's become her standard outfit of jeans and a baggy, shapeless top.

Her hair looks clean but thinner somehow, and hangs listlessly around her face. I wonder where all the fancy hair slides and bobbles are that she used to love to wear.

'Looking forward to it?' I smile, standing back as she sits on the bottom step to put on her trainers.

'Suppose so,' she mumbles as she pushes her feet into her shoes without undoing the laces. I guess feet can lose weight, too.

'I can't wait to see the film,' I say. 'It's getting great reviews.'

It's like I'm talking to myself. I pretend I don't notice her lack of interest and grab the car keys from the hall table.

'Ready?'

She stands up and walks towards me. All her movements are slow, lethargic. As if she hasn't got the energy to do anything.

'How are you feeling now?' I say carefully. 'I texted Miss Diane and she was concerned. She sends her love.'

'It's just a headache.' She frowns. 'I'm not dying.'

'No,' I say carefully. 'That's true. Still, it's obvious you've not felt your best for a while.'

She looks away and falls silent.

On the way to the cinema, I try and engage her in conversation.

'Having your usual?' I say lightly. 'At the restaurant?'

'Oh, are we going there?' She looks out of the window at the people bustling in and out of a cluster of local shops. 'I didn't think we'd be eating too.'

'Well, it's our thing, isn't it?' I glance over at her. 'A film and then a nosh-up?'

'Suppose.' She shrugs without taking her eyes from the window. 'I'm just not that hungry.'

I know that if I refer to her lack of appetite, she'll blow. I can feel it bubbling under the surface. It's so easy for her to counter anything I say. She's got a well-practised pool of excuses and observations, most of which I've already heard: she ate earlier; she feels a bit off; she doesn't fancy food because she has a headache; she's losing weight because of a growth spurt.

It's hard to disagree with any of these perfectly reasonable observations. Except they're not reasonable at all, because I'm her mother. And as her mother, I know there's something very, very wrong.

It's hard work at the cinema, like wading through treacle. Maisie has no opinion on where we should sit, and of course she isn't interested in snacks or sugary drinks before we go in.

Throughout the film, she sits stone-like. No whispering, laughing or nudging me in the funny bits like she used to. Her eyes are unfocused, staring. I honestly begin to wonder if she's in some sort of chemically enhanced zombie trance.

But then she turns and catches me looking, and her eyes flash, registering her irritation with me. She shuffles in her seat, folds her arms and resumes her vacant stare.

Ironically, I soon realise that I've stopped watching the film myself. I'm staring at the screen just like Maisie, but my head is full of thoughts and concerns. I'm not fully present either.

I'm going to have to broach some unpleasant things with Maisie. I have no choice if I want to get to the bottom of her personality change.

I feel afraid of what I might find out.

Does she blame me for her dad leaving? She hardly ever talks about him, or her visits to Joanne's house, if she can help it.

I've tried to encourage her as much as I can without putting her under pressure. It's hard to mention her dad's new girlfriend and her daughter without her eyes growing dark and sad.

CHAPTER 60

Maisie

Nothing seemed to excite her any more. Watching her favourite vloggers on YouTube, listening to Ariana's new album, the tickets Mum got to see Mariah at the Arena in town. It all seemed so… pointless.

All she really wanted to do was stay in her bedroom 24/7 watching films with the curtains closed. She felt safe there, in the dark.

But she'd been starting to feel really unwell. Light-headed and sick, and sometimes her eyes couldn't seem to focus on anything.

She had always liked watching movies, and she still did. She liked the way you could escape your own horrible life and get caught up in the story, in the lives of other people. For an hour and a half, you could actually be someone else entirely.

She could choose the movie she wanted to watch. At school you got told what to do from the moment you arrived until the moment you left. Then when you got home, your parents took over… well, her mum did. Dad lived with Joanne and Piper now.

Every day, it felt like she lost another little piece of him.

When Maisie emerged from the school gates after attending the art after-school club, she had all of twenty seconds before she got into her mum's waiting car, with the questions that never changed from day to day.

How did it go? What did you have for lunch? What lessons did you have?

Maisie knew all the stock answers.

It went OK. I had a jacket potato and salad. Maths, English and science.

Her mum didn't want the truth. Not really.

She didn't want to know that Maisie's whole day had been an ordeal, that she no longer had anyone to sit with at lunch and so didn't even bother going into the food hall these days.

It made Maisie feel sick to think how she used to easily sink a burger with sweet potato wedges and then wolf down a creamy yoghurt and possibly a chocolate bar. Her body had got so fat and flabby, it was no wonder that nobody liked her any more. She couldn't blame Dad for preferring the perfectly slender Piper for a daughter.

Mum and Gran had spent her whole life telling her what to eat, when to eat and how it was vital she had three meals a day. Feeding her greed, storing the surplus calories up like lard under her dry, flaky skin.

She wasn't a little kid any more. Although no one seemed to realise it, she could think for herself and make her own decisions in life.

Yet the more she tried to take control, the more adults seemed to tighten their grasp. She'd tried to explain to Mum that she didn't want to go to Joanne's house or her dance classes any more, and she'd tried to please her dad by being as perfect as Piper.

Nothing she said worked, because nobody ever listened.

The one person who took an interest in her, who pretended in front of others that she was her friend, hated her. At first, when she started being so nasty, Maisie had tried not to listen to the horrible things she said.

But after a short time, she began to see her own ugliness when she looked in the mirror. She noticed her dad didn't seem to want to spend time with her any more. Even her mum got angry at the least little thing.

Literally, the only thing she felt like she had full control over any more was what she put into her mouth.

Maisie felt sure it would solve everything if she wasn't so fat.

CHAPTER 61

Emma

I creep upstairs and stand outside Maisie's bedroom door.

I can't hear the television, or music. The room seems deathly quiet.

I open the door very slowly and see that, as I suspected, she has fallen asleep, fully clothed, on the bed.

The light from the landing floods the room and illuminates her face. Her skin is pale, almost translucent. Dark curls lie fanned on the white pillow beneath her head, and her eyes are closed. I watch as her eyelids flutter like butterfly wings caught in a light breeze.

I draw comfort from this. A sign that she is still in there somewhere, dreaming of happier times we have shared, perhaps. Something more than a narrow chest rising and falling with laboured breaths.

Her body looks so small now, too small to properly match her head. Too frail to do all the things that she used to do now that food has become her enemy.

Food. Always there for all of us; a pleasure, a necessity… at times in my own life, a terrible temptation I have had to fight.

After our visit to Dr Yesufu, I became more aware. I watched how Maisie had become skilled at carefully deconstructing each meal I served so that it looked as if she'd eaten some of it when in actual fact barely a morsel had passed her lips.

Her method became recognisable.

The way she'd spear a clutch of green beans on her fork and flatten her new potatoes. Shunt a chunk of salmon under a pile of untouched dark green leafy vegetables.

An impressively inventive and successful way to decrease the volume of food without actually swallowing it.

But I too have become skilled – in covertly watching her. She has never been fat but was once slightly plump around her middle in a perfectly healthy pre-teen way, with apple cheeks that shone when she laughed.

I've learned to refrain from commenting when the waistband of her smallest jeans bags looser still. When her favourite pink glittery belt can't be pulled any tighter yet is obviously still too big.

After the doctor's advice, I bought her a whole new set of school uniform without comment. Not because she'd outgrown the old one, but because it hung off her now slender frame.

It's all I can do.

She won't talk to me, you see, so I began to gather evidence, adding my daily observations to a heartbreaking, password-protected spreadsheet on my laptop.

Dr Yesufu said it might well just be a phase.

His advice reflected the professional opinions of the numerous eating disorder websites I researched online.

Don't watch her eat.

Don't comment on her appetite.

Don't talk about food or the profusion of perfectly photoshopped celebrity bodies that flood our screens.

Believe me, it's not as easy as you might think; to take action, I mean.

You can't force food down someone's throat any more than you can make them chew and swallow and keep it down. You just can't.

So I have watched as my beautiful, vibrant Maisie teeters on a tightrope. Knowing that any quick movement or panicky shout could send her over the edge.

She's moved just far enough away from the end of the tightrope that I can no longer reach her to pull her back to safety. This bit happened stealthily, the damage done before I even fully realised.

My daughter used to adore dancing and lip-synching in her bedroom to Ariana Grande.

She loved reading and drawing and watching make-up vlogs for teens on YouTube at the kitchen table while I prepared dinner.

Now she sits surly and miserable, staring blankly at the television each night because I insist she stays downstairs at least for a couple of hours. But as soon as she is able, she darts upstairs, keen to be alone again in her bedroom.

I resist the urge to wake her now, to pull her closer to me. To kiss the top of her small, warm head, to breathe in her scent, her life essence. To beg her to *just eat*.

My influence on her has somehow waned to the extent that I can no longer get close enough to help her.

If someone hurts your child by beating them, hitting them, forcing them to act in a way that is obviously harmful, most parents will react in the same way.

But when someone causes such devastating harm emotionally to your child and you can't actually *prove* it, what does that do to a parent? It destroys you too.

I now believe that Joanne and Piper Dent are hurting my daughter in the cruellest way possible. Destroying her self-esteem, her confidence, her enjoyment of life. They've done it while Maisie's father and I were right there by her side.

Have they broken the law? Probably not.

But it's been enough to ruin a life, and whatever it takes, it has to stop.

I feel completely justified in what I'm about to do.

CHAPTER 62

Shaun stands there staring at me as if I've gone crazy.

'For God's sake, Emma, calm down. I can't believe you're saying this stuff.'

'You'd better believe it, because I'm not going to stop saying it until I've got some answers. If I have to get social services involved, then I will. Trust me.'

'So, let me get this straight. You're accusing Joanne and Piper of giving Maisie anorexia?' He shakes his head. 'It's a psychological condition, not something you can catch. It would be laughable if you weren't so serious. You can't go around saying this stuff, Em. You just can't.'

'She's changed! You must see that, Shaun. Our vibrant little girl, full of enthusiasm, full of life. She lies upstairs, listless most of the time now, wasting away in her own bedroom. Tell me that's normal.'

'I'm not saying it's normal. But it's not necessarily anyone's fault. You told me that even the doctor said it could just be a pre-teen stage and she may grow out of it.'

'And in the meantime I'm supposed to just sit back and watch her fading away to nothing? What does she eat at yours?'

'Exactly the same as we do.' He falters slightly. 'I think.'

'It's since you left home and she's been in the company of that woman and her daughter.' I grit my teeth. 'I know they're destroying her. Who is Joanne Dent, really? What happened to her husband?'

Shaun sighs.

'Emma. Have you looked at yourself lately? You're heading for some kind of breakdown, accusing people of all sorts of things, making stories up in your head. Don't you think Maisie feels the pressure of that, too? Even your own mum is worried about you.'

'Don't you dare try and turn this back onto me!' I step towards him and narrow my eyes, wondering if he's been secretly talking to my mum. 'I'm telling you. Someone has got to our daughter. They are killing her right under our nose, Shaun. Literally *killing* her! You need to ask some questions of Joanne.'

He stares at me, says nothing.

'If you don't do it, then I will,' I say.

'You'll do nothing of the sort, Emma. This is gone on long enough.' His jaw sets. 'So far as I can see, the only person who is harming Maisie with your wild accusations is *you*. If you carry on with this paranoia, I might... well, I might have no choice but to seek custody of Maisie.'

'Over my dead body,' I hiss.

He looks at me, a strange expression on his face. Then he shakes his head sadly and walks out of the house.

CHAPTER 63

Maisie

Maisie walked into the tiny foyer and stood outside the doors. She could hear the noisy buzz of voices and laughter from within. Everybody would've arrived for the class now, pulling on their dance shoes and tying their wraparound ballet tops at the waist.

When her mum dropped her off, the thought had crossed Maisie's head to wait for two or three minutes in here to give her time to get out into the traffic and well away from the building before walking out and sitting in the little park a couple of streets away.

But it had started to drizzle with rain, and how would she explain being wet through when her mum came back to pick her up?

She glanced at her watch. Still three minutes until the start of class. They had been late leaving home thanks to Maisie 'kicking off again', as her mum described it.

'What's the matter with you lately, Maisie?' Mum stood in the doorway of her bedroom, glaring at her empty dance bag lying on its side on the floor. 'You're never going to keep your part in the Christmas show at this rate. If you don't buck your ideas up, Miss Diane is sure to notice.'

Talk of the show made Maisie want to throw up, but she'd be asking for trouble if she said as much to her mum, who had invested a lot of time and money in her dance classes. And Miss Diane had expected her to be delighted with her role.

She had to find some way of speaking to her mum properly about what was happening. How the fact that she'd got the lead role was making everything worse. She was still waiting for the right moment.

She couldn't find the words to answer her mum, so she just looked down at her hands and waited for her to go away again. She couldn't help noticing how heavy her heart felt when only a few months ago she would've been bouncing with excitement by the front door with ten minutes to spare before it was time to leave.

But her mum didn't go away. She walked into the room and sat on the side of Maisie's bed, placed her hand on her daughter's shin.

Maisie bit down on her tongue. She could deal much better with her mum when she was screaming at her like a banshee.

'You've not been yourself for a while, poppet. What is it? Don't you like dancing any more?'

This was a surprise. Maisie had assumed her mum just thought she was being stubborn and misbehaving for the sake of it.

'Come on, you can tell me. What's wrong?'

Maisie smoothed a patch of creased quilt cover with the flat of her hand. Was this the right time to open her heart? She didn't think so.

'I just don't... It's not the same there any more.'

Her mum pressed her lips together. 'Is this because Piper goes to all your classes now? You shouldn't let that bother you.'

Easy for Mum to say. Piper flounced around as if she'd been going to the classes for years. Last week, she'd brought in two gift-wrapped rose petal bath bombs for the teacher's birthday and Miss Diane had been apoplectic with delight.

'Maisie?' Her mum squeezed her shin until Maisie looked up at her. 'This has got to stop, love. Tell me what's wrong.'

Maisie's heartbeat began to race and her fingers gathered the quilt into a tight bunch. This did seem like a good moment. Her mum was calm and concerned, and if she didn't say anything, then how could things change?

'I just… I don't think I want to go there any more. They all hate me.'

There. She'd said it. Her shoulders relaxed a little and her fingers released the bunched-up fabric.

She looked at her mum, expected to see a sympathetic smile, a concerned expression. But there was no trace of that.

'You'll get nowhere being a quitter.' Her mum stood up, brushed down her loose tunic top over her jeans. She looked down at Maisie, and when she saw her shiny eyes, her face softened. 'Look, sweetie, I know you're struggling at the moment, but all your classes are paid for in advance until the end of term. See it through and then we'll talk about it, OK? You spend enough time stuck in your bedroom as it is. I really don't think it's a good idea to cut yourself off even further from your friends and hobbies.'

Friends? Didn't her mum listen to anything Maisie said? The nail of her index finger worked its way slowly into the soft flesh of her palm.

'I know I've been busy at work, and it's been hard for both of us since your dad moved out, but we can get through this together.' She sat down on the bed again. 'We both have to be brave and not let circumstances affect us. You hardly see your friends these days and that's probably why you've drifted apart; how about organising a sleepover here Saturday night?'

Was she *really* that clueless when it came to how girls acted with each other?

Maisie managed a weak smile, enough to hide the dread trawling through her stomach at the thought of being forced to invite people and nobody turning up.

'So.' Her mum squeezed her arm. 'Are we agreed? You'll carry on with classes for another six weeks and try a bit harder to reconnect with your friends?'

Maisie looked at her mum's face. She could see tiny lines at the corners of her eyes and mouth.

Dad leaving had been hard on Mum too, she thought guiltily. Maybe her plan wasn't such a bad one after all.

She smiled weakly and nodded.

'Perfect! That's settled then.' Mum stood up again, checked her watch. 'OK, five minutes tops before we have to leave, so get that bag sorted and let's go.'

And that had been it. Six more weeks of dance classes agreed. No more arguments.

The double doors leading to the dance hall flew open now, the hum of voices exploding out into the foyer. Two girls Maisie recognised but didn't know well scurried past her towards the bathroom.

Their heads bobbed closer and they glanced back at her, both suppressing giggles. As they disappeared into the bathroom, Maisie heard a burst of laughter.

They'd seen her now. If she didn't go into class, they might tell Miss Diane.

Steeling herself, Maisie gripped the handle of her bag with one hand and pushed open the door with the other.

As she stepped into the dance hall, the noise surrounded her, invading her ears like a swarm of angry wasps.

Her heart began to hammer and the bottom of her back felt hot and sticky. She always felt like this now when she was in a crowd of people, or first thing in the morning at school when she had to walk into class.

Her chest felt tight, as if she couldn't get enough breath in, and sometimes her face went all red and blotchy. It was stupid. Embarrassing.

Everyone was too busy chattering to notice her. She crept around the edges of the room, trying to mingle with the small clusters of girls dressed in grey and pink.

She used to march in and cut through the middle of the dance hall to where Zoe and Sandeep and the others would be standing at the top, near the stage. But now she avoided that end of the hall as she knew *she* would be there, waiting to make her look stupid.

Halfway up, on the right-hand side, she spotted Julia, and finally she breathed out.

She felt a flicker of guilt. Julia had a much worse time of it here than her. Nasty rumours had circulated for as long as Maisie had attended classes that Julia was really a boy called Julian. She was always alone and never got invited to birthday parties or anything like that.

To her shame, Maisie had joined in with the sniggering sometimes in the past, even though she'd felt a bit sorry for her… him. Whatever.

If Julia could find the courage, then surely Maisie could see it through for a few more weeks.

She sat on the floor and pulled her ballet slippers on, just as the two girls she'd seen in the foyer returned from the bathroom. One of them barged into Julia's arm when she could've easily walked around her.

They giggled as they passed. Maisie opened her mouth to say something and then closed it again. She didn't want to draw attention to herself.

'All line up at the barre, please,' Miss Diane called out, and the room fell quiet.

Julia turned away, fumbling with her pink knitted top, and Maisie saw a tear roll down her cheek like a wet diamond before Julia's hand furiously wiped it away.

'OK, I'm looking for someone to demonstrate the perfect plié.' Miss Diane beamed, looking around.

Not me. Not me. Please, not me, Maisie wished silently.

'Maisie… our lead show dancer this year! Come up to the front.' Miss Diane smiled.

Maisie stepped forward slowly, ignoring the nudges and suppressed giggles from the others. She was taller than most of them and felt like a flabby giant now as she clomped past slim, pretty Piper and the smirking girls who used to sleep over at Maisie's house at weekends.

That was what it was like here when people switched friendship groups. If they decided you didn't fit in, that was it.

Nobody got a second chance.

CHAPTER 64

Emma

Finally, I have the time to spread out the printed copies I've made of the screenshots of Joanne's certificates.

The first one is Piper's birth certificate. Her father is named as Paul James Stafford. I feel sure this must be the man in the photograph I found. Piper's name is documented on there as Piper Stafford.

The second document is a copy of a deed poll certificate dated two years ago, when Joanne changed Piper's surname to Dent. The third and final piece of paper is a copy of Joanne and Paul Stafford's marriage certificate, where Joanne's maiden name is stated as Dent.

I assume there must be a deed poll certificate for her too somewhere, changing her married name back to her maiden name.

It's been a messy process, but now Joanne and Piper are a match-ing pair, with no untimely reminders of Paul Stafford. The man they used to share their lives with, now deceased according to Shaun.

I open my laptop, and remember for the first time that I haven't seen Shaun's laptop lying around since he left home. Joanne bought him some fancy new model, so he left his old one here. I'll have to have a hunt around for it. Maybe we could erase everything and Maisie could use it for her homework, instead of commandeering mine to search various subjects.

I open Google and type *Paul James Stafford* into the search bar. I spend a while sifting through the results and clicking on the odd one that looks promising. But all I get are Paul Staffords who are still very much alive.

I amend my search: *Paul Stafford+death+Joanne+Piper*.

The results load again. This time I hit gold with the first item. A newspaper article from the *Yorkshire Post* loads.

> A man and a young girl have died after falling from a privately owned boat off the North Yorkshire coast. The RNLI confirmed it sent out three lifeboats to rescue the man, Paul James Stafford, from Leeds, and his daughter Bethany, aged ten, who fell overboard from the vessel a few miles north of Scarborough.
>
> Mr Stafford and his daughter were pulled from the sea and flown to James Cook University Hospital in Middlesbrough, where they were both sadly pronounced dead, said North Yorkshire police.
>
> Joanne Stafford, wife of Mr Stafford and stepmother to his daughter, Bethany, was also aboard the vessel at the time and raised the alarm.
>
> The couple have a younger daughter, Piper, who was with a childminder that day.
>
> The Marine Accident Investigation Branch is investigating the fatalities.

My fingers quiver over the keys. I'm in shock as I struggle to join up the dots.

The other child in the photograph... she must be Paul's daughter, Bethany, as referred to in the article. Now tragically dead, just like her father.

I read the report again, slower this time. The heating is on but I feel so cold, my forearms pepper with goosebumps.

It's simply terrible… just the worst thing I can imagine to happen to a family. And I am so shocked that Joanne herself was there to witness the death of her husband and his daughter.

I feel physically sick when I realise Joanne's relationship to Bethany is identical to the one she'll have with Maisie if she and Shaun get married.

Yet, what were originally facts to discover and use against her now feel intensely personal and terribly sad. I feel ashamed of myself for prying but at the same time, I'm filled with a powerful sense of utter dread.

This is not about me, I remind myself. What Joanne went through, I can't imagine. What right have I got to dredge up an incident that she wanted to bury? I'm even beginning to understand why she wants to erase the whole event from Piper's mind.

Still, there's no time for sentimentality here. That's a rule I know well from working in the legal system. I've taken risks to get the information and I need to finish the job. If nothing else, to put an end to the constant wondering about Joanne's past.

I search for more results on the accident, but can't find another article, which is odd.

I'm baffled momentarily, until I remember the 'right to be forgotten' rule. The gappy search results are a perfect example of someone applying for information to be removed.

I happen to know, from previous cases I've been involved in at work, that removing online historical entries is a lengthy process. Each case is dealt with on its own merit and not all requests are approved.

But it seems as though someone who knew exactly what they were doing has done a pretty good job of erasing the accident that killed Paul Stafford and his daughter from the public domain.

I can understand Joanne wanting to forget the terrible tragedy in her past, but effectively attempting to erase it from history seems a step further than most people would venture.

In true paralegal style, and in the spirit of trying every single loose end before giving up, I enter different combinations, different words, that amount to the same question and the same event.

Finally, I manage to conjure a search query that gets me one more result.

A short report loads, which I stare at open-mouthed before sending it to the printer set up in the office upstairs.

It's a follow-up article from the original report of the accident in the *Yorkshire Post*, which confirms that Joanne Stafford, the wife of Paul James Stafford, has been formally questioned by police in relation to his death and that of his daughter.

CHAPTER 65

Maisie

It was hard, seeing Mum and Gran so worried and knowing it was because of her own actions. She'd never meant to hurt them, but she was powerless to make it any better.

She'd become immune to their pleading, their lecturing. The phrases they used to try and scare her held no power over her.

These days, it felt like she was an observer in her own life; as if she were hovering somewhere close without actually being part of herself.

At one time, if she'd had to describe how she felt about her life, she would have said it was like a kaleidoscope of colour inside her head. She loved so many things: music, dancing, reading, school, animals… There wasn't enough time in the day to do all the stuff she enjoyed.

But now? Now everything in her head was grey. Plain, dull grey, no colour, no bursts of excitement. She couldn't remember the last time she'd looked forward to anything; life was just one big ordeal.

She found she had a talent, though. She was brilliant at covering up how she really felt, and had also become a very good fibber, covering her tracks so it was virtually impossible for her mum and gran to track what she was actually eating.

She preferred to think of it as fibbing, not outright serious lying.

She didn't like lying to the people who loved her the most.

She felt certain that one day, if she lost enough weight and looked the way she should do, the pain would stop and she'd be back to her old self. Then everyone would like her again.

One day.

In the meantime, she had a constant battle to hide the true extent of it all from Mum and Gran.

She opened her wardrobe door, stood back and stared into the full-length mirror. One of the tricks she'd learned from the Internet, where there were forums to help people like her, was to pin her clothes, use belts on her jeans and wear baggy tops with two or three layers underneath, so it was more difficult for people around her to see how much weight she'd really lost.

It was easy to spend hours on the Internet in her bedroom now without her mum knowing. She'd smuggled in her dad's old laptop he'd left behind – he had a fancy new iMac now that Joanne had bought him – and Mum hadn't even noticed it had gone from the kitchen worktop.

Mum was always so busy with work, with trying to be the best. Maisie's Internet use was completely off her radar these days.

She shrugged her dressing gown from her shoulders and let it fall to the floor.

Her face contorted in disgust as she scanned her misshapen body.

Her hip bones stuck out, but she didn't really notice them. She was too distracted by the soft pads of flesh just above them. She thought this was what people meant by the term 'muffin top'.

Her thighs were too pale and seemed to balloon out at the sides. They were so fat and wide compared to her ankles. That couldn't be right, could it?

Her skin was blotchy, and if she rubbed it, dry flakes would slough off like fish scales. She felt like one of those shedding amphibians they'd learned about in science.

When she'd tried on the swimsuit to go to the swimming party a few weeks ago, she'd seen Piper's mouth drop open and the glance that had passed between her and her mum.

They'd obviously been shocked at just how fat Maisie still was. Her swimsuit gaped despite its elasticated legs and neckline, but it couldn't disguise the fact that the flesh underneath was like swollen lard.

Piper's arms and legs were long and slender, and she still had a faint tan from their holiday in Gran Canaria earlier in the year. Maisie could see that her swimsuit fitted like a glove, hugging every inch of her perfect body; no lumps and bumps there to reveal.

Piper kept trying to get Maisie to jump into the pool like she was doing, but she knew it was only so they could see how big her legs were and have a good laugh about it.

She made a point of swimming up the other end and keeping out of their way, counting the minutes on the massive wall clock until she could finally get dressed and go back to Joanne's apartment to spend some time with her dad.

After the swim, they'd had to go up to the café overlooking the pool, where the party food buffet was. Joanne ordered her a hot chocolate with cream and marshmallows without even asking Maisie her preference.

'I have a stomach ache,' Maisie told Joanne when she encouraged her to drink it.

Stomach aches were the best because adults couldn't prove you were lying. Even teachers had to give in and let you sit out of PE if you grumbled about the pain for long enough.

When they got back to the apartment, Joanne told them to go and put their wet costumes in the bath while she had a quick word with Maisie's dad about something. She looked meaningfully at Piper as she said it.

'They're talking about *you*, you know,' Piper said spitefully when they were alone. 'Your dad thinks there's something wrong with you, with the way you look.'

Maisie felt like crying, but she jutted out her chin and said nothing. She knelt by the bath and began wringing out her swimsuit, inhaling the chlorine as the water dripped down.

'Nobody even likes you at dancing any more. They all want to be my friends now instead.' Piper tugged the swimsuit out of Maisie's hands and threw it on the floor behind her, standing over her, hands on hips. 'What's wrong with you and your crazy mother? Are you both going mental or something?'

Maisie turned, picked up the wet swimsuit and lassoed it in the air as she stood up straight, enjoying the feeling of satisfaction when it hit Piper in the face like a big wet fish.

As Piper began to wail, covering one eye with her hand, Maisie turned and walked out of the large bathroom and across the landing into the spare bedroom, where she calmly closed the door, sat on the bed and waited for the brown stuff to hit the fan.

CHAPTER 66

In view of what had happened, it was decided that Maisie should go home earlier than planned.

In the car on the journey back, her dad wouldn't shut up about it.

'I don't know what's got into you lately, Maisie. You seem intent on upsetting Jo and Piper, despite them trying very hard to include you in their plans.'

Maisie opened her mouth to speak, but her dad continued.

'It's an awful thing to have to say, but it does make me wonder if your mum is poisoning you against them both. And it's not just me, even your gran is concerned. She spoke to me, you know. She's worried about you *and* your mum.'

'She—'

'There can be absolutely no excuse for violence. You really hurt Piper's face when you slapped her with that wet costume. You could've blinded her, do you realise that?'

Maisie laughed. She couldn't help it. Piper was such a drama queen.

'Enough!' Her dad's cheeks were blooming with angry red blotches and his eyes looked dark and full of unsaid words that would probably make Maisie cry.

She turned her whole body towards the window and stared out blindly until the car slowed and parked up outside her house.

Without waiting for her dad, she flung open the door and rushed up the path, into the house.

She heard her mum call out as she thundered upstairs, but she didn't stop to answer. She ran straight into the bathroom and banged the door shut behind her.

After nearly half an hour of keeping her hands immersed, Maisie pulled them out of the bath to inspect her fingertips. She liked how the water dripped from them, marvelled at how its soothing warmth sucked the moisture out of her skin without her even feeling it was happening.

Her mum had followed her upstairs and tapped on the bathroom door.

'Please don't come in,' Maisie had said calmly. 'I want a bath. I'll tell you what happened later.'

She heard her dad come into the hallway and Mum went back downstairs. Their low, concerned voices became faint and then disappeared as they went into the kitchen. Maisie heard the chink of cups and knew they'd talk in there for a while.

She stared again at her hands. The once smooth, plump fingertips had now transformed into little withered ravines that looked like the dry riverbeds they had seen in Spain on the coach that had taken them from the airport to the hotel. She'd been about six or seven then. Mum and Dad still loved each other and they'd been a proper family with no awkward stuff hanging in the air that nobody wanted to talk about.

Sometimes you couldn't change the things that happened around you, but Maisie was beginning to realise that you could change little bits of yourself.

When your mind felt sad, scared and confused and everyone told you what to do, you still had control of your own body.

You could change small things that adults didn't even notice so couldn't do anything about. For a while, at least, until they realised something was wrong.

Some part of Maisie knew it wasn't right, what she was doing. But she felt powerless to stop. She knew about eating disorders; they'd even had a session about them in school when a lady came in to talk to Year 6 in assembly.

But Maisie didn't care about the label. She just cared about how she felt.

And she'd found she felt much better when she wasn't stuffing her face with food.

Her dad had changed who he was. He acted so differently around Joanne and Piper. He was never tired and took Piper to Sunday league football training every weekend.

He'd never done that when he lived at home with her and her mum.

It was because Maisie was boring.

Maisie was ugly and rubbish at football.

She told her, all the time.

CHAPTER 67

Fourteen years earlier

You hated every minute of it. All that vomiting and purging and starving yourself as a child… it hurt you, set you apart from your peers.

Other children at school know when someone is different. They know when something is wrong, off kilter, but they don't always know why.

But that didn't matter. It was enough for them to isolate, to victimise, to force you to endure years of bullying.

And when you finally left school, it stayed with you. It was so hard to trust people, to make friends. Your worst relationship was the one you had with food, and with yourself.

The habits she forced you to endure somehow became part of you. They became who you are.

At twenty years of age, your stomach is raw, your skin is flaky and spotty, your flesh bags away from your bones. But still, she tells you that you are beautiful.

And you believe her.

When your mother dies, you are bereft. You mourn her, pine for your loss.

But you discover there is one way you can feel close to her again. One way you can be yourself.

You continue what she taught you. You purge, and vomit, and starve yourself of food, the enemy.

Yet better is to come. You find you can pass on your mother's legacy. You can teach another young soul the same secret.

All you have to do is find the right girl.

Someone who is lonely and afraid.

Someone who needs your help to be her best self.

CHAPTER 68

Emma

I'm forced to admit that someone – probably Joanne herself – cleaned up the Internet pretty well in order to get the awful drowning incident forgotten.

The fact is, though, you might be able to erase Google results, but you can't throw an invisibility cloak over real-life historical records.

I tell Mum I have to attend a conference away and she agrees to look after Maisie.

The trip up to Scarborough takes two and a half hours. The traffic during the day is quite light, and although I stick an audiobook on to listen to on the way, I barely take any of it in.

Making this trip was an impulsive decision, but checking out the woman who is almost certain to become Maisie's stepmother is absolutely vital. I know I'm doing it for the right reasons, whatever others might say.

I don't know who I need to speak to or what I'm hoping to find out. But I have to act on this drive, this gut feeling that there will be people there who remember the accident that killed Joanne's husband and his daughter.

I know it's no use trying to get answers from the Marine Accident Investigation Branch; they'll be bound by data protection. But local people are free to talk, if I can just find the right person.

*

Thanks to the newspaper article, I know that the incident centred around the harbour, as well as initially being out at sea. There are bound to still be people around there that remember that terrible day.

After I've parked the car, I walk down there, salty wind whipping through my hair and my ears filling with the screeching of seagulls.

I spot a small café tucked away between the harbour buildings and decide this might be the perfect place not only for a much-needed cup of tea, but also for the lowdown on who I need to speak to.

The jolly plump waitress comes over right away.

'What can I get you, love?'

I order tea and a toasted teacake and we get into polite conversation about why I'm here.

'I'm just stopping off in the middle of a work trip, actually. My friend and his daughter drowned here in a terrible accident a few years ago. I've never been here since and… I just wanted to pay my respects, I suppose.'

Her face grows pale.

'Oh, I'm so sorry to hear that. I wasn't around that day but it was a terrible, terrible thing that happened; people talked about it for years later. Still do sometimes.'

'I wondered… would there be anyone on the harbour who was actually there that day? Who I could speak to, just to hear about it first-hand? It might help a little, with the closure.'

'I think Jack Hufton was down there earlier. He was there that day. Let me see.' She stands on tiptoe and cranes her neck to stare down at the sloping harbour. 'Yes, he's still there, I can see his woolly yellow hat. He'll be going out on the fishing boat any time, though, I should think.'

'Thanks,' I say, standing up and heading for the door.

'Oh! What about your tea and teacake?' she calls, but I'm too focused on the stocky figure in the yellow beanie hat at the quayside to reply.

Jack Hufton turns out to be a bullish man in his fifties with a craggy, weathered complexion. He looks up sharply as I approach him and runs a thick, mossy rope through his hands as he watches me negotiate the harbour slope in my fashionable ankle boots.

The wind whisks hair from my clip and splays it over my face. I forge through the freezing bluster of the wind and instinctively duck as a seagull soars just above my head with an ear-splitting screech.

I'm relieved when the fisherman smiles and I find him instantly friendly and approachable when I introduce myself and tell him the lady in the café said he might be able to help me.

He pulls off his knitted cap to reveal a head of thick salt and pepper hair and accepts my reasons for asking about the incident, no questions asked.

'I'd really appreciate if you'd tell me, in your own words, what happened that day, Jack. I'm after the truth, not just what the papers said.'

'I still have nightmares about it on occasion,' he says softly in his broad Yorkshire accent. 'I'll never forget it, I know that. I'm sorry for your loss.'

I swallow down any temptation to provide him with further fraudulent reasons for my interest and listen intently as Jack provides a concise recap of the tragedy that day.

'I don't like idle gossip,' he begins. 'But you've asked for the truth and there were witnesses here, people I've known for years and trust, who said that the couple had been arguing like cat and dog, even before taking the vessel out.'

'This is Paul and Joanne?' I clarify.

'Aye. Husband and wife, weren't they? So you might say nothing unusual there. My own Mrs can certainly get a bee in her bonnet at times and—'

'They say the sea was calm and untroubled, and yet somehow, Paul's daughter, Bethany, fell in,' I say, purposely getting him back on track. I didn't read that in the online reports but I have to get him to believe I know a bit about the tragedy and steer his memory to certain parts of it.

'I don't know about calm, I reckon it was fairly choppy out there. Anyway, the child should have been wearing a life jacket, calm or not.'

He nods when shock registers on my face.

'That's right, that little lass had no protection out there. She was in charge, the woman; Joanne. It was her boat. She should've known better than to take a child out without observing the most basic safety guidelines.' His expression is grim. 'They said, when she was unable to turn the boat around, she threw a life belt to her stepdaughter and then raised the alarm.' He blows air from his mouth, short and sharp. 'Bit like shutting the door after the horse has bolted, if you ask me.'

'Bethany was the first one in the water, then?'

'Aye.' Jack nods, looking out to sea. 'So they said.'

When he stays quiet, I stare myself for a few seconds, mesmerised by the dark grey water that whips into a maelstrom of white peaks when it hits the harbour wall.

Then Jack tells me that Paul Stafford jumped straight in to try and save his daughter. He had a frozen shoulder, a problem he'd suffered from for some time, and he quickly tired in the cold water.

By the time rescue teams reached the boat and pulled Paul out, he was already dead.

'There was an investigation, of course, went on for a while. It was a very big deal around here and everyone became obsessed with it. Those of us that work on the water felt a strange sort of responsibility.' His voice softens. 'The little lass washed up just over there.'

He drops the rope and points to the slick wet bend of the harbour wall, just over the other side of the slope where we are currently standing.

We're both silent for a moment and I shiver, but not because of the arctic air. It feels like shreds of the horror of what happened still hang in the air down here, worming their way into my very core.

I pull my coat closer to me and try to focus on finding out as much information as I can from Jack while I have the chance.

'You mentioned there was a lot of local interest. Did people suspect foul play?'

'Interest is perhaps the wrong word. People were *concerned*, wanted to know a process was being followed to find out exactly what happened.' He hesitates. 'In their rush to blame, you always get some folks who can be unkind and say some pretty serious things without having any evidence.'

'What kind of things?'

He looks around him and speaks a little more quietly. 'Oh, you know, that the woman had it planned. Joanne. Wanted the kid off the scene.'

'I see.' I manage to say, shivering when I think about the time Maisie spends in Joanne's company.

'The little girl, Bethany, she was Paul's own daughter, you see.' He pauses to think. 'I seem to remember they had a younger child together, who wasn't there that day.'

'Piper,' I say faintly.

'Rumour was, Joanne Stafford wanted rid of little Bethany so she could play happy families with her husband and their own child. So, when Mr Stafford went below deck, she pushed Bethany overboard, knowing the kid wasn't a strong swimmer. Some folks reckon she wouldn't have expected him to jump in after her, what with his shoulder problems and all, but he came back up on deck unexpectedly and that's exactly what he did.' Jack frowns. 'No surprise to me. Any father would do the same.'

'How did these rumours start, if the three of them were out there alone with no other witnesses?'

Jack shrugs. 'Joanne was devastated when her husband drowned. They brought her and the boat back in but she didn't mention Bethany until people started trying to comfort her. Then, they said, she seemed to realise all eyes were on her and she seemed to flick a switch inside herself and suddenly started acting very differently.'

I don't know what to say, so I stay quiet.

'I know it all sounds a bit heartless. But what I'm telling you is first-hand from the folks that were there with her that day.'

He nodded across to the other side of the harbour.

'Joanne stood over there, shaking, waiting while they dragged her stepdaughter out. Apparently, she blabbed stuff out to one of the rescuers, told him what really happened on the boat. That's where the rumours came from; her own mouth. The people around her said it felt like she was acting, playing the role of grieving mother. They didn't find out until afterwards she wasn't the child's mother. She denied it all afterwards, of course. Said it was the shock making her talk nonsense, said she loved the little girl like her own daughter.'

'Was she arrested?'

He shakes his head. 'She was questioned a few times, but her being a lawyer, she just tied them up in knots. No evidence, you see. The folks around here were convinced there'd been foul play, but nobody listens to idle gossip without any substance, least of all the authorities.'

Back home, I thank Mum for looking after Maisie but I act purposely distant.

The way she's started looking at me, the off the cuff comment Shaun made about the two of them speaking… I know I can't share what I found out about Joanne today. Not if, at some point, custody of our daughter is in the balance. Joanne was never arrested nor charged; I can just imagine Shaun using my trip to the coast to prove I'm totally paranoid.

Jack seemed so totally convinced that something didn't add up that day. If she could plan and implement something as terribly callous as pushing Bethany overboard, there's now no doubt in my mind she's responsible for psychologically damaging Maisie to drive her away, make her lose the will to live. Yet the only person who seems to buy into that theory is me.

I need some time to think, time to consider my next move.

'Maisie's been asleep most of the day,' Mum says. 'Or at least she appears to be resting when I put my head around her door. I think if she doesn't improve, I should take her to the doctor's again.'

When Mum has left, I pace the house, debating whether to contact the other partners, Dan and Roy, at work right now, tell them what I've discovered. I know they must be unaware of Joanne's past; they're sticklers for squeaky-clean histories for all their staff.

Still, the echoes of Damian haunt my thoughts. And that strange loose feeling in my guts is back, when I start to wonder if ultimately, I'm to blame for his death.

Plus, Maisie's relationship with Joanne is bound to strengthen as time goes on. She doesn't want to go over to her place right now, but I know Shaun won't accept that for long.

My heart fills with ice when I think about the trips Maisie takes out with them. Shaun mentioning applying for custody of our daughter…

If I reveal Joanne's secret, I have to be prepared that anything could happen. What would she do to protect her past?

The other side of her, the side that I've heard about today, would be capable of anything, I think.

CHAPTER 69

I sleep better than I've done for a while.

I went to bed early last night, but before I did, I took warm milk up to Maisie's room and we talked and I was gratified she actually took a few sips.

I brought the conversation round to her dad, about arranging for him to come to the house to spend some time with her.

'I want to see Dad, I just don't want to see *them*.' She scowled. 'Can he come over soon?'

When I went to bed, my mind felt a little clearer about some things, at least. I felt vindicated now I'd found out Joanne's secret; I always suspected she was hiding something and now I knew.

It felt like I held the cards now. All I had to do was to make sure I kept Maisie away from Joanne's toxic influence, until I decided exactly how I was going to reveal what happened to her husband and his child to the company and, more importantly, to Shaun.

I instinctively knew I had to do so in a way that put me in a concerned light. I knew I had to pick my moment with Shaun, so he could fully appreciate the implications.

Joanne was never arrested, but it was clear to me after my digging around, that she had gone to great lengths to bury her past. Its revelation could well tip her over the edge and expose the real her.

*

When I wake, I feel I should make a real effort to build bridges again with Shaun.

I plan to let him know he's welcome here and that it's by far the best thing for Maisie in getting back to her normal self if they spend time alone for a while. Taking the emphasis away from her lack of eating and lack of friends is what's needed, according to Dr Yesufu.

I've already decided I'm not going into work today. I don't think I can face Joanne and her holier-than-thou act in the office, without blurting something out about what I know. It's vital I choose my moment so she can't wriggle out of the truth.

I'm thinking, instead, if I can arrange for Shaun to come over to watch Maisie while I pop out to the supermarket.

Mum's right. I've let things slip in the house, I know that. On top of this, I'm not eating properly myself, either. How can I expect Maisie to recover her appetite when I've neglected our regular mealtimes or properly cooked food that we can sit down and share together?

It's time I sorted myself out, before I decide what to do about Joanne Dent. Provided Maisie is safe here with me, there's no rush; Joanne's awful past isn't going to go away.

As if on cue, my phone beeps and a text pings through from Shaun.

Any chance I can collect the rest of my papers from the office today?
Perfect! I reply:

Maisie off sch and in bed. Can you watch her here at the house for a couple of hours pls?

A few more exchanged texts and we agree for Shaun to come just after lunch as he's busy until then. Not ideal, but it's the start of me trying to rebuild an understanding between us. I readily agree.

It feels as if things are already on the turn for the better.

CHAPTER 70

Shaun arrives at three o'clock. Far later than we agreed.

I walk to the door, thinking how I've used the extra time wisely while waiting for him to arrive, making an effort to chat to Maisie about the Christmas show and how proud I am of her.

'It's important you don't miss any classes now, so you're the best you can be in your role,' I explained. 'Miss Diane believes in you and so do I. When you show the other girls how brilliant you are, they're all going to realise how silly they've been.'

'I don't feel well enough to go to today's class,' she said quickly.

'That's fine.' I didn't want to push her too hard and besides, I was hoping Shaun might stay for a good few hours.

She brightened a little then and she did show some interest when I suggested we could perhaps get away in the new year to the coast for a few days. Just her and me, wrapped up warm and holed away in a tiny cottage somewhere.

'I'd like that, Mum.' She smiled, hugging her knees to her. 'Somewhere far away from here.'

She ate half a slice of toast in front of me and took a few sips of orange juice. That definitely counted as progress and I can't help drawing parallels with her improvement and the fact I've told her she won't be going to Joanne's for a while.

Shaun looks a bit bashful when I open the door, but I smile and ask him if he'd like a cup of tea before I go out to do the food shopping.

'Oh! Thanks, yes. That'll be nice.'

He seems taken aback by my pleasant manner, as if he expected a dressing down for being late. Perhaps I've been more difficult with him than I'd imagined.

'Alright, tiger?' He walks over to the seating area, where Maisie is lying watching television.

'Hi, Dad.' She turns her face for a kiss and he ruffles her hair.

'Lazy bones, still in your comfies,' he teases her, pulling at her pyjama top. I see his face drop when he takes in how baggy it's getting on her diminishing frame.

Within minutes, they're joking and chatting about TV programmes. This is what they've needed; time together to bond again.

I make Shaun's tea and then I grab my handbag and shrug on my quilted jacket. There's plenty of time for us to chat when I get back and I want to get something nice for tea in the hope he might join us and stay a while longer.

'I'm off to Sainsbury's, I'll be a couple of hours at the most,' I say, kissing Maisie goodbye. 'You two have fun.'

They barely notice I'm leaving, they're chatting so much.

I head for the car, happier than I've felt for weeks. I want my daughter back and nobody is going to stop me doing what I need to do to make that happen.

I get to the supermarket, remember to take the canvas shopping bags out of the boot for once, and open the shopping list app on my phone. The shop is pleasant at this time of day; no rushed lunchtime shoppers or manic after-work visits from people like me. I even start to fantasise what it might be like to sell the house and be able to get a part-time position in a smaller practice so I can be there for Maisie more.

The thought itself seems to spring from nowhere and it surprises me.

My whole life, I've never considered anything less than forging ahead with a steely determination to prove my dead father wrong.

For the first time ever, that approach feels like a cage rather than a motivation. Promotion is not the only gauge of success in this life.

The realisation brings a lightness to my step, melts the heaviness in my chest.

Another job I did this morning was make a list of ingredients for Maisie's favourite meals. If I keep her away from negative people and make delicious food, I reckon she should be on the road to recovery in no time at all.

I'm planning to make a family favourite for tea; good old bangers and mash. Inside the shop, I follow my list, gathering together quality ingredients and basics needed for my badly depleted larder and fridge.

I'm about to pass the wines and spirits section when I impulsively grab a couple of bottles of the red that's on offer on the aisle-end display. Maybe, just maybe, Shaun will appreciate a glass later when we hopefully have a heart-to-heart talk about our daughter and he can see I've changed my curt approach.

If we can both relax a little and really talk honestly, he might begin to wonder if I've got it so wrong about Joanne after all.

I pop the wine in the trolley and when I look up, Sandeep's mum is rushing around the corner like a woman on a mission, clutching an already overfilled wire basket. Her eyes widen when she sees me and for an awful moment I think she's going to ignore me, but I smile and stop walking.

'Seems like forever since I saw you,' I say, my voice upbeat. 'I said to Maisie just the other day, Sandeep really ought to come over for a sleepover soon.'

'That's kind, but...' She transfers her weight from one foot to the other. 'Well, we've all got such busy lives, haven't we? In fact, I'm hurrying now because—'

'Maisie's been in a bit of a bad place, you see,' I cut over her excuse. 'I think she needs to reconnect with her friends and Sandeep was one of her *best* friends.'

'Yes. I do know that.' She's dropped the fake manners now and she plonks the heavy basket down on the floor. 'Sandeep has been very upset, too.'

'Why's that?' I'm wondering if it's all a big misunderstanding and the girls just need us mums to gently encourage them to reconnect again.

'The notes Maisie wrote?' She's staring me out now, eyes popping. 'Sandeep's ballet slipper flushed down the loo?'

'What? I-I'm sorry, I don't know what you're talking about, Sarita.'

'Oh come on, I'm sure you do, but I don't blame you for being embarrassed. Everyone understands Maisie has been affected by her dad leaving and—'

'Now just a minute.' I push the trolley to one side and step closer to her. 'I don't like the sound of this casual gossip about my daughter. You mentioned notes?'

Sarita began to speak mechanically, as if she was going through the motions because I'd asked, but that she was under no illusions I knew all about what had happened.

'Sandeep had a note pushed into her dance bag. It was from Maisie, telling her she was a little bitch and she didn't want to be her friend any more.'

'Just stop right there! Maisie would never—'

'Maisie signed the bloody thing!'

Her fury matches my own. We stand aside as a sales assistant saunters by looking concerned at our clenched fists and aggressive stances.

I shake my head. It doesn't make any sense.

But Sarita's in full flow now.

'Zoe invited everyone to her birthday party, including Maisie. Surprise, surprise, Zoe got a note too, telling her in no uncertain terms to eff off, quote: "I would rather die than go to your crappy little farm visit." Again, she had the audacity to sign it.'

'This is crazy,' I whisper to myself. I grasp the trolley handle for support as I feel suddenly queasy.

'And Sandeep caught Maisie red-handed, flushing her missing ballet slipper down the loo, tears streaming down her face while she did it! She's obviously disturbed.'

My skin feels like it's being grilled. The heat inside me is building.

'So now perhaps you understand why the girls are staying clear of Maisie, Emma.' She picks up her wire basket and pushes her shoulders back. 'Now. If you'll excuse me... I have somewhere I need to be.'

CHAPTER 71

I don't know how long I stand there, in the middle of Sainsbury's; my knuckles are white from grasping on to the trolley too hard and my cheeks feel as if they're blazing. When I come to, I realise I'm drawing some unwanted attention.

The sales assistant I saw earlier has now returned with a man in a suit.

'Are you alright, madam? My colleague noticed earlier that you were—'

'Mind your own bloody business!' I yell and push the half-filled trolley away. I run past them, taking the quickest route through an operating checkout, out of the shop.

I ferret blindly in my handbag for my keys as I rush across the car park towards the car. I feel so sick, Sarita's accusations about my daughter whooshing around in my head.

But she sounded so outraged, so angry on behalf of her daughter… I could tell, as a mother, I'd feel exactly the same if it had happened to Maisie.

Sarita left before I could ask her any questions. Why haven't the other mums spoken to Miss Diane about this? She's had plenty of chances to tell me when I've called in at the studio. Why haven't the other mums – Sarita in particular – walked up the road to my car and asked to speak to me about it?

The biggest question of all is, why hasn't Maisie told me any of this stuff has been happening? It's an enormous burden for a young girl to bear alone, everyone against her.

Her repeated pleas to me, asking if she can stop her dance lessons, fill my ears and then I realise. Piper, or Joanne herself, must have forced Maisie to do these awful things to make the other girls hate her.

I know, from what I found out yesterday, that Joanne will stop at nothing to get what she wants.

And only Joanne Dent would have the power to tell the adults to keep their mouths shut. It's the only thing that makes any sense.

I pull up on the drive and jump out. A wave of heat bursts up into my chest and neck when I realise Shaun's car isn't parked on the road outside the house.

The front door is locked. I use my key and burst into the hallway.

'Shaun? Maisie?'

No answer.

'Hello?' I run from room to room but I already know he's taken her out somewhere.

'Shit!' I stab my finger on my phone screen. Shaun's phone rings but he doesn't answer and it sends me to voicemail.

'Where are you? You were supposed to stay here, Shaun, you knew that! Ring me back immediately. It's important.'

I don't wait long before calling him again. And again. And again. Finally, he calls me back.

'Thank God! Where have you taken her? Is she OK?'

'Calm down, Emma! What the hell is wrong with you?'

'I need to speak to Maisie and you were supposed to stay in the house, you—'

'She's *fine*,' he says, his tone implying I'm being ridiculous. 'She said she felt much better, so I brought her back to Jo's and—'

'What? You had no right!' Infuriatingly, tears begin to sprout. 'You don't know the full story, Shaun. I'm coming over there right now.'

'No. You're not coming over while you're in a state, Emma.'

We both fall silent. A stand-off; our daughter caught in the middle.

And so I tell him. Very quickly, I tell him about Joanne's possible involvement in Paul and Bethany Stafford's deaths.

'I think you need help,' he says after a pause. 'You're not coping and making up these terrible stories—'

'Put Maisie on the phone right now,' I say curtly, swallowing down disappointment at both myself, for rushing the telling of Joanne's secret, and also at Shaun for immediately defending her.

'Maisie's not here,' he says falteringly. 'Joanne persuaded her to go to dance class after all with Piper. I thought you'd be pleased.'

Back in the car, I reverse out of the drive like a madwoman and get beeped at by an oncoming vehicle for my trouble. I don't care. I need to get to the dance school right now and get Maisie back to safety. It's time everybody knows exactly who Joanne Dent really is.

I'd hung up on Shaun and rushed out here, not even checking I'd closed the front door properly behind me. Nothing matters any more, nothing except making sure my daughter is safe and away from that evil cow Shaun has decided to bring into our lives.

I drive to the dance studio on automatic pilot, somehow managing to get there in one piece, although I know by the number of hand gestures and horns beeped, I didn't do it safely.

Just as I turn on to the road, my phone rings, flashes up Joanne Dent's name.

I ignore it. Shaun will have told her I'm on the warpath and she'll be trying to fool me, just like she manages to fool everyone else with her easy charm and clever lies.

I want her nowhere near my daughter from now on. I don't care if I ruin her career and her relationship with Shaun; what she has done is a thousand times worse than Damian did and I dealt with him.

The phone bleeps to inform me I have an answerphone message but I don't bother listening to it. I'll say what I need to when I see her face to face. When she can't wriggle out of the truth.

The class should be in situ now. There is no sign of any of the other parents and yet I spot, with a start, that Joanne's Mercedes is still parked on the double yellow lines outside the foyer.

Maisie's distressed face flashes into my mind and I feel a spike slipping up through my torso, like a blade ripping out my innards.

If she's in there, hurting my daughter, I will kill her.

CHAPTER 72

Maisie

'If you want to run away, I can help you. Maybe you should pretend to do it… hide out somewhere just for a few days to teach your mum a lesson,' she said. Her face looked scary, sort of crazy. And she was standing in front of the door, so Maisie couldn't walk out of the room.

'My mum has done nothing wrong. It would kill her if I ran off,' Maisie said, shaking her head. 'Why do you hate her so much? Why do you hate me?'

'Silly girl. I don't hate you.' For a moment she looked sad that that was what Maisie thought of her. 'But your mum is to blame for all the misery in my life. I hate her, with all my heart.'

A glint of something shone in her hand, and Maisie saw she had a knife.

Maisie gasped and turned to run, but she grabbed her by the hair. Maisie screamed out.

This didn't make sense. How could this be happening?

'My mum will tell the police!'

She laughed. 'The police aren't interested in little girls who stop eating. Nobody made you do that; you did it to yourself.'

'You told me I was fat. Ugly. You told me to cut down, to hardly eat, and the hunger pains would go away.' Maisie's eyes glittered with tears. 'And they did. But something inside of me went away too.'

Suddenly the door opened behind her and Maisie glimpsed Piper's face. Her eyes widened and she closed the door again.

'Beautiful, slim, talented Piper. No wonder your daddy loves her more.'

'He doesn't! Stop saying that. *I'm* his daughter, not her.'

'Where did he choose to live? With Piper, or with you?'

The door opened again and Maisie let out a sob, but the poisonous words continued in her ear.

'Your mother killed my fiancé, did you know that? We were due to be married, had our whole life ahead of us. And now she has to pay for that.'

'Maisie...' a familiar voice said tentatively. 'Are you OK, sweetie?' Joanne stepped into the room and looked at Miss Diane. 'What's going on in here? Why is Maisie upset?'

'I'm just talking to her, that's all.' Miss Diane smiled, moving the knife behind her back. 'I think she needs help, Joanne. She's talking about running away.'

'No!' Maisie dashed to Joanne's side. 'She's lying! She's been saying bad things to me for weeks.'

'I've called your mum and left a message, she'll be here soon.' Joanne put an arm around Maisie's shoulders. 'I think it's time for us to go. Step aside, please, Diane.'

'You! You're just as bad as her mother. You employed her after she killed Damian. I came here to get revenge; started the dance school expressly to get close to her. I won't let anyone take justice for his death away from me.'

'He broke the law, as well you know.' Joanne ushered Maisie to the door just as it flew open. 'We must work within the law, not outside it.'

'Mum!' Maisie bolted out of the door and into her mother's arms.

CHAPTER 73

Emma

I push open the door and fall into the room as Maisie rushes into my arms, sobbing.

I see Joanne's face, her features stretched and pale.

Her mouth is moving but her words are deep and long, too distorted for me to make any sense of.

I feel Maisie's thin, warm body clinging to me and I wrap my arm around her shoulders while I sway with the effort of keeping upright. I feel… so… dizzy and sick, I…

Maisie jumps away as I lash out at Joanne with my free arm, my hand making contact with her face. She staggers back, holding her cheek and then I turn, hearing a roar and fast movement to my other side.

My eyes meet the dance teacher's as she dashes forward and plunges the knife into my stomach, and in an instant, I just know.

All this time, it was Miss Diane, not Joanne, who was trying to destroy my daughter.

As Maisie's screams grow increasingly faint around me, I slide into a dark, silent place.

'Maisie…' I whisper before my daughter's small, frightened face fades away.

CHAPTER 74

Emma

'You've lost a lot of blood,' the nurse says gently when I open my eyes. 'You've been sedated, so you'll feel a bit groggy.

She's holding a tiny white cup and a glass of water. 'It's important you stay calm. No getting excitable.'

I take the tablets obediently and settle back on my pillow. I still feel so very tired.

'If you're up to it, you have a visitor.'

Joanne walks into the room and sits on the hard plastic chair at the side of the bed. The nurse smiles at her and leaves the room.

'Shaun told me… you know about what happened on the boat,' Joanne says.

'I'm sorry,' I whisper, feeling ashamed at the scratch mark and bruise on her cheek. 'Sorry I hit you and accused you.'

'It's OK,' she says, reaching for my hand. 'I should've faced up to all the stuff that happened to me, instead of trying to bury the guilt and pain.'

I nod. I know how that feels.

'You did me a favour, Emma. Forced me to face up to it.' She looks down at her hands. 'I know what the locals thought happened, but it was an accident. And that was the official verdict.'

'I know.' This woman was trying to protect my daughter when I last saw her. If she wanted rid of Maisie, then she could have just walked away.

'The other partners at the firm have been fine with me. They've carried out an internal inquiry into the accident just for the record, but it's cleared me. There's not really much they could do even if they wanted to; there's no evidence I did anything wrong.'

She seems to be labouring the point and it's a strange thing to say, I think.

She holds up her left hand and shows off a sparkling diamond ring.

'Shaun and I got engaged,' she says simply. 'He's been worried about telling you, but I hope you'll be happy for us.'

'Congratulations,' I say faintly. She saved me from the madwoman, hit her with a chair and called the police and ambulance, so I can hardly be trite about it.

'Just before the police arrived, Diane told me she was the one who sent you the note and did all those mean little things at the house. Simply to unnerve you, torture you for revenge.'

I shake my head slowly, hardly believing it.

'She's waited all this time?'

'Set the dance school up especially to manoeuvre herself into a position to destroy you.' Joanne confirms. 'She said she knew it was time for her to act when the rumours started about you and Shaun breaking up because you'd be more vulnerable.'

All this time I've blamed myself for Damian's death, as Diane obviously has too.

But now, it's as though someone has shone a bright light of truth on what happened, and I understand that his decision to end his life was his own.

I did the right thing, and his tragic actions were not my fault.

'Where's Maisie?' I say hoarsely, keen to get off the subject. I'm embarrassed that I got it all wrong, and somehow I have to build a relationship with this woman who is soon going to become Maisie's stepmother.

'She and Shaun are outside, but I asked him to let me just have a few minutes with you first.'

I look at her. She looks thin and pale and there's a manic quality about her eyes today.

'I care about Maisie, you know. I promised you at the beginning that I'd look after her, and I've stuck to my word. It's been difficult, because in some ways you've tried to set her against me.'

'I know.' I stare at the ceiling. 'And truly, I'm sorry.'

'Are you feeling OK now? You had a pretty impressive meltdown earlier.'

I nod.

'I can't really remember much… just a lot of shouting.'

Joanne glances at the door. 'The nurse told me they sedated you, so you'll be confused. I won't keep you long, I just wanted to make sure we're cool now. No more silly fall-outs. Our aim has got to be getting Maisie back to her former self.'

I'm encouraged at the thought of my daughter regaining full strength.

My mind returns to Damian.

'He told me he'd make me pay for what I did one day, you know. When I least expected it.'

Joanne nods. 'And Diane carried out his threat. She wanted to drive you into a mental breakdown through worrying about your daughter. She told me she was abused as a child herself, forced to endure an eating disorder by her own mother. In her own twisted way, it seems like she actually thought she was *helping* Maisie.'

I close my eyes, unable to process such skewed logic.

'But the doctors say Maisie's making great progress now, and you can rest assured we'll look after her until you're strong enough to come home.'

'Thank you.' I reach for her hand and squeeze it.

Joanne bends forward and smiles. It's a strange smile. I think the sedatives are still making me woozy. All her teeth look sharp and small.

'I know... that you know,' she whispers in my ear.

I look at her, unsure what she means, and shake my head.

'I pushed my husband's daughter that day on the boat. Sent Bethany flying to her death.' Her face is close enough to mine that I can feel her hot breath against my cheek. 'She was a nuisance, making our lives difficult. Just like Maisie does now.'

I drift a little, red and black colours swirling before my eyes, then jump as a tall figure looms to my right. It's Shaun.

'Mum!' Maisie rushes in and sits on the bed to hug me.

'Are you OK, Emma? You look as white as a sheet.' Shaun frowns.

'She's sedated,' Joanne says lightly. 'A bit confused, too.'

'She just said... I... take Maisie...'

'Hush, Em, you need to rest,' Shaun says softly. 'You've had a terrible shock, no wonder you're feeling confused.'

'No! I don't want...' Their faces are fading.

'Mum! We're going to the coast,' Maisie squeaks with excitement, pressing her face close to mine. Her eyes twinkle just a touch, and although her face is pale, she looks more like her old self. 'Joanne is going to take me and Piper out... *on a boat*!'

'No!' They're all merging into one, in and out, like the ebb of the tide around me. My own voice sounds strange, sort of far away.

'Don't worry, Emma.' Joanne's face hovers above mine as she bends down and kisses my forehead. 'Maisie and I are much closer now. I'll look after her, I promise.'

A LETTER FROM KIM

I do hope you have enjoyed reading *Closer*, my seventh psychological thriller. If you did enjoy it, and want to keep up to date with all my latest releases, please do sign up to my email list below to be sure of getting the very latest news, hot off the press! Your email address will never be shared and you can unsubscribe at any time. You can also connect with me via my website, on Facebook, Goodreads or Twitter.

www.bookouture.com/kl-slater

The idea for this book initially grabbed me because I am a mother myself. My daughter is a wonderful young woman now, but I can clearly remember her as a ten-year-old. Those pre-teen years are strange for a parent, I think. We see our young person growing, developing their own opinions and preferences, hopefully against the backdrop of parental guidance. And yet ultimately they are still very much a child and need protecting.

Life has a funny way of throwing challenges and complications at us, and I got to thinking about how, if parents are distracted with their own problems, it might be surprisingly easy to take your eye off the ball briefly. Just long enough for a negative influence to sneak in and turn your child's life upside down.

As adults, we like to put the past in a box, control it as we see fit. Sometimes there are happy memories, sometimes events best forgotten. It's a constant source of fascination to me how the past has a bearing on our present, and although we like to think we can set previous bad experiences aside, they have a nasty habit of resurfacing just when we could most do without them.

Another occurrence that contributed to *Closer* was that I happened to watch an emotional interview with a pre-teen girl and her mother who, happily, had survived the child's anorexia and emerged from the other side stronger and chatting openly about their experience.

One thing I took from their interview and from subsequent research on anorexia in young people was that parents very often have an inbuilt alarm when it comes to 'just knowing' something isn't right with their child. Doctors and friends and family may cast doubt because clear, measurable evidence isn't always there, particularly at the beginning of an eating disorder. It's often the pure gut feeling of a parent who refuses to rest that gets to the truth of what is happening in their son or daughter's life.

I chose to explore the mother–daughter bond in writing *Closer*. I do hope you enjoyed taking the journey with me.

If you would like more information about or help with any of the issues covered in the book, there are many excellent resources that can be accessed by searching online.

Closer is set in Nottinghamshire, the place I was born and have lived all my life. Local readers should be aware that I sometimes take the liberty of changing street names or geographical details to suit the story.

Reviews are so massively important to authors. If you've enjoyed *Closer* and could spare just a few minutes to write a short review to say so, I would so appreciate that.

Until Book 8, then…

Warmest wishes,
Kim x

KimLSlaterAuthor

@KimLSlater

KLSlaterAuthor

www.KLSlaterAuthor.com

ACKNOWLEDGEMENTS

Enormous thanks to my editor, Lydia Vassar-Smith, who is always a massive support every step of the way for each new book.

Thanks to my amazing agent, Camilla Wray, for her unshakeable belief in me as an author. Her guidance and advice have been truly priceless.

Thanks also to the rest of the hard-working team at Darley Anderson Literary, TV and Film Agency. Special thanks go to Clare Wallace and to Mary Darby, Kristina Egan, Roya Sarrafi-Gohar and Rosanna Bellingham.

Thanks to *all* the Bookouture team for everything they do, especially to Claire Bord, Leodora Darlington, Alexandra Holmes and the wonderful Kim Nash.

My publisher gave me some incredible news while I was editing *Closer*; I've now sold over a million copies of my titles! I'm so grateful to my wonderful readers and to the incredible team of people at both my publishing house and to my literary agency who work tirelessly to support me in my writing journey.

Thanks as always must go to my wonderful friend and fellow Bookouture author, Angela Marsons, who is always there to share in laughter, tears and, of course, the writing life (until I fall asleep at about 9 p.m.). As promised, Ange, I won't mention the raccoon dressing gown here.

Massive thanks must go to my husband, Mac, for his love and support and for taking care of everything so I have the time to write. To my family, especially my daughter, Francesca, and to Mama, who are always there to support and encourage me in my writing.

Special thanks must also go to Henry Steadman, who has again designed a thrilling, poignant cover for *Closer*, and to the eagle eyes of the book's copy editor Jane Selley and proof reader, Becca Allen.

Thank you to the bloggers and reviewers who do so much to help make my thrillers a success. Thank you to everyone who has taken the time to post a positive review online or has taken part in my blog tour. It is always noticed and very much appreciated.

Last but not least, thank you *so* much to my wonderful readers. I love receiving all the wonderful comments and messages and I am truly grateful for each and every reader's support.

Made in the USA
Coppell, TX
30 December 2019